Take His Likeness

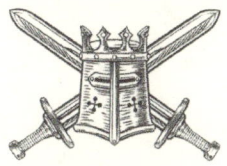

A Pride and Prejudice Variation

by Lyndsay Constable

Lyndsay Constable

Copyright © 2024 by Lyndsay Constable

All rights reserved.

This is a work of fiction. Unless otherwise indicated, all the names, characters, businesses, places, events and incidents in this book are either the product of the author's imagination or used in a fictitious manner. Any resemblance to actual persons, living or dead, or actual events is purely coincidental.

No portion of this book may be reproduced in any form without written permission from the publisher or author, except as permitted by U.S. copyright law.

No Generative AI was used in the creation of this book.

Edited by Katie Jackson – Regency Editorial Services

Original cover art by Jeremy Micheal Elder

ISBN number 979-8-9881820-5-4

Dedicated to my friend Jennifer Bolt.

Thank you for your support, your curious mind, and introducing me to Jane Austen Fan Fiction.

Contents

1. The Insipidness of Apples — 1
2. Inured to Self-Denial — 9
3. A Wish to Forget — 23
4. Extensive Reading(s) — 29
5. Not a Slight Slight — 53
6. Conceited Independence — 67
7. A Most Iniquitous Affair — 77
8. Balm of Sisterly Love — 87
9. Nicholls Has Made White Soup Enough — 99
10. Without Any Intention of Coming Back — 115
11. Find Such a Woman — 123
12. Serious Attachments — 131
13. In the Middle Before Beginning — 139
14. An Attentive Neighbour — 153
15. A Triumph Sadly Lessened — 161

16.	The Pretty Follies That Themselves Commit	167
17.	What a Letter Is This!	175
18.	A Dear, Sweet Girl	191
19.	The Bitterest Kind of Distress	211
20.	Bingley, Master of Subterfuge	219
21.	The Happiest, Wisest, Most Reasonable End	227
22.	Lady Catherine Being of Infinite Use	241
23.	Having Been Taught to Hope	253
24.	Extraordinary Sources of Happiness	269

Afterword	275
Acknowledgements	279
About the author	281
Also by	283

Chapter 1

The Insipidness of Apples

Dull. Heavy, silent, and tiresome. There was a fly upon the window that provided the most entertainment that the wearisome room had to offer. It wandered back and forth, making an endless trail upon the glass in a futile effort to escape into the even duller world outside.

Caroline Bingley envied the fly with its occupation. At least the creature had a goal in mind and was exerting an effort to attain it. She inhaled deeply and let out a sigh into the quiet of the room. The only other sounds were the turning of the pages of a book being read by Mr Darcy, the snores of Mr Hurst, the whipping snaps of the fire, and the exciting, rare collapse of a log in the grate. It was an abysmally stupid way to pass an evening. So far from the rumble of carriages, the theatre, balls, mad crushes at a rout, and the endless pulse of Caroline's lifeblood...gossip.

What could Charles have been thinking? To drag us out here to the wilds of Hertfordshire? To let this decrepit house? Hertfordshire is a swamp of slow-witted, culturally deficient provincials of low connexions. And this house, Netherfield, I am certain it will come crashing down around our ears before the week is out. If he was determined to take a place in the country, he should have at least chosen somewhere closer to the estates of more fashionable society than the savages of this wilderness.

Her eyes narrowed at her brother, Charles, who sat close to the fire, cleaning his gun for tomorrow's hunting. It was a chore that should have been left to the servants. As if to demonstrate his slow slide into the mire of inferior breeding that Hertfordshire was rank with, he had taken up the habit of performing this task himself. Caroline could not help but roll her eyes upward and look away. Her gaze fell upon Mr Darcy, who had glanced up from his book just in time to observe the look of disgust on her face. His inscrutable expression returned to the volume before him with little change. Caroline could not help but blush at the knowledge that she had been caught in a moment of sour humour by the man she was determined to claim as her own one day.

She began to feel the rise of something that ran the risk of turning into one of her famous tantrums. Her sister, Mrs Hurst, and brother, Mr Charles Bingley, both had small scars upon their arms and faces that showed just how dramatic her flights of rage could become. Caroline glanced over at Mr Darcy. Under no circumstances would she allow him to see her temper at such a heated degree. At least not until they were firmly married.

That last thought caused the rising tide of red to dissipate and fade as a small smirk turned up the corners of her mouth. She rose from her chair and strode across the room to sit close by her sister.

"My dear Louisa, can you observe anything better in the quality of this fruit than what we are able to have in London?" Caroline reached for one of the apples that sat in a bowl before them. She twisted it back and forth, mere inches from her face, her reflection shone red on the skin. "Truly, I fail to observe or taste a difference. But then, an apple has always struck me as the most insipid of the fruits. Perhaps it is the nature of the fruit itself and not the poor quality that is to blame. And Hertfordshire seems to be positively rife with nothing but apples."

"Hardly surprising, given that it is late September, a time when most varieties of apples are at their peak of ripeness and therefore harvested in abundance," Mr Darcy muttered without raising his eyes.

Charles, coming to the defence of the apple, leaned over and took it from Caroline's hand and bit into it with an echoing crunch.

"These were picked fresh just yesterday from that little farm down the road. And I happen to think they are delicious. Gordon is the name of the farmer there. Yes. We met him on a ride, did we not, Darcy?"

"We did. The apples are not the worst I have ever tasted."

The room lapsed back into silence after this exchange. Caroline glanced at Mr Darcy, hoping for some acknowledgement of her clever observation. When none came, she pressed her lips together in petulant silence. Louisa straightened her dress repeatedly, apparently not wanting to participate in the great apple debate. After several more moments, Caroline leaned in to Louisa and whispered, "Did we ever find out who started the rumour that Lady Glassly's newest child bears a striking resemblance to that handsome captain from the militia? Captain Moss, was it?"

Thus began a hissing exchange between Caroline and Louisa as they started a round of their favourite game of 'Tail of the Snake'. It was an amusement of their own invention that had been successfully employed to while away a slow hour when needed. They compared notes on a particularly delicious snippet of gossip that was making the rounds and tried to uncover from whom the tale originated.

After several minutes more of whispers, in a somewhat deflated mood, they both realised that it must have been themselves who had started the rumour. It was not nearly as much fun when that was found to be the case because it left little room for speculation as to the reason the rumour was started. If the originator's motives could be guessed, they could often give rise to an entirely new snake of gossip to let loose in the tall grasses of society.

They both sank back into the boredom of the evening with varying degrees of acceptance and resentment.

Finally, Caroline sat up and ventured, "What was your impression of the visitor we had today, Charles? A Mr Bennet, was it?"

"Well, I found him to be a quiet, agreeable man. He seemed to be a bookish sort who might get on well with Darcy, given the chance. And I have the impression—"

"Five daughters!" Caroline trilled with an amused lilt of laughter. "I have had it from my maid, Kate. And Louisa—you will be most shocked—*all* of them out. The youngest is fifteen and the eldest is one and twenty. You would never hear of such an appalling occurrence in London. Their mother must be absolutely desperate to catch husbands for them, do you not agree?"

"They will be on the hunt for agreeable men of fortune, to be sure, sister. I caught a glimpse of Mr Bennet from the window, and his clothes were many seasons past the latest fashions. That can only mean that their fortunes are limited."

"Mmm. Too true. Some of us should be on our guard. It would not do to have them begin to form expectations beyond their own circle. Is that not so, Mr Darcy?"

He looked up at them with a startled air. "Excuse me, I was not attending."

Caroline could not account for it in the least. She was accustomed to Mr Darcy's quiet, detached moods. But ever since he had joined them at Netherfield, he seemed particularly distracted and almost low in spirits. No matter how much she attempted to lure him out in conversation, she could not find out what he had been up to recently. Even her maid had been unsuccessful in worming any insights from his man, Crump. For both she and Kate to fail in sniffing out any truffle of information was unusual. The only thing that they had been able to piece together was that he had visited Ramsgate and then had attended his sister, Georgiana, almost exclusively for several months afterwards. Caroline knew him to be an attentive brother, but this bordered on excessive. Had she not harboured secret ambitions when it came to all things Fitzwilliam Darcy, she would have been very tempted to begin a few rumours in an attempt to flush out the truth. Alas, she did not wish to risk anything of that nature getting back to Mr Darcy.

"And, Caroline," Charles said, undeterred by Caroline's interruption, "you will be surprised to learn that there is some society to be had here after all. Sir William Lucas extended an invitation to us for the next assembly in Meryton. There is sure to be dancing and company lively enough to entertain for the evening. I am quite looking forward to it."

Completely oblivious to the hushed chill that greeted his announcement, her brother happily continued with his polishing and speculation. "It will be some jolly fun to meet the famous Bennet sisters. I have had it from the groom in the stable that they are reckoned to be the loveliest of all the girls in the surrounding counties. And agreeable. *That* will be something for us to look forward to, eh, Darcy?"

"What?" He appeared momentarily confused, then chagrined. "You know how I dislike assemblies and balls."

Charles laughed. "I am well aware. But imagine a room full of pretty young women and no scheming mothers shoving their girls in front of you every moment. Not at all like in London. Surely, even you must see there will be some pleasure in an evening like that. Why, Darcy, I will wager you that I will secure the first dance with the prettiest Bennet sister before you have even—"

"Pretty?" Caroline exclaimed. "Beauty to be found in a place such as this? Charles, do not be ridiculous. I shall guarantee that they are all eyebrows and teeth, the lot of them. They will merely be handsome, for that is the word one uses when attempting to be polite in the face of homeliness, is it not? The word handsome when used to describe a woman can cover a multitude of sins. Would you not agree, Mr Darcy?"

With a studied laugh, she turned her head, anticipating some sharp-witted response from him, but was disappointed once more. He sat watching the fly upon the window with an expression that almost bordered on wistful.

After a dreary evening that had not improved a whit, Caroline sat before the mirror in her room and sighed loudly as Kate brushed out her hair.

"And even Mr Hurst, who can always be relied upon to badger everyone into a card game, was too dull to even make the suggestion. He slept away the time, flopped on the lounge as if he had walked to Bath and back."

Kate let out a small titter as she continued with her long, smooth strokes of the brush. Caroline examined her own face closely in the reflection of the mirror, tilting her head slightly in one direction and then the other. An almost imperceptible change in her countenance had lately given rise to concern. It was miniscule—perhaps even imagined—but worrying nonetheless. It seemed as if there was a certain diminishment in the glow of her bloom. Bloom was that one elusive quality that older women coveted and the young took for granted. A mild downcast of her mouth seemed to be creeping in, slowly and steadily.

Two years. Two years I have been cultivating this intimacy with Mr Darcy, and I seem no closer to receiving a proposal of marriage. I am the epitome of what the future Mrs Darcy ought to be. How does he not see it? I have no flaw that I can detect in form, figure, or character. If I do not see an improvement in his attentions soon, I shall have to...I shall have to...

Her thought spasmed and died, like a horse that collapsed mid-race, leaving nothing behind but shock and dismay. A tightness in Caroline's throat caused her to cough suddenly and grip the end of the table.

"Are you all right, miss?"

"Of course I am perfectly fine," Caroline snapped. "It is this wretched country living that has my nerves on edge. I was not made for this. Were there but some entertainment to be had! Some form of diversion that would help me to cultivate a bit of excitement in the evenings."

"Ah, I see."

A thought struck Caroline. She attempted to give her maid an ingratiating smile as their reflections gazed at each other. This only served to make Kate appear more on edge, like one accustomed to the growl of a dog before it tries to steal a chunk of your flesh. Caroline narrowed her eyes and pressed on. "You have not happened to hear of anything of interest in the area, have you? Anything out of the ordinary that could cheer away the dullness during these long evenings? Hmm?"

Kate broke her gaze away and went back to brushing Caroline's hair a little too rapidly. "Oh, no. I cannot say that I have heard of anything like that. Except... But, no. It would be beneath your notice, I am quite certain, miss. Nothing that would interest you or the other guests."

Caroline spun rapidly in her seat and caught Kate's wrist in her firm grasp that was as quick as lightning. Kate gave a small gasp of shock. Caroline's grip did not loosen.

"Please, miss. I really should not say. It could be thought of as just wrong."

"Now Kate, you know that you can trust me implicitly. You remember well how I managed to smooth over that little misunderstanding you had with the head footman at my brother's house in town? We would not want any knowledge of that to become common tittle-tattle, now would we?"

Kate, though not the quickest of girls, appeared to comprehend her mistress's nature too well not to recognise the threat.

"I would simply love to hear any information that you may have," Caroline purred in her smoothest voice.

With an air of resignation, Kate sighed and began to speak very softly. "Well, if you go into the woods just a little ways from here..."

Chapter 2

Inured to Self-Denial

Threadbare and barely presentable.

Those were the only descriptions fitting for the pair of gloves that Elizabeth Bennet was gingerly pulling on in preparation for a walk. If she gave in to her more impulsive nature and yanked them on—as she may have done in years past—another tear would appear that might prove to be a tear too far. Thread and a needle could procure a miracle healing only so many times before the strength of the fabric itself was beyond redemption.

Elizabeth sighed as she held the other glove up to the light coming in through the window, observing far too much illumination through the material to convince her that they would last for the winter season. For the past year, the finances of her family and the Longbourn estate had sunk so low that Elizabeth had insisted that castoffs from her older, taller sister Jane skip herself and go straight to Mary, the third eldest Bennet sister. Any concern that Jane expressed about Elizabeth's wardrobe was laughed away with a joke from Elizabeth and the prediction that their fortunes were sure to turn at any moment. Elizabeth was likely to be agreed with on this point by their mother who believed that an enormously wealthy husband must be in the near future for Jane, her eldest and most beautiful daughter.

Such liveliness could be easily maintained in the presence of others, but when Elizabeth kept her own company, shadows of worry and doubt darkened her thoughts. For only Elizabeth knew how truly bad the finances really were. Mrs Hill, the Bennets' housekeeper, suspected the real extent of their troubles and did everything in her power to keep household expenses low. Hill frequently received gifts of money from Elizabeth to help reduce the cost of groceries for the entire family. And only Hill knew how Elizabeth obtained the money. No one else was privy to the secret, not even her beloved sister Jane.

Their father, Mr Bennet—after having seen several of his unwise investments shrink his estate further from its original, modest size—had retreated from the world into his study and only made the social calls that were the bare minimum expected from the local gentleman of standing. He proclaimed himself in possession of a genuine treasure in Hill when he was never called upon to increase the budget needed to feed five growing daughters. All of his curiosity had retreated to books. If any of the pressing concerns of daily life were put before him, he would shrink away further into his shell. It was just as well, for Elizabeth suspected that if her father knew she was contributing to the household funds with her secretive business, he might be shocked out of his hermit-like existence in outrage. She was genuinely concerned that if Mr Bennet was spurred to action in an effort to salvage and expand what little of the estate that was still profitable, he might pursue yet another speculation that would lead to irretrievable financial loss.

Based on his recent effort to visit the new tenant of Netherfield, Elizabeth supposed that even her father saw the advantage of introducing his daughters to an unmarried man of means. She smiled privately to herself.

Her mother had been so persistently forlorn by the fact that Mr Bennet had not yet called upon the recently arrived Mr Bingley that it was perhaps also his desire for tranquillity that had spurred him into this unusual show of gregariousness.

Elizabeth scurried out of the house unnoticed and briskly made her way to the home of her closest friend, Charlotte Lucas. The air was sharp and it chilled her throat with the promise of the coming winter months. The trees breathed with the hollow rattle of leaves preparing to abandon their safe harbour for a solemn adventure.

At Lucas Lodge, Charlotte shared with Elizabeth the latest news to be had from Netherfield. "My father invited the new tenants to the assembly next week, so we may have a few more partners to even out the poor odds of eligible gentlemen to ladies."

"It is unfortunate that the neighbourhood seems to be in constant need of eligible gentlemen. Mama will be positively beside herself in anticipation. What more can you tell me about our new neighbours? You know Mama will question me relentlessly."

"I am sorry, for I have little else to add. The rest of the party was not available both times my father called. It was only he and Mr Bingley who visited together."

"Does that not seem odd? I heard from Hill that there are more ladies and gentlemen in residence. It would seem usual for them to also make the acquaintance of the neighbours, would it not?"

"I have the impression that, though Mr Bingley is genial and social, the rest of the party are very fine and may think the local society beneath them."

"Really? Did your father say as much?"

"No, indeed not. You know my father...he had nothing but good things to say. It was the impression I received from the details of his remembrances."

Elizabeth had to bite the inside of her cheek to repress the desire to laugh. If Sir William Lucas had ever expressed an insight as sharp as the one his daughter had just shared, it would have shocked her to the core. His ability to approve of every single person he met, no matter how sneering they might be towards him, was profound. She knew both herself and Charlotte were gifted at discerning the true character of people, but it was a skill that few others in their families possessed. Elizabeth held her aptitude for sketching the nature of people to be far superior to Charlotte's—a blessing for which she was grateful, for her full belly every night depended on that particular skill.

Charlotte and Elizabeth parted, both anticipating the assembly more than usual since it would have the enhancement of new faces. The society of Meryton was so small, any addition was a point of interest that would provide hours of conversation thereafter.

Elizabeth made her way home, eager to inform her mother that the party from Netherfield would be attending the Meryton assembly. Hopefully, that would divert Mrs Bennet's nervousness from the endless speculation of how and when her daughters could be spontaneously thrown into the path of Mr Bingley, to the problems of what they should wear for the momentous evening. Perhaps they would know more about the new neighbours by then.

With a deep breath, Elizabeth cleared the speculations from her mind by bringing her attention to the clouds racing overhead. While passing through a meadow at the boundary of the Gordon farm, she spied a young woman in the fine clothes of a London lady's maid dashing into the apple grove towards the forest beyond. Elizabeth sighed and hurried her steps home. She did not want to miss out on the chance to make a small profit.

She met with Hill in the main hall and mentioned sighting the lady's maid, who surely worked for one of the new ladies at Netherfield, and the direction she was walking.

"Tell Mama that I have a little headache and do not wish to be disturbed. And that you heard that the party from Netherfield will be attending the assembly. It should distract her from now until the moment we attend." Elizabeth pressed her bonnet into Hill's waiting hands.

"Miss Lizzy," Mrs Hill said with a hand resting on Elizabeth's forearm to detain her briefly, "you be on your toes if you start having dealings with that Netherfield bunch. They're from London and may have more shrewdness about them than the local folk. It would not do to have you exposed. I do wish you could give all this up. I begin to rue the day that I first taught you the art."

"Never mind that, Hill. It may be that these high society ladies will have deep pockets that will help keep the larder filled through the winter."

Elizabeth lifted her skirts and bounded up the stairs two at a time. Once in her room, she turned the key to lock the door. Her mother would be too distracted to seek her. And, supposing a sudden wave of maternal concern did sweep over Mrs Bennet, Elizabeth knew that she was her mother's least favourite daughter and was least likely to be intruded upon. The only sister who regularly sought Elizabeth out was Jane, who was so very respectful of her privacy that she rarely bothered Elizabeth when she was in her room. It was usually Elizabeth who sought out Jane for companionship. Her younger sisters, Mary, Kitty, and Lydia, were all too absorbed in their own wildly divergent interests to seek any sort of camaraderie with Elizabeth. Lydia and Kitty's interests were strictly confined to men, gowns, bonnets, and gossip. Mary preferred her own shaky attempts at the pianoforte and her contemplation of a Fordyce essay on the evils of novels on the fragile minds of delicate young ladies.

Elizabeth dressed in her most ragged, dark blue gown, then ensured that her bedroom door was securely locked. Crossing her small room, she paused near the wall and lifted the corner of a rug with a small string attached to it. There was a well-worn groove in the floorboards beneath it that she hooked her index finger under. A very narrow trapdoor that ran parallel to the wall lifted up. Elizabeth took a small lantern and stepped noiselessly down into the hole, gently shutting the door above herself. Though her figure was reckoned to be lithe and slim, it was a tight fit even for her.

Elizabeth balanced on the rickety, slim staircase. In the dim light, she spied the end of the string and pulled it down until the door above was concealed again by the rug. If anyone should enter her room, it would appear relatively normal, with just the rug slightly askew. All would think she had taken another one of her rambles and neglected to inform anyone else in the house.

Elizabeth held the lantern before her as she carefully made her way down the stairs. She believed the extremely narrow passage ran through an unusually thick wall that separated the parlour from an alcove where the piano was kept. It was fortunate that Mary was so regular in her practice on that instrument, for Elizabeth was certain there were times when any slight noise she made was concealed by her sister's playing. Other times it was attributed to mice. But the secret passage did not terminate at the priest's hole at the bottom of the confined stairs.

Another narrow passage, lined with stones, could be revealed by shifting several planks sideways, like sliding open the bolt of a lock. A tunnel ran under Longbourn and out to the forest beyond. It was another tight fit, but Elizabeth could just make her way along it, lantern extended forward to light her way, ducking her head, and hunching over. Whoever had been the Catholic relation in the distant past of the Bennet family and had seen fit to provide this escape route for the local priest, must have mistakenly reckoned that clergy were no bigger than a street waif. Elizabeth's slight frame could just barely make it through the tight, damp walls. It was fortunate that she had no fear of confined spaces, unlike her mother and sister Jane.

Pressing forward, her back began to ache and small tendrils of sweat trailed down her forehead, despite the cool in the tunnel. Every time Elizabeth made this trip, she could not help but imagine the terrible fear that must have gripped the heart of the priest while he travelled this path. It was truly a trial, but since discovery would probably have led to death, it was a trial worth facing. There was a fork in the tunnel before her and, without hesitation, Elizabeth took the path on the right. At last, after at least twenty minutes of rapid scurrying, she saw the slats in front of her.

One by one, she moved the horizontal boards to one side, then left the tunnel. Placing her lantern upon the dirt floor, Elizabeth turned and replaced the slats so that they resembled a rickety wall of the cottage. She brushed the dirt off her hands and turned to a set of dark, voluminous robes that hung on a hook on the wall. After sliding into them, she lowered a black veil down over her face. Using the lantern she had brought, she lit a small fire in the fireplace of the tiny stone cottage that she was in. The dry sticks took immediately and bloomed into a warm, cheery blaze. She added several sprigs of dried mint that were hanging from a bunch on a rafter above. This was the signal to all who approached the one room, stone cottage that she was officially open for business.

Elizabeth went to the one window beside the thick, locked door. The window had a wooden shutter that she lifted out of place to reveal sturdy steel bars covering the outside. Making sure her heavy veil was firmly in place, Elizabeth sat in her wooden chair and asked in her most husky, whispery voice, "Yes?"

The lady's maid whom Elizabeth had spied entering the apple orchard appeared before the window, her wide eyes filled with uncertain terror. The young woman looked to be about nineteen, no older than Elizabeth herself.

"Are you the—the lady who reads on the cards?"

"Yes. I am that, child."

"And you tell people what is to come for them? What has not happened yet?"

"If they like it. Do you seek my services, my child?"

"I was not certain I was in the right place…there did not seem to be anyone within."

"I am here now, as you see."

The girl fidgeted and seemed about to run. Her courage at approaching the stone hovel in the middle of the woods had probably used up every little ounce of bravery within her.

She would not have come here on her own volition. If she is from the Netherfield party, it is likely this young woman rarely leaves London. If she was born and raised there, small patches of woods such as these must seem the most awful of places, filled with unseen monsters. No. She does not strike me as the type to have made this journey willingly. She is a lady's maid. She is here because of her mistress. She is more frightened of her mistress than of the horrors of the forest and of me. Her mistress must be a powerful character. Why would a lady such as she send her maid on such a foolish errand? The lady in question is either bored or in love. Or both at once.

With a frustrated sigh—for Elizabeth had not paused long enough to take some refreshment back at Longbourn or to grab one of the seed cakes she kept here for her peckish moments—she decided to give the frightened girl some small encouragement. "Would you like your future told? Though I think you are here as a messenger for another. Your mistress, perhaps? Am I right?"

The girl looked at her in absolute astonishment. "Yes!" she squeaked. "How did you know?"

Simple observation, my dear. And a knowledge of the nature of people, Elizabeth thought, but would never say out loud. "I am very gifted with the second sight," she muttered darkly with a small, amused smile on her shrouded face.

The maid looked utterly awestruck. She reached a trembling hand into the sleeve of her cloak, pulling out a small sack of jingling coins. "I am to buy something from you. But it is not for me, it is for my mistress, I assure you. I would not have you thinking I purchase this for myself."

"I understand completely."

"Do you have any love charms? Something to cause another to fall in love with you?" she asked in an embarrassed whisper.

"But of course, my child." Elizabeth reached under the sill of the window and pulled up a little satchel. It was a snippet of a lovely castoff of lace and green satin that was bound at the top by a deep red ribbon. It contained little more than mint and rosemary. Some salt at the bottom gave it some heft and, as Hill had instructed her, "keeps the fairies from meddling with the purpose of the thing. It would not do to have the intended fall in love with the wrong person because meddlesome fairies like to have their jokes at our expense." Elizabeth did not agree with Hill's assurances that fairies were real and living in the haunts of Hertfordshire, but it was futile to debate with the good woman on this point, as Elizabeth had learned from experience.

Elizabeth slid the modest pouch along the sill and under the bars of the window to the young woman outside. "It is imperative—"

"Imperative? What does that mean?"

"It is *important* that the charm is close to the skin and the heart of the one you wish to entrance with your charms."

"Lawks, old woman!" The girl tittered. "As I said before, it is not for me. La! What a thought."

"Well, whomever it is for, the one who seeks to capture a heart must say the name of the one they hope to catch three times while holding the charm in their palm. Then place it as close to the person as may be. An excellent spot is under a pillow or the mattress of the one who must fall in love."

The lady's maid looked at the bars and then back at Elizabeth. "Why do you have these bars on the windows?"

"Sometimes people do not like to hear what I have to tell them."

The girl's eyes widened even farther as she slid a coin to Elizabeth. She put the satchel of herbs in her sleeve and hurriedly turned to leave.

"Oh!" she exclaimed, running back. "My mistress would have tanned me alive if I had forgotten. You are to be at Netherfield tomorrow evening. Do you understand?"

"And what is my payment to be?"

The girl plonked the coin bag on the sill. Elizabeth's eyes widened at the thought of all the extra food that would afford. Not to mention a new pair of gloves for her to wear at the Meryton assembly. She would no longer risk raising eyebrows at her less than adequate wardrobe.

"That is half. The rest is to be yours when you complete your card readings for the party at Netherfield."

Bowing her head and placing her hand over her heart for an extra bit of drama, Elizabeth said, "It would be my very great honour."

The poor, pale servant girl lifted the hem of her skirt and rushed away. Elizabeth shook her head in sympathy for the slight thing who must have a true harpy for a mistress. The coin bag felt wonderfully heavy in her palm as she lifted it up and down a few times. Real money. That was something to be celebrated. Usually, the locals paid her with a dozen eggs, fresh apples, or a green goose freshly killed. She did make coins now and then, but never had her talent for picking up gossip and sketching peoples' characters brought in a satchel this full to the brim. Elizabeth smiled at the thought of adding to it tomorrow evening.

But then the smile faded as she realised that she had never laid eyes on these people before. She would not have the benefit of observing their actions and conversations daily. Her knowledge of any gossip about them was almost nonexistent. Elizabeth had extensive, intimate information, from the lowliest scullery maid to the gentry of the land for miles around, thanks to Hill, her own natural curiosity of people, and a memory that could recount details of the neighbourhood's history.

Suddenly, Elizabeth had the sensation of butterflies in her stomach at the prospect of a true test of her abilities. She inhaled deeply, closed her eyes, and thought of what she already knew.

At least one of the ladies of the house is a silken dragon to make that poor servant girl brave her fear of the forest to come to the hut for a visit. And the lady in question is most likely in love, the main reason people seek the advice of someone like me. The love charm is surely for her. Mr Bingley was to have a sister to keep house for him as I recall. The lady could not be in love with her brother; therefore, it is one of the other gentlemen in the house staying as a guest. The gentleman in question is either not returning her affections or is too shy to display them. So one of the male guests is either of a quiet nature or recalcitrant of her overtures. Mr Bingley, on the other hand, has declared how much he loves dancing and has eagerly accepted Sir William Lucas's invitation to an assembly. I think I can assume he will be of an open, happy nature. However, is he intelligent? Surely, a wealthy, single man would not openly declare his fondness for dancing to be repeated around a neighbourhood certain to be filled with single, young women and mothers eager for a rich son-in-law and not expect to be stalked like a fat stag. Hmmm. Either he is too exuberant for his own good or else very stupid. For one can be intelligent, but heedless. But one can also be jolly, but stupid. I shall know within a few moments of meeting him which he is, I am certain.

After gathering her thoughts, Elizabeth felt more at ease to meet the next evening with confidence. What was one more reading? She was as proficient at this as one could be.

Elizabeth stood and moved to the side of the stone chimney. The river stones were stacked together and narrowed upwards and out through the dense thatched roof. She reached to the side and took one particular stone in her hand. When pulled down and to the left, it slid away with ease. Behind it, in a little nook within the wattle and daub wall was the bundle that held the true tool of her trade.

She removed it and gingerly unwrapped the stack of thick, ancient cards. The hand-painted images upon each card were still vibrant, though Elizabeth suspected that it had been at least a century since the artist who painted them had placed his brush upon the thick board. Based on the style of the images, she guessed they must have been made in Italy and executed by a talented painter. The top two happened to be the images of Il Papa and La Papessa. Not for the first time, Elizabeth marvelled at how such an oddity came to be hidden away at Longbourn.

Hill had been the one to gift them to her after she had discovered that Elizabeth found the entrance to the priest's hole. Elizabeth had been a young lady of thirteen when she discovered the trapdoor in her bedroom floor. It had taken her only a few additional trips to find the sliding slats that opened the false wall at the bottom of the stairs and to venture down the tunnel. Knowing that Hill had been at Longbourn for so very long, she would not rest until the mysteries were explained. That was when Hill had shown her the cards and the trick of the hut. Elizabeth's great-great-grandmother was the last Bennet who "had the gift for seeing in others what they cannot see themselves." After Hill taught her the little she remembered of the meaning of the card pictures, Elizabeth had begun to practise and before long was setting small fires in the fireplace of the hut again. Word spread in the county of Hertfordshire, and Elizabeth had a fairly steady stream of customers, from the gentry down to chambermaids. Fortunately, the cottage lay on a neglected strip of land, part of a nearby estate that had been tied up in a legal dispute for several decades and was of no real consequence to the squabbling parties. Mr Bennet's father had sold the cottage and land in his youth to cover some debts. Added to that was the reputation for being frequented by ghosts, and the local population held it in some fear. Her own father never gave any credence to any of the stories of the cottage, so never bothered to venture to it to determine the validity of the tales that were whispered.

After making her way back to Longbourn through the tunnel, Elizabeth joined the family for the evening meal with a happy heart and that small satchel of coin already placed in the hands of Hill. Elizabeth had only kept out enough to supply herself with a new pair of gloves for the assembly.

The only one of her family who ever questioned these occasional absences was dear Jane.

"Are you quite recovered from what ailed you this afternoon?" Jane asked as they retired to the parlour.

"Yes, I needed a little quiet to recover myself after that long walk this morning. You are well aware that I occasionally ramble too far for my own good. Besides, I had promised a letter to our little cousin, Hattie. Aunt Gardiner is quite insistent that Hattie improve her penmanship, and I am happy to oblige the poor girl with long tales about my adventures. How her eyes must roll when she receives one of my letters!"

Jane shook her head with a laugh. "I am sure you are mistaken about that, Lizzy. Our young cousins hold you in high regard."

"Then my secret plot to overthrow you as their favourite Bennet cousin is quite on schedule. It is only a matter of time before I receive far more adoration than you from the little scamps of Gracechurch Street."

"Oh, Lizzy! I know you jest." Jane laughed. Elizabeth was glad that Jane seemed to have forgotten some of her concern. But she had to be careful around Jane, for though Jane was all that was sweet and good, she was no fool. It would be easy to make that mistake, but Elizabeth knew better.

That night, Elizabeth went to sleep, excited and frightened. True adventure was so seldom a visitor here in the sleepy, rolling hills of Hertfordshire that Elizabeth could not decide which was the stronger emotion for quite a while. It was only after a long sigh and a smile at the thought of her family finally affording some of their favourite foods that Elizabeth was able to drift off with a full stomach and a happy heart.

Chapter 3

A Wish to Forget

A dispirited Fitzwilliam Darcy gazed out at the steely light that tried so valiantly to break through the drizzling, low clouds of the early morning. The candle upon his desk was close to extinguishing after burning through the night.

Darcy sighed. There was no mistaking the weary tone of it. The bleariness he felt in his eyes spoke of another restless night. The sheets of paper in front of him were not nearly as filled as he had anticipated they would be by now. One was a letter to his sister, Georgiana. But his courage to complete it had failed him. It petered out after several lines of asinine observations. He had promised to write to her faithfully, but the words stalled at the tips of his fingers as drops of ink waited patiently to be freed from the pen.

So, in frustration, he had started a very different kind of letter, thinking that would be the solution to his trouble of getting words upon paper. A letter to his steward was a standard, common enough task that Darcy usually enjoyed. Not now, though.

Darcy leaned his head back against the chair. His eyes ignored the unfinished work before him. The dull sunrise just outside the window was all he had the energy to attend to. He slipped his hand under his nightshirt and rubbed the skin just over his heart, hoping to relieve some of the tightness there. But nothing eased it.

Coming here was a mistake. Hertfordshire was a mistake. I should return to Pemberley and be near Georgiana. It was my carelessness in her supervision that brought about this calamity. If I had only— What would my parents think of me? I have failed them. It was only through sheer dumb luck that further tragedy was prevented. I, who laughs at dreams and intuitions, had felt that something was wrong. And it was due to that intuition that Georgiana was pulled from Wickham's power at the last possible moment. I am a fool. I am undeserving of the responsibilities that have been entrusted to me. I should not have left her alone at Pemberley, even though she implored me to give her some time to recover in solitude. I should not have listened. Bingley begged me to come here and see Netherfield, but I should have refused. I should be by Georgiana's side, watching her, protecting her, keeping her in perfect safety. I should—

Self-recrimination could be an exhausting activity, and Darcy's nodding head told him that he had worn himself out thoroughly. He dozed lightly until his man, Crump, entered the room to ready him for the day. It was only when Crump started back from the empty bed and let out a small gasp of surprise that Darcy jolted fully awake in his chair.

"I apologise for my minor outburst, sir. I was surprised by your medicinal remedy. I mistook it for a mouse." Crump sniffed audibly, his disapproval causing Darcy to blink rapidly to awaken. "I shall replace it."

Darcy rubbed his forehead and then his eyes with the palms of his hands. His groggy mind was in no mood for the excellent manners of his valet.

"What the devil are you on about?"

Crump slowly turned, with one arm extended, until he was facing Darcy. From his pinched thumb and forefinger, a small satchel dangled, as far from his body as he was able to get it. Despite his thoroughly foul mood, Darcy could not help but smile at the barely repressed look of disgust on Crump's face.

Darcy grabbed the small bag from him and examined it closely. A waft of herbal smells drifted up to his nose. It was a bit of lace and fine fabric tied up with a red ribbon. The only scent he could truly distinguish was of mint.

"It was under your pillow, sir."

"What is it? Something to keep the bed from becoming infested with vermin?"

"I think not, sir."

Darcy looked up into Crump's face. Was there the slightest upward curve of his mouth?

"If the chambermaid did not put it under my pillow and neither did you, then who did and for what reason?" Darcy demanded, beginning to feel a rather desperate need for a cup of coffee.

Crump cleared his throat discreetly. Darcy knew this was how the man prepared himself for the telling of uncomfortable news.

"Yes?" Darcy demanded again.

"I believe, sir, it may be a charm of some sort."

"A what?"

"It was discussed—in the servants' quarters, you understand—that Miss Bingley's maid, a rather lovely young woman by the name of Kate who was a little overly excited from her adventure, visited an old woman who lives in a hut in the woods a few miles from here. She sells charms and reads cards. Kate arranged for the old woman to entertain here tonight and made an additional purchase of this charm to aid her mistress in her, well...her fondest of hopes."

Darcy was certain he must look as horrified as he felt. He glanced at Crump, at the satchel in his palm, and then back at Crump. Crump wisely kept his face a mask of benevolent passivity.

"Are you seriously telling me that Miss Bingley had her maid put a love charm under my pillow?"

"So it would seem, sir."

Darcy flung the satchel into the fireplace. It smouldered for a moment on the red embers before blooming into a flame. A cloud of minty smoke drifted up. Darcy stood and angrily pulled his nightshirt off over his head. He balled it up and threw it in the chair before the desk. His unfinished letters fluttered upwards for a moment as if attempting to take flight before resettling back into stillness. Darcy breathed deeply, eyes squeezed shut, hands on his hips, naked as a robin as he battled to control his fuming temper.

"Crump?"

"Yes, sir?"

"Never mention anything about this to anyone ever, either to me or in the servants' quarters."

"Of course, sir."

"Right. I am ready to dress."

Darcy tried to get through the day with as few encounters with Miss Bingley as possible. Every time they were in each other's company, however, he could not help but notice there was a certain anticipatory sharpness in how she watched him. He was accustomed to her persistent observations of his sitting styles, the rapidity of his writing, his techniques for holding books, and how often he might sneeze during a blustery day. Miss Bingley was eager to offer him helpful advice on any topic in which he might have the slightest interest. He was inured to all that nonsense. But the predatory way she observed him today was truly unsettling.

There was no doubt in Darcy's mind that Miss Bingley wished to catch any glimmer of change in him. Had the fragrant trinket worked? Had she struck upon a minty machination that he would not be able to resist? Would he soon be sweeping her into his arms?

Darcy, still feeling the ill effects of another sleepless night, was in no mood for this increased surveillance. Like a rabbit being sniffed out by a hound, slowly and methodically, while hiding in a hedgerow. He went on a long ride for much of the day, hoping to both tire himself and to avoid the focused eyes of Miss Bingley. Perhaps, Darcy reasoned, if he rode far and hard, he would fall into an exhausted sleep tonight. He did not return until late in the afternoon.

Bingley greeted him as he came into the hall. "Thank goodness you arrived! We are dining earlier this evening, for Caroline arranged for some after-dinner entertainment. I will admit that my sister can be overstepping in her plans on occasion, but this sounds like jolly good fun."

"Let me guess. An old woman is coming to tell us all about ourselves."

Bingley's eyes widened. "Darcy! How on earth could you have possibly known that?"

Darcy slapped his gloves into his palm with an exasperated air. "Oh, I do not know, perhaps I have the gift of foresight and it ought to be me whose palm you cross with silver."

"Be serious! Did Crump tell you? You have quite a treasure there, Darcy. He always seems to hear and see things. Sometimes I suspect that is why you appear to be far and away the cleverest one in the room."

"Or maybe I *am* the cleverest man in the room. Look, Bingley, I shan't take part in all that silliness with the fortune-teller, so count me out."

Bingley looked crestfallen. "Oh, but you must! Caroline insists that everyone visit the woman in private. She has quite the buzzing bee in her bonnet about the entire thing. You know she will hound me endlessly until you relent. So, if you could just spare a few moments? As a favour to a friend? Hmmm?"

Darcy sighed, too weary in spirit to resist. He often felt sorry for Bingley, having two such sisters to deal with. Especially as the most difficult one appeared to be reaching a point where the possibility of her remaining permanently unmarried and on her brother's hands was becoming more of a sure reality.

Though Georgiana has caused me so much worry and sorrow these past months, I am grateful to have a kind, bright younger sister. If I had sisters such as Bingley has, I may have fled the country.

"All right, Bingley. As a favour to you, for the sake of your peace of mind, I will have my future told by the sibyl of Hertfordshire."

Chapter 4

Extensive Reading(s)

Elizabeth fidgeted with her veil, moving it to settle just so over her face. Her first reading away from the cottage in the woods and her first glimpse of the much-discussed new residents of Netherfield had her in a state of high anticipation. The only disadvantage was that she would be unable to share any observations from her clandestine visit to Netherfield with Charlotte or Jane. That was unfortunate, but such things could not be avoided. Even if the neighbourhood had been in full possession of all to be known of Mr Bingley and his guests, Hill had frequently reminded her of the impropriety of sharing anything that was discussed during a reading. It was a breach of a sacred trust, not to be attempted. So, Elizabeth was resigned that she would have to pretend surprise during the Meryton assembly and behave as if she were laying eyes upon the party for the very first time.

Elizabeth glanced around the Netherfield library. She shifted her weight in the chair and pulled at the long, baggy black gown she was wearing, adjusting it more comfortably. The room was set just as she had discussed with Hill earlier. Though she wore a veil and an old, black bonnet with long sides, the lighting of the room and placement of the chairs were of paramount importance. Elizabeth's chair was angled so that the low fire was just to her back and side. The only other illumination in the room was one candle placed on a table directly behind her chair. Anyone sitting in the chair opposite her would be also looking towards the only lights in the room. It would add to the obfuscation of her face, if any were so bold as to study her intently.

Typically, people were hesitant to look directly at her when she was dressed as the old woman. It was as if they were very slightly scared of her, the way one is scared of a horse that has a bad reputation for startling and kicking out. Fear could be a powerful persuader.

Elizabeth smiled to herself as she recalled the time that Sir William Lucas had come to visit her little cottage to gain insight into a rather large investment that he was contemplating. Unless she was very much mistaken, he had been trembling slightly as she laid the cards down under the bars of the window. She had wisely interpreted the cards in a way that would make him more cautious of future investments, for the thing sounded rather ridiculous to her. She did not think that lemon mines in southern Spain was the actual way that the fruit was obtained. The last thing she wanted to see was her friend Charlotte Lucas plunged into poverty by the poor investments of her father. Charlotte was quite brilliant, but her father had gained his fortune through luck and being in a fortuitous place at a propitious time rather than due to any greatness of mind.

Elizabeth sighed, grateful that she could claim at least one intelligent parent. Her father only lacked any ambition or foresight that could have taken advantage of his natural quickness. She tried not to dwell too long on anything that approached the recrimination of her father. As much as her mother regarded Elizabeth with indifference, her father looked on her with pride. So it made her uncomfortable to examine the ways in which he could have been a better provider to the Bennet family and the Longbourn estate.

As she looked around, the shelves of books in the library were just barely visible in the dimness. Elizabeth would have loved to pass each row and truly examine the collection, for Netherfield had been shuttered for so long that this was her first time in this room. She thought she could just make out some titles of poetry that would have been pleasant to crack open, when a shuffle just beyond the library door caused her to shift back deeper into her seat.

And so it begins, the very first reading.

A tall, imperious woman with one long, burgundy feather shooting up from her hair entered the room. Her matching gown was of the finest quality, and her hair was artfully coiffed. There was a slight upturn of her nose and stony set of her lips that gave an observer the impression that a cat had used a corner of the room for a chamber pot. She had an air of perpetual disapproval.

Elizabeth was grateful for the veil as she could not help but smile slightly. She thought the woman would have been extraordinarily beautiful but for that sour visage.

So this is the lady who commanded her frightened maid to come to my cottage. Of course she would insist on being first. She will gleefully tell everyone else any little thing to discredit me or use any dowdiness of my appearance as a source of merriment for the others. I hope the man she has her sights on can discern these qualities in her. But perhaps he is equally unpleasant and they are well suited to each other. Only time will tell.

Without being asked to enter farther, the woman marched in and sat opposite Elizabeth, ramrod straight in the chair, and looked down her nose. Her glance fell on the small table between them and the cards upon it, then back up at Elizabeth. Her eyes flashed, prepared to be angered or disappointed, or perhaps both at once. Elizabeth allowed the silence to spread. It was always a way to test the nature of the person. How did they respond to silence?

After a few more moments, a blush of anger spread across the woman's fine cheeks. "Well? I am the sister of the master of this house, Mr Bingley. I am Miss Caroline Bingley, and if I am not very much mistaken, I have paid you quite well to come here this evening and provide us with some diversion from—" She glanced around the room in undisguised disgust. "—from the tediousness of this awful place."

Well, Elizabeth thought to herself as she grasped her deck of cards from the table, *there are no hidden layers to be peeled off this onion. That makes my job easier.*

Elizabeth cleared her throat and did her best impression of a severely sore throat. "You must prepare a question in your mind, but keep it to yourself," she rasped out. "Some matter you wish to have guidance on. The cards will provide clarity."

"Do you mean to say that it will not be the future you tell me? Really? That seems like an unfair exchange. I was under the clear impression that you were to provide insight into the future. Not some sort of advice that I could ask a dozen friends for. All of them much *cleaner* and more well informed than the likes of you, old woman."

Elizabeth sighed and pressed on, knowing that there was no chance that Miss Bingley would storm out. If she did, she would miss out on a delicious story to be told and retold to the wealthy, bored members of the London *ton* during the approaching winter season. Elizabeth shuffled the cards, offered the deck to Miss Bingley to cut, which she did as if they were drenched in blood, and then peeled off the top three cards. Carefully, Elizabeth placed them in a line in front of her and studied them in silence.

"Well? Tell what there is to tell, old croaker, before I have you tossed out on your ear," Miss Bingley demanded.

"The cards must be allowed to speak to me in their own time. Otherwise, it may encourage an unfolding of events that could prove disastrous. You would not wish your concern to have a disastrous outcome, would you?"

That took Miss Bingley down a peg. Her colour paled slightly. She attempted a genuine smile—*attempted* being the key word. "Oh, take your time, take your time. I was merely hoping to move things along."

They both leaned over the cards and looked in silence. After another minute, Elizabeth pressed back in her seat and templed the tips of her fingers. This posture always conveyed a sense of a trance that people found very in keeping with the moment. She locked her eyes on the very first card in the row of three and let her gaze unfocus and her breath slow.

Elizabeth deepened her voice so that it would sound grave and wise. "The first card is the Knight of Wands—he is mounted on a mighty steed, setting off for adventure. The mountains behind him are the things that he will attempt to conquer. This card represents your past. You have been on the precipice of staking claim to new territory or a new partner. If you are in search of a husband, the mountains may indicate conquests that may occur in your very near future."

There was little mistaking the instantaneous, blushing glow on Caroline Bingley's face. It was crystal clear that this woman was on the hunt for a very particular gentleman. The love charm of salt and mint had been for the underside of the mystery man's pillow.

I have indeed struck upon it. That is the reason I am here this evening. Although the glow on her cheek can hardly be called love. It more resembles the look of Sir William Lucas's favourite hunting hound when he is lording over a juicy piece of chop. It is a look of proud possessiveness, not a heart burning with passion.

"The next card is the Six of Wands." Elizabeth brought her finger down upon the second card in the row. "It is again a man on a horse, riding through a crowd of his peers. He looks proud, yes? The crowd is praising him. They admire him. He has prestige and honour above the crowd."

"And the card represents?" Miss Bingley asked, breathlessly anxious.

"It is more how the present moment is unfolding for you. This is how you see yourself now, how the world sees you."

A smug smile crossed Miss Bingley's lips. Whatever or whomever she had been scheming for, this reading seemed to be confirming every belief she had. Every desire was there before her, and it was clear that she found the prospect glorious.

But now Elizabeth studied the third and final card—a thorny patch that she must tread carefully around lest she get stuck and bleed. It was good her face was so shaded, for her brows were knit together in thought. Miss Bingley was obviously a terror in the finest lace. Should Elizabeth read this card absolutely truly, her fee would be withheld. She knew it in her bones. That was the kind of woman who sat opposite her. The words needed to be vague and like a cloud passing in the sky. Miss Bingley's imagination could project upon the words what she wished.

"And the final card? Old woman, are you awake?"

"Ah, forgive me, my throat has become parched. Perhaps you could bring me some watered-down wine? I am not as young as I once was for such readings."

Miss Bingley brought her finger down upon the last card with a forceful thud. "What is the meaning of this final card?"

Elizabeth looked down at The Tower card. Calamity. Drastic, unexpected change. Unforeseen forces that one cannot predict. The card pictured a tall tower being struck by lightning and two people falling to the earth, helpless and doomed. "It is a sign of change. Sudden change."

Miss Bingley frowned. "Good change?"

"It could be, yes. All change is good to some and evil to others."

Elizabeth could see by the narrowing of Miss Bingley's eyes that she was on the verge of losing out on the rest of her coins. So, she rallied her thoughts and proceeded with extreme caution. "But, judging by the most wonderful, the most excellent cards that came before it, in my humble opinion, it will be a change for the good."

But for whose good, that has yet to be seen. It would be wise for me to stay quiet on that particular point.

Elizabeth had said enough, for this woman probably believed that the sun and moon had been created for her convenience. Miss Bingley stood immediately, no longer even looking in Elizabeth's direction. There was an air of confidence that caused her to appear even taller than when she first came into the library. She was a general who had no fear as to whether she would be victorious in an approaching battle.

Without a word to the hunched, veiled figure before the fire, Miss Bingley turned to leave. There was no acknowledgement, gratitude or—much to Elizabeth's concern—jangling purse of coin.

As Miss Bingley grasped the handle of the door, Elizabeth asked, "May I have a small glass of watered wine? To coat my throat before the next reading? I would be so very—"

The door slammed shut, leaving Elizabeth alone in the dim library.

"—grateful," she muttered to the empty room.

The next to enter the library was a tittering, shorter, plumper version of Miss Bingley. Not as beautiful or elegant, but they were clearly related. Elizabeth guessed this was a sister or cousin of Mr and Miss Bingley. She was gratified that her assumptions proved correct when the visibly nervous woman introduced herself.

"This is so terribly exciting. I am Mrs Hurst. My sister Caroline was so clever to think of this for the evening's entertainment. It will be so much fun to tell our acquaintances of it when we return to London. Only a few of our circle have ever had a card reading before. It is very in fashion at the moment. Only the most terribly elegant have had a reading, it is so rare to find a teller to read the cards. I must tell you that I am so very concerned about my husband, Mr Hurst. I am always worried that he will meet with an accident when hunting. Guns misfire so very often, do they not? Or when he is riding. Horses are so cruelly skittish, when a sudden noise disturbs them or someone accidentally steps out into the path before them, even if it is no more than a lady out for a stroll! Or when he is out playing cards with friends. Would it not be terrible if he were called out for a duel? A matter of honour to be settled? How sad I would be if he were shot through the heart! I do so worry about him. I suppose he could be accidentally killed by an acquaintance while they were out shooting, do you not agree? One does hear of such things occurring. And then London itself can be so very hazardous for men who like to be in their cups once in a while, not that I am saying that Mr Hurst drinks to excess. No. I would never *say* that. But even a few drinks can cause the most upstanding of men not to notice a runaway carriage. It happens far more frequently than one would suppose. Just crossing the street and—well, you know. Ha, ha! Suddenly some poor widow must plan for a funeral and the mourning clothes. Black does not become me at all, but one must adhere to the standards expected."

By the time the woman stopped talking, Elizabeth was more than a little concerned over the well-being of Mr Hurst. Was it typical for wives to speculate so endlessly on their husbands' future death? Elizabeth reflected on her own mother and her persistent fretting about the encroaching hedgerows if Mr Bennet should die before his daughters were married. She considered asking Jane or Charlotte about this later, as it seemed to be a topic of importance to wed ladies. Though, in defence of Mrs Bennet, she did not ever recall her mother creating so many macabre scenarios when discussing the subject. Underneath the bickering and complaints, there did seem to exist a begrudging affection between her mother and father.

Elizabeth wanted this reading over and done with as soon as possible. So, after a very rapid card read in which accident, calamity, or fatal tragedy played no part, she ended the session. A visibly disappointed Mrs Hurst rose to leave.

"Could you perhaps send in a glass of wine?" Elizabeth asked. "Very watered-down, of course. The work of interpreting the cards can make the throat dry. I would be so thankful."

"Not a single accident. I cannot believe it," Mrs Hurst muttered to herself as she left the library without a thank you or a tip.

Elizabeth sat back in her chair and groaned in frustration, for she was truly becoming quite thirsty. It was turning into a long evening of tiresome, conniving people to deal with.

"What? Hallo, there! Has no one brought you food or drink? I apologise. What a neglectful host I am, to be sure. Do forgive me, yes?"

A handsome, young man with a broad smile and sandy locks popped his head back out of the library door and hallooed for a servant. To Elizabeth's relief, she heard an order for refreshments to be served.

"Quite an oversight on my part, I assure you. We cannot have a guest labouring away without a chance to refresh themselves, can we?"

"Thank you, young man."

The man—whom Elizabeth immediately put down as none other than the famous Mr Bingley—sat down opposite her. His ready smile and open countenance were infectious. She could easily imagine him announcing to everyone how very much he loved to dance. Beneath her veil, she could not help but smile back at him.

"I say, this has been one of Caroline's better ideas. What a jolly way to pass an evening. Though the quiet of the country does not bother me half as much as it does my sisters. They are very much at home in the noise and smoke of London. Which, I confess, I do enjoy up to a point as well. But it is so beautiful here in Hertfordshire that I can imagine no better place to live."

A servant brought in a tray with refreshments for Elizabeth. But, not wanting to lift her veil and risk Mr Bingley glimpsing her face that was decidedly not old and wrinkled, she decided to wait until his reading was finished.

After the servant had departed, Mr Bingley clapped his hands together with a laugh and said, "Shall we begin? Do not feel the need to hold back, if you see anything unpleasant! I am able to tolerate bad news very well indeed."

"I have no doubt, young man," Elizabeth muttered as she shuffled the deck three times. "Now, clear your mind of all other thoughts and—"

Mr Bingley had closed his eyes tightly. "I say, that is rather harder than you would think it would be. Just when one thought is swept away, another comes and replaces it. It is rather like trying to bail out a boat with just your hands. I think that it is far more difficult a task to clear one's mind than one would assume. I have so many thoughts, racing one after the other—"

"Young man, you will achieve your goal more rapidly with the aid of silence. Now, clear your mind and focus on what guidance you seek. A subject that you desire clarification about."

With his eyes still squeezed shut, he nodded rapidly. "Right!"

Mr Bingley was charmingly candid and enthusiastic. He was such a contrast to his sisters, it was difficult to believe they had come from the same family. But then her uncle, Mr Gardiner, was very different from his two sisters, so it was not a wholly uncommon occurrence.

"Please, open your eyes and cut the deck, trying to keep that thought in reach."

The gentleman did as he was told, and Elizabeth laid out the three top cards.

The first was the Ace of Stars. "A new path has opened to you in the recent past. Do you see the hand holding the star? That is it. The fields behind it are fertile and lush. Your new path is verdant."

"Netherfield, surely. We very recently moved here. It must be Netherfield of which you speak."

Elizabeth could hardly keep from laughing, for Mr Bingley was at the edge of his seat in eagerness. This session was a refreshing balm after his wearisome sisters.

"The second card is The Hermit. How you are now, at this very moment. It is an old man in a robe, holding a lantern. He is alone, but that does not necessarily mean that he is lonely."

He frowned. "But I am not at all like a hermit. My friend Darcy would say that I seek out company far too much."

Darcy? Perhaps that is the name of the man for whom Miss Bingley is buying up love charms. Hmmm. I wonder if he shall make an appearance next? He must be rather handsome to excite such a fervour in such a lady. Or else he is extremely rich. Or both. Miss Bingley does not strike me as one who would settle for anything less than her own quite high standards.

"You misunderstand, young man. The card does not tell who you are, merely what you are experiencing at the present moment. Are you not more quiet in your life here in the country?"

"Why, yes, I am more subdued. There are no social calls every day or events every night, so I suppose I am living a more hermit-like existence."

"And you see the lantern the old man is holding? He is lighting the way for others. Are you showing others how to act? How to proceed?"

Mr Bingley looked thoughtful for a moment, then grinned broadly. "I should think it may be the other way around! For my sister Caroline is always telling me *what* to do. And Darcy is considered a very respectable gentleman whom she would like me to emulate. You know, buy a grand estate, consult with others as to the best way the country ought to be run, make clever business investments, that sort of thing. I do not quite see how I could possibly be guiding them in any matter of importance."

"Perhaps you are wise in other ways that your family and acquaintances are not. Such as wisdom, matters of the heart, compassion."

This gave Bingley pause. "I suppose, if I do stop to think on the subject, that it is I who is most enjoying the country living here. Getting out every day, hunting up something for dinner, buying a large basket of fresh apples from the farm next door, polishing my gun at night. Yes, I think I see your way of thinking on things. I do enjoy my time here and wish the others could be as appreciative. So, in a way, I suppose I am lighting the way." His expression took on a wistful look as he paused and gazed into the fire, then said, "The only thing that would make it perfect is the pretty face of a loving wife to greet me in the mornings when the birds are singing their loudest. I should very much—" Mr Bingley looked back at Elizabeth with a blush on his face and a shake of his head.

"Pardon me, I did not intend to wax on about such a delicate subject. It was unconscionably rude of me. Pay no heed to my ramblings."

"It is to be expected, young man. You are gazing at your inner landscape and finding what pleases you and what does not. It is a good thing, not a bad thing."

He eagerly leaned in towards the third and final card on the table. "And that one?"

"That is the Two of Swords." Elizabeth leaned back, weighing her words carefully, for she had the impression that this gentleman could be easily swayed by the words of others and she did not wish to speak anything that might be too persuasive upon his judgement. "The woman is holding two crossed swords. But she is blindfolded. She is unable to fully see all the facts before her or where each path will lead. The two swords indicate that two paths will open before you. One path is full of logic and sense. The other path is for your intuition. It is usually advisable to follow the second path, which is also the way of your heart."

"Well, I'm not sure what *that* is about. Hmmm."

Elizabeth shrugged and held her hands, palms up, over the cards. "Perhaps the decision is not before you. Yet."

"Ahhh, I see. Very good. This has been the most interesting evening. I should allow you time to refresh yourself before the next one is sent in.

Thank you." He rose and turned to leave, his face bright with the fun of the reading.

Mr Bingley paused at the door. "Did my sister Caroline pay you yet?"

"No. The rest of the coin she owes has not been passed to me."

He dug in his pockets for a moment before placing a very tidy sum on the table near Elizabeth. It was much more than what his sister had intended to pay, she was certain.

"Thank you so very much for your generosity, but I must protest. It is too much that you give to me."

"Not at all. Do not think upon the matter, it was well-earned, I assure you. Thank you for the jolly evening. What fun! I think I have much to ponder."

After a quick drink and a bite of the fruit and bread that were on the tray, Elizabeth stood for a moment to stretch her back. Being constantly hunched over, in the aspect of an elderly woman, could become wearisome. A rattle of the door handle caused her to sit suddenly back down.

Will this be the mysterious Mr Darcy of whom everyone speaks so highly? A man who advises and leads? A serious man held up as an example for the gregarious Mr Bingley to emulate? A man handsome or rich enough to make the shrewish Miss Bingley insensible? For it is clear that she must have her cap set at him.

The man who entered was red in the face, overweight, and had a distinctly bleary look in his eye.

Ah. No. This must be Mr Hurst, whose wife hopes for accidents and misfortune so that she may once again be on the hunt for a husband. Poor fellow.

Mr Hurst sat and took a swig from the glass of port that he had brought in for himself. He made a sloshy wave over the cards. "None of that nonsense for me, thank you! If I do not come in here for a few minutes, those ladies will berate me till I am forced to go to bed early. Poor Darcy, they are wearing him down right now."

Elizabeth obeyed his wishes, and they sat in silence for a few moments.

"Too bad a good game of cards cannot be had with those things," Mr Hurst said with a nod at the deck.

"Oh, but it can. The cards were first created long ago in Italy for the purpose of playing a game. Let me explain the rules to you. You could easily modify a deck you have in your possession to suit as this one does."

This caused Mr Hurst to perk right up. He and Elizabeth spent a very pleasant half an hour going through the rules of the ancient card game and trying out a few practise hands. At the end of their time, Mr Hurst had a twinkle in his eye and a laugh in his words.

"I am very eager to show the lads at my club this new game! Or perhaps I should say a very old game, yes? It will be quite the thing, I am sure. Old Rollins will not be able to dupe me quite so easily with this one."

"I am glad that you are pleased, sir."

Mr Hurst tossed a coin on the table before straining himself up and out of the chair.

"Thank you, sir. You are most kind. May you have good fortune and no accidents in your future."

Elizabeth was truly beginning to feel quite fatigued. Never before had she been in the character of the fortune-teller for so long. She hoped that she would be able to catch a glimpse of this mysterious Mr Darcy, give him a quick reading, and be on her way.

A knock at the library door made her start. No one else had knocked.

"Please, do come in," she said in her raspy voice that was uncomfortably scratchy.

The door opened and the profile of a man was dimly lit by the light of the weak fire and the single candle. In that one, unforeseen moment, everything changed. Where Elizabeth's steady, constant heart had once been, there was a wild, winged thing that beat and fought against her cage of ribs. The violence of the sensation caused her to hold her breath. Her veil hid her look of astonishment as she openly stared at him. He stood at the door, hesitating.

Then he spoke in a rich, deep voice that vibrated through her entire body. "May I enter, madam?"

Elizabeth could only nod and gesture towards the chair opposite her. He strode across the room. She could not recall ever having seen a man so handsome, gentlemanly, and tall. He was dark and stately, but there was a curve of his lips that hinted at a gentle, loving nature deep within. Every fold of his cravat was meticulously in place. The black curls of hair were swept to one side in an effortlessly casual, but controlled manner. His dark eyes spoke of a mind that dwelt on many subjects with depth and consideration. He sat down, crossed both his legs and arms, and sank back into the cushions of the chair.

Elizabeth's breath came back to her in a sudden rush. It felt like the very first breath she had ever truly taken in her life. The man looked at her with concern.

"Are you unwell? Should I fetch someone to attend to you?" he asked, peering at her through the veil, obviously unable to make out any distinguishing features upon her face.

Elizabeth could barely compose a thought to respond with. His eyes were rich and fathomless. She felt herself bound by his gaze, unable to think clearly. For the first time ever, her mind and body were shaken to the core by a man in whose presence she had not spent more than a few moments. All of the novels she had read of love instantly and irrationally springing upon a person finally made sense. She no longer thought of those descriptions with incredulity and mocking doubt. With every impulse of self-preservation she possessed, Elizabeth made herself recall her surroundings and her present circumstances.

"I am well, Mr Darcy," she whispered shakily, no longer having to make an effort to disguise her voice.

"I see others have mentioned me earlier this evening," he said dryly as he let his gaze wander to the fireplace and the shelves of books. "I cannot say that I am particularly surprised."

He stood suddenly and moved to the fireplace. "An evening chill is in the air. If you will permit me, I will place another log on the fire."

"Thank you, that is very kind. I was becoming cool." Elizabeth felt a tremble through her entire body, though whether it was from cold or the presence of this man, she could not say. As a flume of sparks rose up from the log he placed down, his face was warmly lit and any hint of chill in her body was rapidly replaced by a surge of heat.

Once the fire had been stoked back up to a small blaze, Mr Darcy sat down and turned his gaze towards her. Elizabeth forced herself to squeeze her eyes shut and calm her heart. She knew the most important thing for her to do now was to gather as many titbits of information as she could by simply observing him in the steady silence. She opened her eyes. Mr Darcy was now staring at the fire, seemingly forgetful of the woman who sat across from him. But Elizabeth could tell by the sagging of the skin around his eyes and the occasional flare of his nostrils that something was weighing heavily on his mind. As his gaze stayed on the fire, it was clear to her that many thoughts raced through his brain, urgent and troublesome. These subjects obviously brought him no pleasure. A full minute passed in silence. The occasional pop of the fresh log in the fire as it tried to catch fully echoed through the library. The only other sound was their breath. Once, Mr Darcy's breath started to race, his brows furrowed, and he looked as if he would gladly wish to outrun something that plagued him.

Elizabeth, compelled to comfort him by a desire that was entirely new to her, said, "Something presses in on you, from all sides, I think. It is not a happy thought. There is a darkness to the burden which you carry. The burden is heavy."

Mr Darcy turned his head towards her, his brooding parted by a startled look. "Is that what you guess?"

"It is what I know. The face of a person, even the most taciturn, can tell much. If one is willing to watch."

Elizabeth waited, her breath held.

Will the next words out of his mouth be outrage and anger? He will be difficult to anticipate. The waters in him are deep and quiet, but that can drown one in an unexpected eddy of turbulence.

With a slight grin, Mr Darcy said, "I imagine after many decades of telling people what they want to hear so that you may anticipate a larger payment, it has become second nature for you to glean as much as possible through observation. A fine lady would claim that she is a student of sketching the characters of others."

"I am no fine lady, as you see." Elizabeth smiled to herself at the truth of this confession, with or without her disguise. "But some of what you say is the truth."

With a start, Elizabeth realised that more time had passed than she had perceived. She noticed that she craved to be in this man's company for as long as possible. The longing was so strong, it ached through her entire being. She chased this notion away and brought herself back to the reason for her visit to Netherfield.

"You must bring to mind a particular situation that you wish for clarity on. If there is a certain worry for which guidance would be of aid. Bring that into your mind, clearly and focused."

For just a moment, Elizabeth thought she saw the merest hint of true concern race across his countenance. But then, the mask of stolid indifference returned.

He is closed off, arms crossed, legs crossed. The bridge is up and the portcullis is down. He is a sceptic. Good, that is far more challenging than the wide-eyed girls who come to me without a doubt in their minds. But there is more than mere scepticism—he is protecting himself. There are shadows under his eyes that come from more than one sleepless night. Worry has left a crease on his forehead. Concern. But for what? He is obviously a man of some means; his clothes are well made, but understated. That gives the impression of one who appreciates wealth, but does not hold it above all else in importance. So the worry is probably not money. What would worry a man such as him—comfortable, handsome, intelligent? An obligation. A responsibility. Not of something, of someone. A friend? Unlikely to cause such deep discomfort. Family? A parent? A sibling? Perhaps. Perhaps a sister. Or perhaps an aunt or mother. A man such as him would feel particularly protective of a female relative.

"Shall I see what the cards have to tell us this evening?"

"If you wish," he replied in a nonchalant manner. "I have to have something to tell those ladies in the other room, so you might as well ply your craft in earnest."

"I understand that the ladies were quite persistent in their demand that everyone partake in this diversion." Elizabeth bit her lip. In her newly turbulent mood, she had slipped into speaking in a manner that was not quite consistent with a bedraggled fortune-teller who lived in the smoky cottage. She noticed that Mr Darcy sat up straighter and regarded her with increased interest. Elizabeth felt a blush of anger flash across her cheeks at her own folly.

"It is to be expected, I suppose, with a novel experience such as this," he said. "I am certain that the two ladies you met with previously will retell this adventure many times at balls and parties filled with friends and acquaintances. By the dozenth or so narration, you will have been endowed with fantastical powers and a magical appearance."

"I suppose I am flattered that, in the retelling only, I shall perhaps have wings on my back and flames from my nose."

Mr Darcy laughed and relaxed farther back into his chair. Elizabeth felt even more drawn to him now that she witnessed a flash of merriment in his face, no matter how fleeting. The thought enveloped her that nothing in this world could be more pleasing than watching this reserved man smile broadly and laugh loudly.

Five minutes alone with Mr Darcy and you forget all of your skills! Get a hold of yourself before you accidentally betray something about your true identity. You have seen a handsome face before.

It was true that a handsome face was nothing new to Elizabeth, but it was the combination of all Mr Darcy's qualities that was the fresh experience. She had to remind herself that all he saw was an old woman. He had no idea that beneath this veil was the second—or perhaps third or fifth, according to her mother—most beautiful Bennet sister.

Elizabeth shuffled the cards with shaky hands and let Darcy cut them. Then she drew the top three cards and laid them side by side. She glanced up to see that, though Darcy sat far back in his chair, limbs still crossed before him like weapons, his eyes were focused intently on the little table.

"The first card is the King of Swords. He sits alone on his throne with his sword in his hand and the crown upon his head—decisive, in control, independent, capable, and in his element. In relation to your concerns, this is the past. You have always acted with your strong hand ruling above your heart. Logic and adherence to the rules directed your actions and probably served you well. You have been stern, honest, honourable, and disciplined with your responsibilities, yourself, and your fortune. Although you may have seemed cool and unconcerned to others, that can sometimes hide that you can truly feel quite warmly."

Elizabeth paused and glanced up at Mr Darcy. His face was unreadable, but the glint in his eyes told her that he was listening very closely to her every word. His lips were slightly parted as his breath came in short bursts.

"The second card is The Hanged Man. He is hanging by one ankle, upside down with his arms tied behind his back, from the branch of a tree. He is helpless and bound. This is the present. You may be indecisive, uncertain, and powerless to act on the thing that concerns you. It is a time that you must use to develop patience and wisdom so that you will make the proper decisions in the future. But the inability to act as you wish and even the possibilities of humiliation and embarrassment can cause you pain in the moment. Use this time wisely so that you will be better prepared for future problems."

Elizabeth again dared a glance up. There was a steeliness in Mr Darcy's eyes, as if he was indeed gathering some inner strength to him. She thought that it must be very unpleasant to be opposed to this man if he felt he was acting justly.

"The final card is the Seven of Cups. That means there are many possibilities that will open up to you for the future. Unexpected paths that you could not have previously imagined. Some of them will lead to earthly things such as riches and power. But if you are humble, selfless, forgiving and, most importantly, willing to follow your heart and not your head"—Elizabeth pointed at the cup at the very top that appeared to glow more brightly than the other six cups on the card—"you will make the best choice for your happiness and to live up to your highest destiny. Although, perhaps, it may not be the path you could have predicted for yourself."

She glanced up at Mr Darcy and discerned a chaotic blend of emotions running through him. Though his tightly clenched jaw let none of them show upon his face, his eyes told of a battle within that ranged from hopeful to anger. Elizabeth quietly sat back and allowed the man to study the cards at his leisure.

Both of them sat silently as the light of the fire waned further into darkness. Finally, Mr Darcy raised his eyes to Elizabeth, his brow furrowed.

"Who are you?" he whispered.

Elizabeth swallowed hard, knowing what she had told him had cut close to the bone. "No one of importance, sir. Just a hungry woman telling what the cards have to say so that she may earn her bread." She felt no guilt in this admission since it was so very close to the truth.

Mr Darcy stared so unceasingly that, though she knew her face was obscured by the veil and dim lighting, Elizabeth felt increasingly uncomfortable. She greatly desired to shift in her chair or stand and walk about the room, but she knew well that a mind such as his would become suspicious by any sign of discomfort. She forced her muscles to be still and her breath to be calm.

Finally, Mr Darcy blinked and stared into the fire.

"There were some true things in what you said," he muttered in a hushed tone. "But I do not believe in mystical arts."

Elizabeth shrugged. "That is your decision alone to make. I believe that most people hear what they want to hear. They only hear what serves to carry them further to their chosen goal. Very few people actually listen rather than just hear. The very wise among my visitors attempt to listen and understand. Then they learn what they need to know about themselves. There is little mystery or mysticism to it."

Mr Darcy looked at her in earnest for another period of silence. Then he stood so suddenly that she almost startled back.

"I think you are saying that in order to truly benefit from this time with you, a person must be able to hear even that which is unpleasant or not anticipated. Perhaps those things were already within and looking at them can be an uncomfortable experience."

Elizabeth could only give the smallest of nods.

"I thank you for your time, madam. This has indeed been surprisingly interesting."

He reached into his pocket, then laid several coins upon the table.

"Sir, Mr Bingley has already been very generous."

"I can easily believe that to be so. But still, I appreciate your time and wish you the best. The past half an hour has been very..." He paused, a small smile turning up one corner of his mouth. "It has been very enlightening, thank you, madam. Good evening."

Mr Darcy gave her a small bow and left the room. Elizabeth let out an enormous exhale and, smiling, picked up the coins. They twinkled in her palm from the glow of the fire. But she barely saw them as the emotions of the past half an hour washed through her.

Such a man as he, I have never seen before! I wish I could have been dressed as myself and spoken as myself. Perhaps, when he sees me as I truly am, and I am able to speak freely as Elizabeth Bennet, he may want to converse further. Maybe we will even dance together.

She smiled broadly at this idea. *Dancing with Mr Darcy.* It sent an unexpected curl of shivers coursing up her spine. She reached out to gather the cards from the table. The image of passing Mr Darcy slowly during a long set—taking up his hands in hers, their bodies nearing and pushing away from each other, almost touching during each thrust and retreat of the dance—made her pause. Suddenly, she realised that she was looking forward to the Meryton assembly as she had never anticipated a dance before. More specifically, Elizabeth was wishing with an eager, hopeful heart for a particular handsome, stately dance partner.

Is this how Kitty and Lydia feel when an assembly approaches? No wonder they are nothing but smiles and giggles for days beforehand.

Chapter 5

Not a Slight Slight

Elizabeth could feel the trembling of her hands as she entered the Meryton assembly. She squeezed them tight together in an effort to quell their shaking.

"Lizzy," Jane said, "you look so very beautiful tonight."

"Thank you, Jane. I would return the compliment, but it is such common knowledge that you are an exceptional beauty that I feel silly repeating it. I would not want to be accused of lacking in conversation, only able to parrot what many have said before me."

"Oh, Lizzy, you do make me laugh."

The two sisters held hands as they walked across the large room to greet Charlotte. Elizabeth could not help but glance around, not wishing to miss the moment when Mr Darcy entered the room. The buzz of speculation from the surrounding crowd was louder than usual as all in attendance were awaiting the arrival of the party from Netherfield. Those few who had been witness to a Mr Bingley sighting were sought after so that they may repeat the very same information that had already been told and retold. Elizabeth smiled as she thought of the very intimate setting and conversations which she alone had shared with Mr Bingley and his party.

Elizabeth was all too aware that her heart was achingly taut with expectation. The chatting of the people around her became an indistinguishable wave of sound. Her thoughts of the last several days had always strayed back to the image of Mr Darcy, his face warmly illuminated by the dying fire in the Netherfield library, gazing at her, his lips parted in anticipation of what she would say, waiting. It was humiliating to her pride to have to admit that she might have been mistaken to dismiss those stories of a sudden revelation of love. It seemed to her very possible that if she did not catch a glimpse of Mr Darcy again and soon, she might start to develop one of those vague brain fevers that heroines brought low by disappointment fell under.

"Do you not believe so, Eliza?" Charlotte had asked.

"Pardon?"

"Are you feeling well? Though you look as handsome as I have ever seen, you are distracted. I think you have hardly heard a word spoken this evening. You must be feeling well, though, for you have a beautiful glow upon your face."

"Thank you for the compliment. I finally decided to take the advice of my mother and took particular care of my toilette this evening. She cannot accuse me of being neglectful of my appearance when the Netherfield party descends from their golden chariot. And as for your observation of my thoughtlessness, it is merely because I have a powerful curiosity to see Mr Bingley and his party after such an enormous amount of tittle-tattle."

"So much anticipation and gossip. It is remarkable that Mr Bingley and his sisters and friends have not fled the countryside."

"But that is often the advantage of being the object of wagging tongues, is it not?" Elizabeth replied. "You are frequently unaware of the chatter that you yourself create. A water-tight barrel of blissful ignorance surrounds you."

"Are you suggesting that if we all want peace and quiet, we should act in a way that gives rise to rumours?" Charlotte asked with a twinkle in her eye.

"Oh, no!" Jane chimed in. "Surely not. It is one of her jokes, that is all."

"Of course, my dear Jane," Elizabeth said as she gave her sister's forearm an affectionate squeeze, "I do endeavour to avoid being the cause of gossip."

Truly, I try harder than anyone can possibly realise, Elizabeth thought to herself as she recalled her late-night scramble back to Longbourn. It had been frightening, but the money she had made in one night would ensure that her family would eat very well through the approaching winter and that a few additions to her own wardrobe would keep her appearance above reproach. She had already purchased new gloves; however, she had not had the opportunity yet to replace the very worn fan that she had brought this evening.

A hush descended as the doors opened and Mr Bingley and his party entered.

"So it is but two ladies and three gentlemen, not the dozens of ladies that were spoken of. So much the better, for we are always in need of more gentlemen to even out the number of available dancing partners," Charlotte whispered to Elizabeth with a small laugh.

But Elizabeth could hardly attend to what her friend was saying. At the sight of Mr Darcy, her heart leapt. He was just as handsome as she had remembered. Perhaps even more so. There seemed to be an increase in the colour of his cheeks, as if whatever had been tormenting him had subsided in its power. His gaze wandered over the room and paused for the merest second on Elizabeth before moving on. Mildly disappointed, she dropped her eyes in an attempt to disguise her blush of embarrassment. It was no more than her sensible side had expected. But her romantic side had secretly hoped for a grand, spontaneous gesture worthy of swoons and sighs. After reading so many novels, she had held out a small wish that he would be instantly overwhelmed by her potent charms, rush over, and sweep her up in his arms. Now that her much more practical side was reasserting itself, she smiled at her own folly and shook her head with a small laugh to herself. Perhaps the evening would present an opportunity for her to be introduced to him properly, with no veil over her face or coarse voice to disguise her identity. But that was all she could hope for.

Mrs Bennet and the rest of her daughters joined Elizabeth, Jane, and Charlotte. Once she had her brood fully assembled, Mrs Bennet hissed out the particulars of the impressive fortune of Mr Bingley and the even more formidable estate and wealth of Mr Darcy. Elizabeth sighed in embarrassed annoyance. Her mother silenced her chatter when the two gentlemen approached them. The brief introduction of the Bennet ladies to Mr Bingley and Mr Darcy was propitious for some and melancholy for others. Mr Bingley immediately requested the honour of the next dance with Jane. Mr Darcy behaved as if the cornice moulding that circled the room was the most fascinating thing that he had ever laid eyes upon and decidedly did *not* extend an invitation to dance to any of the Bennet sisters.

The gentlemen moved away from the Bennet ladies. Mrs Bennet was dismayed for a few seconds at the prospect of such an eligible bachelor as Mr Darcy not succumbing to the superior allurements of at least one of her daughters. But Mrs Bennet—in keeping with one of the few traits she had in common with Elizabeth—chose to focus on the positive of the situation. The qualities of Mr Bingley were exalted loudly and the shortcomings of Mr Darcy were labelled and discussed with vehemence.

"We know nothing of Mr Darcy's life before his arrival in Hertfordshire," Elizabeth interjected when her mother paused to draw breath. Her remembrance of Mr Darcy's reading and the haggard aspect to his handsome face provoked her to come to his defence. "Perhaps he is not as amiable as he usually is due to circumstances of which we are unaware. I agree that he appears to be a very proud man, to *that* opinion there can be little argument. But even the proudest among us bear trials that cannot always be known to the rest of the world."

"I concur with Elizabeth," Mary chimed in. "Passing judgement on our fellow man must be done sparingly, lest we ourselves become the object of judgement."

"Yes, Mary. Thank you."

Mrs Bennet's eyes sparked with a rapacious twinkle. "My dearest, sweetest Lizzy. Have you heard something about Mr Darcy that the rest of us should know? Please, child, if you have any information to pass along, you must do so at once! Your mother demands it."

All eyes were suddenly upon Elizabeth. She resisted taking a step back, away from her mother. "I-I was speaking in general terms," she stammered out. "There is no harm in him that I know of, other than an apparent dislike of dancing. For that, we can hardly put him in the pillory."

Mrs Bennet pursed her lips tightly, as if thinking that perhaps a dislike of dancing *was* indeed a reason to put a wealthy, eligible young man in the pillory. She swiftly lost all interest in Elizabeth and began to advise poor Jane in a very loud whisper about how she ought to conduct herself when dancing with Mr Bingley. Elizabeth left when Mrs Bennet began to demonstrate a demure look from under lowered lashes, unable to bear witness to the spectacle of her mother any longer.

Elizabeth found an available chair and sat, hoping to remain obscure for a time as she observed the newcomers with interest. The actions and speech of the Netherfield party were, initially, very different from what she had experienced with them when she had been in the disguise of an old fortune-teller. But upon closer observation, she was able to once again clearly see the true nature of their characters. Miss Bingley was barely containing her sneers of disapproval as her eyes constantly wandered to wherever Mr Darcy happened to be in the room. Mr Hurst was trying to gather enough people to get a card game started. Mrs Hurst spent most of the time vapidly arranging and rearranging her bejewelled wrists and fingers. Mr Bingley was apparently relishing every dance, particularly the ones with Jane. And Mr Darcy. Her heart gave a shocking lurch whenever her eye fell on him. He stalked the perimeter of the room, tall and handsome, looking very much as a noble lion must when warily avoiding a possible trap. He occasionally stopped to speak briefly, but only in the form of a curt acknowledgement when spoken to.

As Mr Darcy made his way to where Elizabeth sat, she took time to smooth her hair, run a palm over her skirt, and make sure her frayed fan, which had a large rip directly in its centre, was firmly closed. He stood with his back to her, absorbed by the activity of the room. Her hope that he would turn and speak to her began to falter.

Just then, Mr Bingley approached Mr Darcy and began to admonish him into fraternising and dancing. Elizabeth was able to hear them quite well and could not help but laugh to herself at the contrast in their personalities.

"You simply must dance. I insist, Darcy. I hate to see you standing about in this stupid manner," Mr Bingley exclaimed.

When his friend quietly pointed out Elizabeth and recommended her to his notice, Mr Darcy responded, "She is tolerable; but not handsome enough to tempt *me*; and I am in no humour at present to give consequence to young ladies who are slighted by other men."

Elizabeth's heart flattened under the weight of Mr Darcy's flip, dismissive judgement. This was a crushing moment if ever there was one in her young life. Here, finally, was a man who truly and deeply interested her. Not just in appearance and standing in society, but in his mind and character. Even if he had not been the richest, most handsome man in the room, she had liked him for himself. His intelligent eyes. His understanding of things left unsaid. His courtesy to her as an old woman, not worthy of consideration by others in his party. A more austere nature such as his could not help but fascinate Elizabeth's naturally lively one.

A red haze of hurt and humiliation began to creep into the periphery of her vision. Elizabeth blinked rapidly. Her entire focus came to rest on the shabby tip of her closed fan as if her life depended on it. All those little lines, separating and organising the folds of the fan into order and calm loveliness. Each section of it was aloof and closed from the others. At the heart of the elegant folds of fabric lay a great rent, hidden away from the outside world. She felt the tide of tears that threatened to flood her face recede as her eyes kept still upon the shut fan. Its symmetry and linear nature were all that she could cling to so that a sob did not escape her throat.

Elizabeth breathed deeply and looked up after she had arranged her visage into something placid and serene.

If I keep this to myself, the fact that this man considers me to be slightly above nothing, I shall go mad. I may burst out into a ridiculous fountain of tears. Where is Charlotte? If I make this slight an object to be laughed at, toyed with, amused by, I will no longer feel this wretched pain. It will become an intriguing diversion, as a cat plays with a loose feather. If I make Mr Darcy's public, vocal insult into one of my amusing stories, all shall have a laugh and I will keep my mind calm and steady. My silly heart will begin to forget about this foolishness and come under some sort of order again.

Elizabeth sprang up when she spotted her friend on the other side of the large room. With a rapid pace, focused eyes, and head held high, she strode past the very man who had just—moments before—uncaringly visited such cruel havoc upon her heart, mind, and soul. Briefly, she wondered why fate had dealt such contrary cards to her. Yet she welcomed the small flame of hatred that kindled in her heart and fanned it proudly, determined that it might burn away her tender feelings towards a most undeserving gentleman.

In Darcy's chest, the modest, delicate bloom of affection began to germinate. A wave of scented air filled his senses as the lovely young woman walked mere inches before him. The smell of something sweet, but spicy. His eyes followed the scent and noticed her slim figure and the way the candlelight shone upon her dark, glossy hair. He casually wondered if her hair was curly like that when all let down, cascading over her bare shoulders in the middle of the night. His hand wanted to know what it would feel like to sweep those curls off her shoulder as much as his lips suddenly demanded to know exactly what those bare shoulders would taste like under a torrent of soft kisses. His focus drifted down to notice the almost imperceptible sway of her hips and the strength of her stride. A stride so long and bold must be powered by well-turned legs, slim and firm to the touch.

With a burst of self-consciousness, Darcy ripped his gaze away from the retreating form of Miss Elizabeth Bennet.

It was Elizabeth, was it not? Not Mary? Or Lydia? He frowned as he tried to recall the litany of female names that had assaulted him while being introduced to the vast, intimidating wall of Bennet women.

Yes, Elizabeth. Miss Elizabeth Bennet. That was certainly the name of the lady who just passed. Darcy had begun to meditate on the possibility that he may condescend to ask her to dance when he happened to look up at the very moment when something amusing Miss Elizabeth had just said caused her and her friend to laugh. Miss Elizabeth's gaze fell upon him. Remarkable and fiery, her dark eyes held him helpless. Darcy, for the first time in his recollection, started to blush.

He looked away and began to stalk the room again. That small, timid seedling of regard for Elizabeth Bennet began to spread its roots at an alarming pace. Darcy knew he should kill it. He knew he should smother it before it took hold. But something stayed his hand. An image of a card with seven cups came to mind. Many unexpected possibilities.

I can hold this Hertfordshire girl in some regard while I am here. There is no danger in that. I can admire her without raising her expectations. All must be well aware that my stay here is brief. She should know better than to anticipate anything like real feelings from someone of my standing.

Darcy paused. With amazement, he realised that several minutes had passed since the last time he had felt the heavy mortification of failure in his guardianship of his most precious responsibility, his sister Georgiana. The sight of Miss Elizabeth had done that. Her eyes had accomplished that. He smiled as he stopped next to Miss Bingley.

"Can you believe we are spending a perfectly wonderful evening in this horrible wilderness, Mr Darcy?" Miss Bingley asked behind her raised fan. "I am quite ashamed of how very much Charles seems to be enjoying himself. I can hardly discern one beautiful face in this sea of coarse provincials."

"Indeed," Darcy mumbled in response, not thinking in the least what he was saying. In his experience, Miss Bingley always expected a reply and could berate one endlessly until she received it.

"I see we agree on this point, Mr Darcy. I was concerned you may become enamoured of one of the Bennet girls, just as Charles seems to be."

"That is hardly possible."

Miss Bingley smiled smugly as she watched her brother pass with his partner, Miss Jane Bennet. She sighed. "I suppose this will lead to one of Charles's tedious little infatuations."

"Perhaps."

"You must promise me that you will help in making him see reality if he truly becomes attached to this one. Agreed?"

"Mmm," Darcy responded. He was still too consumed in thinking about Miss Elizabeth to fully attend to the conversation. His small sound of concurrence seemed to be enough to satisfy Miss Bingley.

Darcy's thoughts were meandering in the thin, beginning mists of a hopeless fog of yearning. He was looking forward to a conversation with Miss Elizabeth. Then he could set his skills in motion. By distilling and examining every aspect of her countenance, conversation, manners, and accomplishments, he was certain to find something to smother this feeling of warmth that was beginning to take hold of him. It was a dangerous strategy, for the very process of attempting to discover and hold her faults up to the light could cause his heart to fall irretrievably into her possession. But Darcy—having never been in love before—considered that impossible.

His eyes hungrily sought Miss Elizabeth out so that he could begin his catalogue of her defects. He stared at her profile as she laughed at something a gentleman said to her. Something that, if Darcy had dared to approach her, he himself could have said to her.

I am certain that I could make her laugh like that, given the chance. Her eyes would twinkle up at me with the same delight. I mean, really, what could that clod of a fellow possibly have said to her to cause such amusement?

Darcy straightened his spine in indignation. Some new sensation in his chest—a kind of sour restlessness—resembled what he had read of jealousy. The urge to make himself the only object of Miss Elizabeth's regard burned in him. Her laugh should only be for himself. Her eyes should only be observing him. Her rapt attention should only be for his conversation.

Darcy admonished the stupidity of what he was experiencing. There was no place for jealousy in his breast. Not when London was teeming with women ready to be his wife at a moment's notice. He recalled the King of Swords from his card reading with that old woman. The King had been calm, rational, in total control, and…alone.

That last thought caused him to frown.

Late in the evening, Darcy lay in his bed, staring at the tapestry above him. He tried to recall every angle of Miss Elizabeth's face. The lilt of her laugh. The spring of her step as she danced with some lucky fellow. Those dimples in her cheeks.

No matter at what angle he held her up, or how he pierced her with his discernment, he could find no fault. Of course, Darcy could find fault with her in accordance with the current standards of what was considered beautiful by the ever-changing whims of society. Her head was held too high, almost teasingly defiant. Her jaw could be called strong. She did not possess that melting, tired, submissive slouch in the current style that ladies tried to imitate. Her breasts were too small and pert, like Artemis of Ancient Greece, not full and heavy and threatening to spill out of her dress at any moment. Her sudden laugh lacked that learned, practised, descending scale that was acquired by ladies who had attended a finishing school. Her smile was broad and beaming and not in the least bit demure and reluctant.

With a groan, Darcy rolled over and forced his eyes shut. A wave of exhaustion washed over him. For the first time in months, he drifted into a deep, sound sleep without tossing for most of the night. Many hours passed and he was not tormenting himself about how he had failed as a guardian and brother.

In the morning, he felt a giddiness as he opened his eyes. The world was in a tumble. Things were disjointed, floating and flipped. The tree before him had its roots covered in leaves and reaching into the blue sky. Then Darcy realised that he was hanging upside down, several feet off the ground. One of his ankles was bound by rope to the branch of a tree. He was swaying and turning. Struggling, he attempted to reach up and untie himself. But his wrists were tied behind his back. His struggles became frantic, causing him to twist and turn even more.

He stopped. With a flash of clarity, Darcy comprehended that he was the living image of The Hanged Man in the fortune-teller's card. He groaned and then laughed at the utter ridiculousness of the situation.

"Hallo? Is anyone here who could give me a hand?" he yelled into the wilderness.

From the trees before him, there was movement. Someone was approaching, clad from head to toe in white robes, their face hidden by a white veil.

"Do you think you could help me? I seem to have been detained without remembering exactly how I got here in—"

The figure unsheathed a sword and walked steadily towards him.

"Now, look here, just cut me down! I am Fitzwilliam Darcy, master of Pemberley and—"

The figure ran at him, sword raised high overhead. Darcy struggled against the ropes until his wrists felt as if they would bleed. The figure swung the sword violently.

Darcy fell to the ground with a crunching thud. He spat grass and dirt from his mouth. With his hands still tightly bound behind him, Darcy twisted himself awkwardly onto his belly to look up at the person. He felt a surge of anger and opened his mouth to curse the fellow for doing such a clumsy job of it.

But there was no fellow at all. It was Miss Elizabeth Bennet. She was now in a loose, low-cut tunic of white, bound at the waist with her legs fully bare—the image of a Grecian forest nymph. The thickness of the fabric was so slight that he could see every curve of her body as if the material were not there at all. The sword was now a longbow that she leaned on as she looked down at him with a happy smile on her face. The smile held kind amusement in it, not ridicule or triumph. Darcy could not help himself. He smiled back.

Darcy wormed himself up into a seated position and caught his breath. Looking up, he said, "Thank you. I am in your debt."

Without a word, she bent down and cut through his wrist bindings with a small knife pulled from a sheath that hung on the belt at her waist.

"Again, thank you. How terribly awkward. I cannot imagine how—"

As he massaged his wrists, she took his cheek in her hand, lifted his face up towards hers, and planted the softest, most delicious whisper of a kiss on his explaining lips. In the silence of the kiss, an explosion of warm dizziness encased Darcy's mind and limbs. As she pulled away, laughing, Darcy reached out to try and grasp her and pull her in close for a return kiss. But she was as swift as a doe in springtime. She sprang up and ran to the edge of the forest.

"You will have to do better than that to catch me, sir." Her lean legs flashed as she bounded over some branches and out of his sight. Without another thought, Darcy stood and ran after her.

She was always just out of his reach. Just when he thought he had lost her, he caught sight of some of her curly hair from behind a tree, or the gentle sway of her thin tunic through the brush. Her laugh was always just beyond the next swell of the forest floor. Frustrated and desperate, he continued to pursue her. He was far less nimble than her in the thickness of the forest. With a startled yelp, Darcy caught his foot in a root and plummeted down into darkness that seemed to extend out endlessly through the ages.

With a jolt and a yell, Darcy sat up in his bed, panting.

Chapter 6

Conceited Independence

An invitation to dine at Netherfield from Bingley's sisters, a downpour of cold rain as she travelled there, and a chill that had been working on her all the previous day had grown into a terrible cold for Jane. Elizabeth stared at the little note in her hand, anger at her mother bubbling up and flooding her cheeks with heat. Mrs Bennet had absolutely insisted that Jane travel by horse, increasing the chances of an overnight stay at Netherfield and more opportunities for the beauty of her eldest daughter to intoxicate the senses of Mr Bingley.

Elizabeth had wanted little time in preparing for her muddy walk to Netherfield to nurse her sister back to health. As she tramped her way through the soggy fields, her desire to be of service to her dearest sister was at direct odds with her desire to avoid virtually every inhabitant of Netherfield. Mr Bingley was always gracious and cheerful. But the thought of enduring conversation with his sisters was depressing. Added to this misery would be the very difficult, close proximity to Mr Darcy, the man who had thought her company little better than reprehensible at the Meryton assembly. Elizabeth sighed as she pushed through a turnstile. Her boots slipped one way and then another in the mud, and—by sheer luck—she did not plummet face first into the muck.

Feeling genuinely tired and more than a little cross, Elizabeth finally arrived at Netherfield. All the inhabitants were stunned when she was shown into the breakfast-parlour. She knew, in the minds of those assembled, that her appearance must appear almost feral. But she was only there for the sake of Jane, so it was more of an annoyance than a genuine concern. Mr Bingley was all graciousness and offered her some refreshment, which Elizabeth declined.

"Such a long walk, Miss Elizabeth!" Miss Bingley exclaimed. "How did you ever manage it?"

"It matters little. I am accustomed to the surrounding country, therefore navigating it is no great trial for me. It was indeed muddy, but I survived, as you can see."

Miss Bingley raised a critical eyebrow as her gaze travelled down to the hem of Elizabeth's dress. Elizabeth knew that the thread of the gown would not be at all visible through the liberal splattering of mud. Her cheeks burned at the idea of being a surprising morning diversion for a woman such as Miss Bingley, a thing to be ridiculed and pitied. Mr Darcy suddenly stood with his cup of tea and went to the window that looked out in the direction of Longbourn. His action had the unexpected result of causing a sinking feeling in Elizabeth's heart.

I must appear so wild and shocking that he cannot bear to witness me standing here! How could I ever have imagined him to be a man worth my consideration?

"It is a fine thing indeed that you have come to check on your sister," Mr Bingley exclaimed. "It matters not how many fields and woods you had to traipse through, would you not agree, Darcy?"

Mr Darcy, keeping his stance of stiff formality at the window, replied in a stilted voice, "It is as you say, in the aim of being of aid to one you care about, I am certain that the fields and woods were no great trial for Miss Elizabeth."

"I am positive that if *my* dear Louisa were to take suddenly ill, I would willingly go four times as far, through the most difficult terrain that one can imagine! Boulders, wild animals, vast creeks, they would be nothing at all to me," Miss Bingley volunteered, seemingly eager to prove just how little she thought of a long walk through lanes of mud and fields of suspicious bulls. "My sisterly affection would give each step strength and purpose. Would you not say the same of me, Louisa?"

Mrs Hurst had been busy managing a thick layer of jam onto her toast and not attending to all that was being discussed. She looked up, confused. "I beg your pardon, what was that you said about boulders, sister?"

Miss Bingley gave her sister an angry glare as Mr Bingley moved to escort Elizabeth out of the room, to her immense relief.

"If you find that your sister is too ill to be removed today, I absolutely insist that you remain here at Netherfield to help her feel more comfortable. Why, I can send for your clothes in a moment."

"You are kindness itself, Mr Bingley. I thank you. But I would not wish to be an inconvenience."

"Nonsense. Anything to help your sister feel better, I will gladly do."

Elizabeth thought she heard a loud groan of annoyance from Miss Bingley as she and Mr Bingley walked out of the breakfast-parlour.

That evening, once Elizabeth saw that her sister was well into a sound sleep, she slipped downstairs to join the others after dinner. A game of cards had begun while Mr Darcy wrote a letter, and Elizabeth picked up a book. She was more than able to hold her own in cards, but the possibility of losing even a small sum of money terrified her. Although she was confident she would have been able to win frequently against Mrs Hurst, Miss Bingley, and Mr Bingley, she was not so certain about Mr Hurst. She recalled very clearly how rapidly he was able to pick up the card game she had taught him during their reading.

Elizabeth moved towards the couch with the novel she had selected. Grateful that Mr Darcy was seemingly taking little interest in her—or anyone else in the room—she settled down with the book open before her. She had been slightly concerned that her voice might remind those present of the fortune-teller from the evening of readings in the library, but apparently her performance had been so well-executed that no one suspected her.

Mr Hurst, brows raised at the book in her hands, said, "You prefer reading books to cards? That is rather singular."

Her hope to settle in quietly without drawing the notice of anyone in the room was clearly not meant to be.

"Miss Eliza Bennet," said Miss Bingley, "despises cards. She is a great reader and has no pleasure in anything else."

Elizabeth had to stop herself from laughing aloud. *If they only knew how untrue their statements are!*

"I deserve neither such praise nor such censure," Elizabeth said. "I am not a great reader, and I have pleasure in many things, including playing cards. I do not wish to enter into a game that I cannot see through to the end. If Jane has need of me, I wish to be untethered so that I may leave to attend her at a moment's notice. It would be an unkindness to the other players to disrupt the game, so reading seemed to be a better way for me to pass the evening."

"Jolly sensible of you!" Mr Hurst burst out in a rare show of emotion. "I applaud your respect to the sacred bond of a card game. It is a sort of temporary link that should not be broken, even under the most dire of circumstances."

"Speaking of cards," Miss Bingley hurriedly said, no doubt to shift any focus off others and back to herself, "I am eagerly anticipating the next time I see the Viscountess Bramerly. She has been so vocal of the time she received a card reading from that old Italian woman who was travelling through London. It created quite the fashion of having one's fortune told, and now I will be able to inform every one of our acquaintance that I have done the same as Lady Bramerly. She may even wish to discuss the experience with me."

"I had not thought of that, sister! To gain an invitation to a dinner with her would be the making of our Season. We must let everyone know of our adventure once we return to London."

"What say you, Mr Darcy?" Miss Bingley asked with a flutter of her lashes. "Shall you be informing all of your acquaintances of what happened during your reading?"

"Certainly not," he said firmly, not looking up from his letter writing.

"Did she say nothing to you that was pleasant?" she pressed on with a seductive pulse to her tone. "Do you have something wonderful to anticipate in the near future?"

Whatever the future is for Miss Bingley, it does not appear that Mr Darcy will play a large role in it. I am surprised that such a seemingly sharp woman would be so unaware. It is plain to anyone who possesses sight that she is not at all as alluring to him as she seems to think.

Elizabeth had to chide herself at this thought. Had she not felt herself to be desperately in love with Mr Darcy until his openly rude statement about her at the Meryton assembly? He was handsome, intriguing, and intelligent. But none of those qualities could overcome his blatant disregard for the feelings of those around him. At least she had that benefit over Miss Bingley; she could honestly view Mr Darcy's flaws as clearly as she witnessed what there was to admire in him.

While Elizabeth observed those around the card table, an unexpected surge of heat up her neck caused her to shift her gaze back to Mr Darcy. He was staring at her intently. When their eyes met, he startled and returned his attention to his letter.

"What was or was not said by an old woman," Mr Darcy muttered with an angry edge in his tone, "attempting to fill her belly by diverting us with a novel amusement for an evening is hardly worth discussing further. She said nothing worth repeating."

"I am not frightened of you, Mr Darcy," Miss Bingley exclaimed, teasingly. "You may turn your nose up at such pastimes. But if Lady Bramerly sees fit to spend her time in the company of a card reader, then it is good enough for me. Such an endorsement by one of the most illustrious members of the *ton* can hardly be looked upon as trifling in consequence."

Mr Darcy did not take the bait offered by Miss Bingley and kept his focus on his letter.

Miss Bingley took this opportunity to turn her attention back to Elizabeth.

"Surely, Miss Eliza, you have visited the fortune-teller and had your cards read? It would be impossible that you could keep away with her being so close to Longbourn."

"Indeed, I have never met her. But I have heard that she is remarkably perceptive."

Mr Darcy had his full attention turned back to Elizabeth. "Do you say that you do not believe that those cards or the old woman herself hold some sort of particular power?"

"I think I would be more willing to say that the cards themselves hold little or no power out of the ordinary. Most of what is witnessed during one of those visits may probably be attributed to the woman's ability to perceive what she can of the character of the person before her. If one takes time to study how a person is dressed, in what way they enter a room, whom they make an effort to speak to, how they hold their body when sitting in a chair and believing themselves to be unobserved, much can be inferred; all of these things can give as much insight into the disposition of a person before a single word is spoken."

"I say!" Mr Bingley exclaimed. "You are quite the studier of characters, then, are you Miss Elizabeth?"

Elizabeth sensed Mr Darcy's eyes burning into her and knew herself to be on very treacherous ground. It would be unwise to mention anything that might lead him to suspect that it was she who had read the cards for them that night. He was sharp. And for Elizabeth, as accustomed as she was to being the cleverest one in the room, it would take extra caution on her part to not raise his suspicions.

"I claim no such thing," she continued, dropping her gaze modestly. "I was merely making an observation as to how this old woman you speak of may have gained what appeared to be special visions into your character and what you believe your future may be. A good deal of the strength of her abilities may also lie in whether the person sitting across from her is persuaded by superstitions or not."

"So, it is your assertion that if the person receiving the reading gives no credence to superstitions, the woman has no powers other than that of keen observation," Mr Darcy said.

"If I were to meet this woman, I would assume that most of her supposed abilities lie in her perceptions and conclusions and that there is little or no magic in the entire process."

"Well, I think that we ought to look to our betters—such as Lady Bramerly—for guidance on such matters," Miss Bingley stated in a matter-of-fact tone. "*Lady Bramerly* claims the fortune-teller whom she visited was positively supernatural in her statements, so I am inclined to follow where she leads. *You*, Miss Eliza, have so little experience moving in such circles, I hardly expect that you can understand such a thing as heeding the actions and authority of a viscountess."

A chilled silence followed. Mr Darcy looked at Miss Bingley with thinly veiled disgust.

"Besides," Miss Bingley continued, unaware of how few desired her further comments, "she is so very elegant and accomplished, I am certain Lady Bramerly possesses the skills of sketching characters and would be able to tell if a card reader was a fraud. It is something that one expects in an accomplished woman."

"So, we must add sketching characters to the accomplishments of a lady, eh?" Mr Bingley asked, chuckling and clearly eager to change the subject. "They all paint tables, cover skreens, net purses, and claim far more abilities than I can name! And now they must be able to sketch a person's character."

"There must be much more than painting, netting, and guessing at characters to make an accomplished woman, Bingley," Mr Darcy said. "I cannot boast of knowing more than half a dozen, in the whole range of my acquaintance, that are really accomplished."

"Nor I, I am sure," said Miss Bingley.

"Then you must comprehend a great deal in it." Elizabeth could not stop herself from directing her curious gaze at Mr Darcy. An intense desire to know what he comprehended as the ideal woman had seized her. Despite all of her sound and reasoned explanations to herself as to why she should detest Mr Darcy, Elizabeth still found her heart racing when they were together in company.

"I do," he replied.

"Yes, of course," cried Miss Bingley. "A woman must have a thorough knowledge of music, singing, drawing, dancing, and the modern languages, to deserve the word. And to this, she must possess a certain something in her air and manner of walking, the tone of her voice, her address and expressions, or the word will be but half deserved."

"And she must endeavour to improve her mind through extensive reading to truly earn the title of accomplished," Mr Darcy said.

"And, let us not neglect the art of taking a person's likeness by observing their speech, dress, mood, and physiognomy," added Elizabeth with a sly smile. "Goodness! We have assembled such a very lengthy list of what is needed in an accomplished woman that I now no longer wonder at your knowing *only* six, Mr Darcy. I rather wonder at your knowing *any*."

"Are you so severe upon your sex, as to doubt the possibility of all this?" Miss Bingley said while staring daggers at Elizabeth.

"I not only doubt the existence of such a woman, I believe that there is no possible way for such a creature to ever have existed, even in the annals of all the mythologies of the world. Not even one of the goddesses of ancient Greece could claim half of what we have just listed."

Despite a general outcry from the ladies at the card table of the unfairness of this declaration, Elizabeth held the very earnest stare of Mr Darcy. She thought she could detect the beginnings of a startled blush rising in his cheeks as he held her gaze. Despite her own body returning the call with heat spreading across the flesh of her chest and up into her face, Elizabeth still held his stare, defying him.

"Here now," Mr Hurst called out. "This is a rummy way to conduct a card game. Let us bring the talk back to kings and queens and leave off this chatter about purse netting and painting."

Their focus returned to the card table. Mr Darcy blinked several times and broke off his gaze from Elizabeth. He renewed his letter writing with fierce alacrity. Elizabeth held her book up before her face, pretending to continue her extensive reading. She could not help but observe Mr Darcy several more times over the top of her pages. He did not look up again. His face still had a reddish hue as his pen raced across the paper.

I cannot make him out at all, Mr Darcy is that much of a puzzle to me. One moment, we converse rapidly and deeply, the next he avoids me completely. Perhaps I have finally met one whose likeness I cannot take.

Chapter 7

A Most Iniquitous Affair

Father would never have condescended to make this admirable gesture of familial reconciliation. Oh, if Father could see me now, he would yell and proclaim what an ass I am! He would not have understood that, as a clergyman under the patronage of the Right Honourable Lady Catherine de Bourgh—Mr Collins paused in his endless inner monologue of self-congratulations long enough to sigh reverently at the mere thought of the name of that great lady—*it is my sacred duty to extend the olive branch and select a wife from among the five daughters of Mr Bennet, our cousin, to atone for the entail of Longbourn to me upon his death. Lucky girls. For one of them to be my wife and receive the great honour of the condescension of Lady Catherine. To hear how a house ought to be properly run, to receive extensive advice on where and how to purchase mutton, to know which breed of chicken will produce the eggs with the yellowest yolks. They have no concept of the great honour which is about to be bestowed upon one of them. I hope a conflict among the Bennet girls does not develop. For what will I do if they all fall in love with me? There will certainly be broken hearts, tears, and vexation at not having been chosen by me. They may turn their fury upon each other. Perhaps my cousins will even fight amongst themselves for my hand in marriage.*

For reasons that he did not fully comprehend, Mr Collins smiled slightly at the image of five beautiful young women bickering and, perhaps, even exchanging blows in an effort to be his most favoured. After several minutes of this happy possibility racing through his mind, Mr Collins' sense of propriety chastised him that this was not the most appropriate thing for him to meditate on.

A jolt of the carriage as it hit a bump in the road brought his attention back to the present. He placed his hand on top of his hat to keep it securely in place. At long last, the estate of Longbourn, long denigrated by his father as being a worthless property full of crumbling buildings and ghosts, came into view.

To his own credit, Mr Collins proudly realised that his father had been wrong. This was a revelation that had become common as he was more in the world and away from his miserly, cruel father. He stored it away in his mind as yet one more sin to hold over the memory of the elder Mr Collins.

Mr Collins ran his eyes past the trees that lined the drive, over the stables, barn, and to the manor house itself. It was a very respectable sort of estate, several centuries old, that would suit his disposition to the letter. It was a mere sheep shed compared to Rosings, the home of Lady Catherine de Bourgh, but it was grand enough to satisfy Mr Collins's desire to move up in the world and in consequence.

It will do very nicely. The only ornament it lacks is a gentlewoman who is accustomed to the neighbourhood and will not object to taking on daily tasks of maintaining such an estate house. She must be beautiful. And docile. And lively at the correct times. And quiet at the correct times. And not too thoughtful upon matters of great importance. And willing to be guided by me in all things. And she must inspire in me a passion of affection so that we may extend the family name through the begetting of progeny. But she must not be so alluring that she may be considered an inappropriate choice of wife for a clergyman. Yes.

To his utter delight, the Bennet family was before the house, ready to welcome him into their hearth and home. And—even from this distance—Mr Collins did not believe it would be difficult to select one of the five daughters who satisfied his notion of a charming yet modest beauty. He congratulated himself yet again on the brilliance of this scheme. As the young ladies came into better focus, he also felt a rekindling of the secret yearning for the possibility of a confrontation between the sisters that might very well end in a tear or two of a gown. But, he did not raise his hopes too high on this possible outcome. Still, one never knew…

"…and it was Lady Catherine herself who advised me to…take a wife." Mr Collins glanced around the table filled to bursting with his lovely, young cousins and smiled contentedly.

"And was this sage counsel from Lady Catherine a recent occurrence, or did you meditate upon the best course of action for quite some time?" Mr Bennet asked, quietly enjoying a glimpse into the life of his cousin's son.

"I can assure you, sir, that I did not trifle for a moment and began to set into motion efforts to follow her advice immediately. That very day, in fact!"

"Excellent. How very reasonable of you, sir."

"During this time of uncertainty, with the war against France raging, Lady Catherine believes it is of the utmost importance for those of us in positions of consequence to set the proper example. It is imperative to lead the flock in an image of good living that is in contrast to the immoralists across the Channel."

Though there was little chance of his words not being overheard by all at the table, Mr Collins leaned in to a mildly surprised Mr Bennet and whispered, "For, as Lady Catherine herself has informed me, the French are using every weapon at their disposal in an effort to turn the tide their way. Even *magic*."

"Napoleon has gone about the French countryside to recruit the fairies and gnomes, eh?" Mr Bennet asked, clearly trying to keep a serious countenance during this silly turn in the conversation.

"And, as I informed Lady Catherine, it would be our sacred duty to bring all of them to the stake to roast for these egregious crimes." Mr Collins nodded in self-satisfaction.

Elizabeth's insides burned with outrage from this man sitting in their dining room, making such a sweeping judgement about the people in an entire country. The rest of the Bennets might not realise it, but there was a priest's hole in their very house that testified to the fearful, mortal danger that their own ancestors had lived through before they converted to the Church of England.

"But is it certain?" she declared more loudly than she had intended.

Mr Collins looked at her as though appalled, mouth agape.

"Is Lady Catherine certain in her information regarding the use of magic by the French? For, correct me if I am wrong, but would it not be an act of bearing false witness to spread such claims if they are untrue? And even if the claims are true, surely it would be unjust to punish the citizens of an entire country for the crimes of a few."

Mr Collins seemed to stagger back in his posture, as if he had been dealt a slap upon his cheek. His mouth flapped in a fish-like manner for a few moments before he returned his gaze to Mr Bennet.

"Would you not agree, Mary?" Elizabeth pressed on, turning towards her younger sister. "You were expressing yourself quite well on the dangers of precipitous judgement of our fellow man just the other day."

Elizabeth was surprised when Mary appeared to be flustered by conflicting emotions and could only look down at her plate. Elizabeth had to resist the urge to sigh in frustration. The one time she was counting on Mary to come to her defence with some blazing insight of theological brilliance and her sister could only shuffle her potatoes about on her plate like a shepherdess busy with her flock.

"Some of your daughters express their opinions in a very outright manner, sir," Mr Collins murmured to Mr Bennet in a hushed, scandalised tone.

"I have always encouraged my girls to think for themselves. My efforts have met with mixed results. Jane and Elizabeth have the most rational minds of the lot, but then again, the other three are still quite young."

A glad rush of happiness filled Elizabeth at her father stepping in to support her in his modest way. But then she glanced back at Mary and felt sorry that their father had not included her in his list of thoughtful daughters. It must have mortified Mary to not be grouped with her elder sisters after she had made such a concentrated effort to educate herself. Elizabeth had always found it unfortunate that her father did not make more of an effort with Mary, who, given some direction and encouragement, might very well develop a more cultivated mind.

Mrs Bennet appeared to realise that Mr Collins—unlike her husband—was not the sort of man who appreciated a lively mind and challenging conversation. Her eyes went back and forth between Mr Collins, Jane, and Elizabeth as a look of concern spread upon her face. Frequently during the meal, Mr Collins had been watching Jane in a doe-eyed fashion. Elizabeth was certain that her mother would rather direct Mr Collins and his flattering comments away from Jane, as her hopes for Mr Bingley as a son-in-law held precedence over any other potential suitor.

"Mr Collins," Mrs Bennet exclaimed, "once we retire to the sitting room, would you care to hear some music? Mary is said to be the most accomplished girl in Meryton. And Lizzy plays as well."

"That would be kindness itself, ma'am. Does my cousin Jane play also? She has such an angelic countenance, it would seem fitting that her voice would match it in melodiousness."

"I do not play, sir. Not a note. Neither upon an instrument nor with my voice," Jane said with a gentle, but assured tone.

"Ah, well, I am sure that you have other, more suitable talents, of a nature that is not quite so—dramatic and, well, exhibitionist in nature. Talents that are demure yet pleasing, with manners of accomplishment that are distinguished, but not as openly..." Mr Collins's brow contracted as he appeared to battle a confusion of thoughts about how to form compliments of Jane's lack of musicality in a way that flattered.

Elizabeth had to cover her mouth with her napkin to smother her desire to laugh.

"But, as I said, Mr Collins, *Elizabeth* and *Mary* both play and sing," Mrs Bennet stated firmly.

Elizabeth, horrified at the thought of appearing in an attractive light before Mr Collins, demurred and said that she felt unequal to entertaining.

"My throat is taxed and weak, so you must excuse me from playing this evening. Besides, my skills are meagre indeed compared to Mary's. We had much better listen to her excellent playing. Mary? Will you be so kind as to play for us this evening?" Elizabeth pointedly glared at Mary in an attempt to drop their cousin's attention like a hot potato on her plate.

To Elizabeth's exasperation, Mary demurred as well with a tense shake of her head. Elizabeth imagined that Mary was having an ethical battle within herself as to whether it was better that she should appear modest or not hide her light under a bushel.

"I-I do not think exhibiting my-myself and my skills in front of our company this evening is appropriate," Mary stammered out. "I would not wish to appear immodest before a clergyman. Modesty in a woman is the highest virtue that she can hope for. Please forgive me if I beg off as well."

"It is not immodesty to exhibit a talent that serves to entertain and uplift those around you. Something as wholesomely innocent as playing upon the piano can hardly reduce the opinion of you in a person of sense." Elizabeth made a stealthy glance at their guest, unconvinced that Mr Collins could stake a claim to any modicum of sensible understanding.

"Please, do reconsider, Mary," she hissed, becoming annoyed.

Mr Collins did not appear to have been following the general tone of the conversation. For he inexplicably exclaimed with a broad smile, "My dearest cousins, there is no need to quarrel amongst yourselves! I am happy to be entertained by all of you, only please be patient for my attention. The last thing I would be desirous of is for all of you lovely ladies to fight for *my* preferment. Indeed, I would not wish to see that at all."

The entire table was shocked into silence. Every face wore an expression of either incredulity or puzzlement. Lydia snorted a laugh into her napkin. Elizabeth kicked at her under the table while shooting an admonishing look at a similarly amused Kitty beside her. Jane stared down at her plate in blushing mortification. Mr Bennet had to press his lips together severely to keep any chuckle from escaping.

So, in the end, no one played a single note. Once the party had assembled after dinner, it was suggested that Mr Collins should read aloud as the safest way to pass the evening. He perused the selection of lending-library books upon the table as if they were live serpents.

"Novels?" he declared. He turned towards Mr Bennet and asked, "Are you not concerned that *novels* will have a bad influence on the minds of these delicate flowers?" Mr Collins swept his hand around the room at all of his cousins.

"They read as they choose, sir. One of the paths to education is developing the ability to discern the good from the bad. Therefore, I allow them to read the great, the good, and the spoilt porridge and allow them to form their own judgements. A thinking mind capable of refined discernment is a skill whose blessings can give comfort through the most—ahem—trying of times."

Mr Bennet sat down and opened one of his own volumes. It seemed that he was beginning to tire of such a wealth of foolishness that was Mr Collins and hoped the spine of his book would redirect that young man to look elsewhere for conversation. At this moment, Mary meekly approached, holding a book out to Mr Collins.

"Ah! Fordyce's *Sermons To Young Women*! There is an excellent selection within these pages on the evils of novels to the delicate feminine mind."

Lydia looked about the room with the desperation of a caged animal before Jane quietly placed her hand on her young sister's arm to calm her. Elizabeth sat up straight as an arrow, attempting to make amends for her earlier outburst of thoughtful observations on the nature of judgement. She watched closely as Mr Collins cleared his throat and riffled through the book, obviously hunting up a very specific passage to read aloud.

Triumphantly, he placed his finger upon a page, looked at the pile of novels on the table, and then glared at each young woman in the room.

He cleared his throat again and began his recitation. *"We consider the general run of Novels as utterly unfit for you. Instruction, they convey none. They paint scenes of pleasure and passion altogether improper for you to behold, even with the mind's eye. Their descriptions are often loose and luscious in a high degree; their representations of love between the sexes are almost universally overstrained. All is dotage or despair; or else ranting swelled into burlesque."*

A snorted burst of laughter erupted from Lydia. "Dotage or despair? Oh, Lord!"

Mr Collins did not raise his eyes from the page, but pressed on in his overwrought tone until Elizabeth began to feel a small pain swelling behind her eyes. She soon gave up all pretence to attentiveness and leaned back in her chair with her eyes closed, wondering when was the earliest time she could plead weariness and retire for the evening.

Chapter 8

Balm of Sisterly Love

It was dreary for a week. The increasingly rainy period meant that Elizabeth and her sisters had to endure long stretches of time with Mr Collins indoors. If it had not been for the forthcoming ball at Netherfield to distract and absorb some of the energies of her youngest sisters, Elizabeth thought they might have all gone mad.

Elizabeth, dressed in her dark shrouds, poked at the smouldering fire of mint and sticks that took some of the chill out of her little cottage. She had retreated to her room with the claim of feeling low so that she might be here to receive any customers. The money was not desperately needed, but Elizabeth was in desperate need of a break from Mr Collins. It had not escaped her notice that she herself was frequently the intended recipient for the majority of his delicate compliments.

She sat at her window and looked through the bars at the very light drizzle that was coming down. As usual, when Elizabeth was alone and unoccupied, her mind wandered back to that paragon of mystery, Mr Darcy. She could not make him out at all, and this frustrated her to no end.

Her time at Netherfield nursing her sister Jane back to health had been a confusing mix of interactions with Mr Darcy. He would spend almost an hour ignoring her when they sat alone in the library. Then, later that same day, he would seem to seek her out for conversation. Was that to incense Caroline Bingley for a bit of fun? Was it only to pass a slow hour before retiring for the evening? His motives were increasingly mysterious to her.

And then there was that time he had actually asked her to dance at the card party. Was it because he felt shamed into it by Sir William's pestering? When she refused, he appeared not at all disturbed or forlorn. But then Charlotte pointed out that Mr Darcy glanced at her a great deal during the course of the evening. Much more than he had looked at Caroline Bingley, his supposed amour.

And poor Mr Wickham! How could anything justify Mr Darcy's treatment of the handsome young man who had recently taken a commission in the militia? Mr Wickham's outpouring of his history and the mistreatment he had received at the hands of Mr Darcy had shocked Elizabeth to her core. There was no circumstance that she could even begin to imagine clearing him of the guilt of having treated such an amiable youth in that malevolent manner. How could anyone deny him his proper living in the church? Leave him destitute and friendless? Her heart, so recently inflamed by Mr Darcy, had transferred a slim wedge of that warmth to Wickham. Her original strong attraction to Mr Darcy had, by now, almost completely transformed into zealous disdain. Elizabeth was looking forward to the ball at Netherfield more than ever as the prospect of dancing again with Wickham was first in her thoughts.

Elizabeth rubbed her head, not accustomed to the sensation of her mind failing her at untangling a knotty problem. A twig snapped in the distance. She sat up tall.

Into view came three figures. With a sinking heart, Elizabeth realised it was merely her sisters, Jane, Lydia, and Kitty. They approached her with a storm of shrieks, giggles, and shoves between the youngest two. Jane hung farther back, obviously only there to accompany her youngest sisters and to prevent any sort of calamity. Elizabeth groaned as she hunched over and readied her voice to be raspy and unrecognisable. Her two youngest sisters had visited her once before in the cottage, but Elizabeth had given them such an uneventful reading that Lydia had declared it a waste of her coins. It was fortunate that they did not come to visit her more often, for there was always the fear of being discovered that ran below the surface of every reading.

It was a wearisome hour of reading fortunes for Kitty and Lydia—the snickering, the poking at each other, the genuine fear in Kitty's eyes. And, as Elizabeth accepted her payment, the knowledge that the coins were from their pin money and would go back into the running of Longbourn. It was a fruitless afternoon, but at least it was far from the company of Mr Collins.

The other silver lining that came from the encounter with Lydia and Kitty was hearing Wickham's name repeated often by Lydia. Elizabeth also took the opportunity to emphasise the sensible and rational in the cards before her in an attempt to encourage Lydia to cultivate a mind that thought deeply on consequences and self-reflection. With Kitty, Elizabeth told of the great benefit of rising above the influence of others and becoming an individual with an independent will. She hoped this would encourage Kitty to seek less guidance from Lydia and to trust her own natural sense more frequently.

"Oh, la!" Lydia said, laughing. "This was far too much like a sermon and not at all like what I was hoping for. You could at least have told me whether Wickham prefers lighter or darker hair. He cannot love red hair, for that would be silly. Harriet will be so jealous, as she is far too afraid to come here for herself. There is nothing to fear. I am not at all cowed by you, old woman. I shall have a good laugh at Harriet for her silliness. I do not even care if Papa scolds me for wasting my coin as he did last time."

"And I shall tell Maria Lucas," Kitty crowed. "She would never think I was so bold as to come here. Perhaps I will convince her to accompany me one day."

"No, Kitty. You had much better to bring Denny or Carter here. For perhaps the old bag will tell them that one of them should marry you and that Wickham should marry me! Then we shall both be married far before Jane and definitely far before Lizzy and Mary. What a laugh we shall have then. The youngest of the girls married before the eldest!" Lydia cackled loud and long.

Elizabeth, in an effort to support this rare moment of independence from Lydia, said to Kitty, "I would be pleased to offer my services to any of your friends, my dear. You have a sweet face and a kind heart."

Kitty brightened considerably at this meagre scrap of praise. Lydia looked peevish at not being praised for her appearance as well.

"I shall tell anyone who asks that this is a waste of time and to save their money. You preach far too much on serious matters and told me nothing of the men of the militia that is worth a farthing. Come, Kitty."

Not even bothering to consult Jane as to whether she wished to have a reading, Lydia grabbed Kitty by the wrist and began to drag her bodily away.

"And the other young woman?" Elizabeth asked, adding an extra layer of gravely phlegm to her voice. "Does she wish to see what may lay before her?"

"I...well, I really do not think I should."

"It will be completely free, my dear."

Jane looked up at the retreating figures of her younger sisters, back to the window, and then stood, considering.

"Perhaps some other time," Jane said as she turned to join Lydia and Kitty.

After Jane left to follow their youngest sisters back to Longbourn, Elizabeth prepared to close up the cottage for the day and take a real walk since the rain had mostly subsided to a wafting mist. As she lifted the wooden shutter up to seal off the window, she saw a flash of red through the bare branches of the trees. One of the militiamen was approaching from the direction of their encampment. With a flutter of heat to her cheeks, Elizabeth realised it was Wickham.

Her smile was broad while she quickly pulled her veil back over her face and excitedly waited for the handsome officer with whom she had so recently become acquainted. Wickham had made it perfectly clear over the course of their brief acquaintance that he enjoyed her company above the company of any other young lady. He had confirmed this by confiding in Elizabeth the very scandalous way that he had been treated by his childhood friend, Mr Darcy. Her temper rose as she pondered how Mr Darcy had destroyed Wickham's prospects by depriving him of a good living within the church. Anytime she was in the company of Mr Darcy and she felt some rise of her former, wild infatuation for him, Elizabeth had only to remember his cruelty to Mr Wickham and his degrading comments about herself to cool any former heat.

"Are you the fortune-teller who reads the cards that I hear about?"

"Yes," Elizabeth rasped as she swept her arm towards the stump before the window. Pausing, Wickham pulled out a cloth to cover the wood so that he might not sully the seat of his pants.

"You had better be worth the coins, old woman. I should hate to have to report you to the local magistrate."

Elizabeth startled back. She was not prepared for such rough usage by a man whose company and wit she had enjoyed. No one had ever come so close to a threat before. Most were scared that she possessed some sort of ability to lay a hex upon them, so they kept their tongues in check, even if they were not always entirely happy with their reading. Besides, since the local magistrate was Sir William Lucas, Elizabeth was not overly concerned that anything would be done that might require effort and would risk the wrath of the local population. She knew very well that people would not take kindly to the loss of their local card reader.

Wickham leaned his elbow onto the shelf and glanced at the iron bars that covered the window. "Is this to prevent unhappy customers from throttling you? I am not sure it would work with me," he said laughingly.

"Sometimes, people are not entirely happy with what the future may hold for them. I am but a layer of the cards. I have no influence over which are dealt or to whom. I treat all my visitors with equal respect and honour."

Wickham snorted and crossed his arms before his chest. "Are you meaning to tell me that you have never before dealt cards from the bottom of the deck? I imagine that happy customers are more likely to pay well. Would it not make your purse heavier to deal cards with nothing but propitious meanings?"

Elizabeth was starting to become incensed. She was accustomed to episodes of mild scorn or laughing doubt. She did not mind such things in the least. But to sit there while he implied that she might outright cheat customers was intolerable.

"That thought had never crossed my mind. It may be that it says more of the person making the suggestion than the one dealing the cards."

His eyes narrowed. Wickham stared hard at Elizabeth, as though trying to catch something of her face under the veil. She then wielded her most effective weapon against difficult customers—an uncomfortable silence. The sounds of the forest rustled around them for a few moments. A rook cried loudly from a nearby tree.

Suddenly, Wickham let loose a laugh and waved his hand. "I was in jest, old hag! Do not take offence, I beg of you. All was in jest, I assure you."

Elizabeth relaxed. She was glad that his sharp words were but a show of his humorous side. His handsome smile and twinkling eyes left her ready to laugh aloud herself. It was terrible that a happy nature such as his had been so mistreated and so misunderstood by Mr Darcy.

Imagine if he had been treated with kindness by Mr Darcy after the death of his father! But I am certain that awful man could not bring himself to see that Wickham has qualities that he could only dare to hope for. Such amiability—I am sure Mr Darcy would not have thought of jesting with me in this way. I am sure Mr Darcy would have found fault in the hardness of the stump. He would have shouted at the rook to be silent. Mr Darcy would have—

"So, should we begin?" Wickham asked.

Elizabeth was startled out of her reflections. She had been so lost in thought about the many defects of Mr Darcy, she had quite forgotten about the task at hand. She shuffled the deck with alacrity, hoping the fast action would also shuffle off thoughts of Mr Darcy. Wickham drummed the tips of his fingers upon the roughhewn ledge as he watched the cards intently.

"You should bring to mind that which you desire to have clarity on. A certain problem, your profession, or"—she almost sent the cards scattering as her fingers failed her—"your love life."

Wickham laughed aloud once more. "Trust me, crone, I need no help in that last area. In fact, sometimes it can be quite the opposite. Ladies do enjoy my company..."

Elizabeth frowned slightly. An image of Wickham, surrounded by young women at a card party, came to her mind. She had to admit that her two youngest sisters left little doubt as to their preference for his company.

It is well that Wickham is all goodness. Such a man could easily deceive women into behaving in a way that could ruin their reputations.

"Do you have in mind what you wish to ask?"

"Yes. Should I tell you?" Wickham queried with a small smirk.

Elizabeth paused. Customarily, she would have said no. Would he enquire after the state of her own heart? Was she first among all the ladies vying for his attention? He left no doubt in anyone's mind that when he entered a room, it was Elizabeth whose company he sought. Still, the urge to know for certain was too great and quickly mowed down any scruples that dared to rise up in a weak protest.

"If you wish the reading to be as accurate as possible, then yes. You should tell me what is in your mind."

She bit her lip with a twinge of guilt. It was wrong to use these moments to gain insight into the hearts of others, but her curiosity to know if she was high in Wickham's thoughts overtook her.

"Mary King."

"Pard— What?"

"Mary King! Is she pining after me?" Elizabeth gathered her scattered thoughts as she shuffled the cards. Mary King was a young girl who had just arrived in Meryton to spend time with her uncle. Lydia had proclaimed her freckles and reddish hair hideous, but Elizabeth remembered Mary King as being a pleasant-looking young woman with nothing remarkable about her countenance. However, Wickham had danced with her, which was enough to unleash the wrath of Lydia's acrid tongue.

"...Lizzy, it is fair of me to point out her faults. Why should Wickham dance with her when he could have me as a partner? Or even you? Mary King is short, plain, and dull, dull, dull! I should think Wickham would require her to have a great deal more than an inheritance of ten thousand pounds to tempt him into dancing and laughing with the likes of her. How could he even look at her when I am several inches taller and without a freckle upon my cheeks?"

"This…Mary King, you said? You wish to know her heart?"

Wickham burst out laughing. "Of course. Will she accept a proposal from me? Would she elope with me?"

"Ahhh, you love her."

"Maybe, maybe not. Why speak of love when a woman can have many allurements? Her fortune is enough to raise the heartbeat of any poor soldier such as myself. I will be comfortable for a while, and she will have a very handsome officer to parade around upon her arm. Marriage to her shall suit the both of us. That is, until her funds run low and she becomes more of a chore than a pleasure. Then I—"

Elizabeth's throat had tightened so very much in mortification that she began to cough.

"I say! Don't die on me before you have told me about these silly cards," Wickham exclaimed, getting to his feet. "Here, drink this."

Wickham slid a thin flask through the bars. The tears rolling down Elizabeth's cheeks and the veil blurred her vision so that she took it without thinking clearly. She brought the flask up under her veil and took a sip, supposing it to be water or a wine. An explosion of hard liquor burned down her throat. She wheezed in an inhale and a wash of dizziness passed through her. But the refreshment—whatever it was—worked its magic and she did stop coughing. Feeling light-headed, Elizabeth thrust the flask back through the bars.

"Look here, I need to return in a bit. Can you hurry this along?"

Elizabeth recovered her calm. The cards were dealt, and she was surprised by what lay before her. There, as the very first card, was the King of Swords, exactly like Mr Darcy. But it was reversed. Elizabeth deliberately kept all of her cards scrupulously upright. She did not like the idea of reading reversed cards. She knew their meanings, but Hill had told her each reader of the cards must one day decide for themselves whether or not to read the cards when they were upside down. For some reason—perhaps it was her natural inclination to make merry of life no matter how difficult the circumstance—Elizabeth had never dealt any reversed cards. Until now.

"I like the look of *that* fellow there!" Wickham said as he pointed to the King of Swords. "Look at the crown on his head! And sitting on a throne. Is that me?"

"It represents your past." Elizabeth paused.

"That is unfortunate. It should be my future!"

Elizabeth remembered the words she had used when the card was upright during Mr Darcy's reading.

Responsible, honourable, truthful, and controlled. The reverse is so very different. Selfish, manipulative, impulsive, and a waste of a good mind.

"It tells of a past that has been focused on your own survival. Your sense of your own comfort and security is very powerful. You are able to persuade others to do as you see fit, as you think is for the best."

She waited with her breath held. Rather than being insulted, Wickham just nodded absently, obviously seeing nothing in what she just said to disagree with. Elizabeth exhaled, relieved. It was the kindest interpretation that she could conjure of the reversed King of Swords. Her relief was replaced by a nagging concern that this was how Wickham viewed himself and he thought little was objectionable to it.

"The next is the Seven of Wands. It shows you should stick to your course. If you apply yourself, you could go far and be successful."

"With Mary King?"

Elizabeth rolled her eyes. She had been hoping to encourage him in his profession. He had always spoken of himself as very capable and brave, more so than his fellow officers. She knew Wickham was particularly proud of his superior horsemanship.

Was he bragging without just cause and I was too aware of his handsome face to notice?

"It was meant to be in your profession, not in matters of your heart. If you apply yourself earnestly in your profession, you have the ability to go far."

"Oh, that is not about my love life? That is unfortunate, is it not?"

Not wishing to dwell on this any longer, Elizabeth pointed to the last card. Again, it was reversed. Upright, it meant skill, ability, and creating a fortune for yourself. But reversed, it signified trickery, a wasting of talent, and lost opportunities to make a fortune.

"The Magician. It means that, in the arena of your heart, you should be wary of what is not real in the days to come. Perhaps you have some knowledge that is not actually true. It is a warning that you should pursue a higher type of love and not lose any opportunities to better yourself as a man."

"Are you saying that Mary King does not possess the fortune that she had been rumoured to have? I say, old woman, thank you so very much. Before I convince her to run off with me, I shall have to question her closely about what the exact amount of her inheritance was. She is such a silly chit that I am sure that shan't be a problem."

Wickham pulled out his flask and took a long pull from it.

"But," Elizabeth said, hoping to press home some of the advantages of behaving honourably and rising in his profession, "I think you do not see that this is a chance to change your fortunes for the better. It only takes some determination and—"

Wickham waved his hand before him, signalling to Elizabeth in no uncertain terms that her opinion was no longer wanted or needed. He stood and straightened his jacket.

"Be seeing you. Thanks for the intelligence, old woman."

Wickham strode off in the direction of the barracks. Elizabeth watched his form disappear into the forest, her mouth open, eyebrows raised. When he was gone, with a humph of discontent, she sat back in her chair and brooded. Then she sat bolt upright.

"He did not pay me," she murmured. Standing and leaning against the bars of the window, she shouted out, "You did not pay me, sir!"

The silence of the trees was the only response. A pattering of rain began again and Elizabeth groaned in frustration and slammed a palm upon the sill. The cards jumped slightly. Puzzled, she picked up the first and last card, examining them closely.

"Now how on earth did you two become reversed? All of the cards in my deck are always right side up."

Elizabeth picked up the rest of the deck and fanned them out before her. The other seventy-six cards were all upright. She shrugged as she gathered them back up and placed The Magician and the King of Swords on top, upright and proper.

Chapter 9

Nicholls Has Made White Soup Enough

The ball at Netherfield was prepared for and anticipated by the ladies of Longbourn for a myriad of reasons. Elizabeth was certain the primary reason Mrs Bennet anticipated the ball was so that the number of witnesses of Mr Bingley's regard for Jane could increase and declarations of future marriages expounded upon. It was all very well and good for Mrs Bennet to observe some look or word in the privacy of a drawing room corner, but that was not nearly so satisfactory as being able to exclaim loudly and bring it to her neighbours' attention much like one might ignite a mountaintop beacon to communicate with a neighbouring valley. Their mother was a whirl of exclamations, advice, curls, and petticoats for several hours prior to leaving.

Lydia and Kitty had their own ecstasies to shriek about behind closed doors. The prospect of so many officers packed into one location with so many opportunities to dance had them in shrill raptures. After an unaccustomed bout of mathematics, the two girls had concluded that the eligible men would outnumber the unmarried ladies by ten to one. Or was it one hundred to one? At least by quite a lot in their estimation, and that was something to be excited about; in their opinion, too often the ladies were numerous and the handsome gentlemen with muscular calves were far too few.

Elizabeth could perceive that Jane was nervous, but also excited. It seemed to her that Jane had recently come to the conclusion that she was indeed very much in love with Mr Bingley. Elizabeth was certain that Mr Bingley felt the same.

Mary was sorting her sheets of music for the dozenth time. There would most likely be a hue and cry for a song to be performed by the more accomplished ladies of the local society. And Mary would be at the ready with grim determination. Her troops had to be in order and prepared to heed the call of their commander.

Unlike the rest of the house, Elizabeth was a confusion of feelings. She was still looking forward to seeing Mr Wickham again. The initial hurt over his single-minded enquiries about the fortune of Mary King had been completely forgiven. Who else but she could comprehend the anxiety of not being secure in fortune? Of course he wanted to marry money. Of course he was interested in having his future secured. Of course the penniless daughter of a local gentleman would not be in his consideration as a future bride. They could still meet in society and enjoy a dance and lively conversation, even if that would be the length and breadth of their understanding.

On the side of her more unpleasant reflections, Elizabeth knew for certain that at least two of her dances were to go to Mr Collins. And then there would be Mr Darcy to contend with. His eyes would be spending far too much time on her, judging her hair, her dancing, her gown, and perhaps even her thoughts. At least Mr Wickham would be there to ease the discomfort of these prospects, and this brought a smile to her face more than once.

I am considered more than tolerable to Wickham, at least. We have no future together, but regardless, it gives a young lady a distinct satisfaction to have her company sought out by the most handsome man in the militia. I am not above having my vanity fanned by Mr Wickham after such a trampling as it received by Mr Darcy.

Elizabeth took a few minutes to gaze critically at her reflection, trying to discern what exactly had offended Mr Darcy to such an extent that it drove him to make such a hurtful, public declaration. Although she did not consider herself to be a great beauty, she could find nothing to vindicate the sneering words of Mr Darcy.

Tolerable. Not worthy of either admiration or scorn. Just a shapeless burden to be borne.

With a touch of melancholy, she made the final adjustments in her hair of the delicate, white flowers and new ribbon.

Darcy scoured the crowd as it slowly trickled into Netherfield. The Bennet family was at the forefront of his mind. They were a troublesome, loud troupe who spoke too freely of opinions that should be saved for private airings. The reasons for his attentiveness at spotting the Longbourn tribe were twofold. Firstly and foremost, he was concerned for his friend Bingley.

I have never seen a person so unmindful of his heart. But this latest flight of fancy for Miss Jane Bennet is the most serious case of ardour I have ever seen in him. He even talks of marriage.

Darcy sighed with exasperation as he left his position of watching the front door and went upstairs to a window that looked out over the approaching carriages. The parade of country locals who disembarked their vehicles would pause to stare wide-eyed at the facade of Netherfield illuminated and grand in the dark of the evening.

"Look at how they gawk. I am all amazement at these unmannered provincials," Miss Bingley proclaimed as she quietly sidled up next to him. "Observe Sir William Lucas, how he stares. And to think he had the temerity to suggest that Louisa and I needed his help in society. Observe how he gapes, how ridiculous."

"Their wonder is understandable. I suppose the surrounding area has grown so accustomed to Netherfield being in darkness and shuttered that it is a surprising transformation for them."

"I agree, it is too amusing."

"Should you not be greeting the guests at the door?"

"If this were a ball of some consideration—with guests of note—I would be attending to my duties with much more earnestness. But here? In Hertfordshire? It is a lark of my brother's, nothing more. Besides, Louisa is there with Charles. Speaking of Charles—" Miss Bingley paused and laid a light set of fingertips upon his upper arm. He resisted the urge to recoil. "—I am so glad we have a moment to confer. It is of the utmost importance that we closely observe my brother. Do not allow him to sneak off alone with Miss Bennet. Should a proposal be allowed to occur, we will regret it to no end."

Darcy nodded absently. He was not fully attending to her whispered instructions, for his heart had leapt to such a height that attention to anything else was impossible. He recognised the Bennet carriage coming down the drive. His first mission of closely observing Bingley was completely forgotten when his second mission demanded his full attention.

I will enjoy the company of Miss Elizabeth this evening. I will even ask her to dance. Again. She refused me once at that small party at Sir William's, but that was understandable, even admirable. For there it was such a mess of moved furniture and rolled-up carpets that it bordered on improper. And her sister Mary was playing so dreadfully that dancing to that music would have been an embarrassment for both of us. No, she was correct in declining to dance that evening. It was sensible and dignified of her. But she cannot refuse me this evening, for everyone will be dancing. It is a ball. There are proper, professional musicians. It is what is expected. I will finally have my dance with her and be done with it. It will be my last time to observe her faults and follies so that I may leave Hertfordshire with equanimity. Then I need never see her again. She will be erased from my mind.

Ever since he had that strange dream, Elizabeth had been a regular visitor to both his nocturnal and sunlit thoughts. A flush of warmth began to creep up his neck and face.

"...and it will be well to be gone from this rustic swamp within the next few days."

"What?" he snapped, realising that Miss Bingley had been speaking while his thoughts were much more pleasantly engaged with Elizabeth Bennet.

Darcy turned his head to see how very close Miss Bingley had come during this secluded, little conference. Her eyes were dilated and her lips parted; her face had a warmth to it as well, as her gaze drifted down to his lips.

He looked away quickly and exclaimed, "Ah, there is the Bennet carriage stopping now."

They both observed the endless line of daughters that emerged. Darcy felt his breath catch as Elizabeth appeared. She looked up. Their eyes met.

The remembrance from his dream of her standing over him with bare legs and laughing eyes engulfed him, causing him to inhale sharply.

"I agree, Mr Darcy. All five out at once! Utterly ridiculous. It is as if I am observing a line of ducklings waddling after their mother. How amusing they are," Miss Bingley cried, oblivious to the true cause of Darcy's discomfort. "That would never occur in London. Can you even imagine?"

"Excuse me," Darcy muttered as he bowed curtly and walked away towards the front door. Darcy took the stairs two at a time down to the main hall, arriving just in time to observe Mr Bingley escort Miss Bennet and Miss Elizabeth into the ballroom. He felt a very unjust anger at his affable friend bubble up within him.

"Too right, Mr Darcy. We should be more vigilant." A slightly breathless Caroline Bingley drew up by his side and looped her arm through his as she steered him towards the ballroom. Darcy had to restrain the impulse to shrug off her cloying weight so that he could approach Miss Elizabeth solo. It seemed he was not to be so fortunate, and he resigned himself to escorting Miss Bingley instead of Miss Elizabeth forward through the crowd.

"What a handsome pair they are," Sir William exclaimed to Mr Bennet as Darcy and Miss Bingley walked by. "Both are so excessively dignified. It would be a common sight in the highest ranks of society, I assure you, but to see it here in Hertfordshire is a rare occurrence. Capital! Such elegant comportment, such an excellent pairing of dignity and grace."

"They are indeed exceedingly tall," Mr Bennet replied dryly.

Darcy did his best to ignore the blaring compliments from Sir William Lucas. He hurried his pace so that Miss Bingley may not notice his words, but there he miscalculated her ability to latch onto any small imagining of the two of them being intimate.

"How droll Sir William is!" she said. "I must say that he grows on me. His powers of observation are acute, in their way. To think that *we* struck him as a handsome couple."

"I believe I saw your brother and Miss Bennet go out onto the terrace. Perhaps we should separate until they are rediscovered."

"Good Lord, nothing is worse than a terrace. It promotes shocking intimacy that practically begs for proposals. I will investigate at once."

"Excellent. I will walk past that row of potted plants in case I was mistaken. They could be concealed there."

"Yes, do that. Greenery is also notorious for providing cover for making offers."

Miss Bingley gave him a curt, conspiratorial nod. Darcy wiped the back of his hand across his forehead as he watched her disappear into the crowd. Once Miss Bingley was safely out of sight, he turned to track his true interest.

Walking casually, Darcy pressed his way through the throng of officers and locals, keeping his eyes locked upon the spot where Miss Elizabeth was having an animated conversation with Miss Lucas. The young ladies leaned their heads towards each other, framed by the lush greenery of the plants.

"I am inconsolable, Charlotte," Elizabeth moaned. "I was so looking forward to dancing with Mr Wickham and now to discover that he is not even here."

"I know how much you have enjoyed his conversation, but given what you have told me about his supposed history with Mr Darcy, it is hardly surprising that Wickham was too frightened to come this evening."

"What can you mean by 'Wickham's *supposed* history'? He gave facts, locations, names. And his way of conveying it all was so artless and sincere. Do you mean to imply that he had not been completely honest?"

"We know little of him, Eliza. As we also know little of Mr Darcy. With so few other people to either verify or counter the facts we have been given, it is difficult to know what to believe."

"We have several facts. And add to those facts the impressions and deductions that have been formed after witnessing the conduct of both gentlemen and I believe we can draw a clear conclusion that one is horrid and the other is wrongly maligned by fate and the vindictive nature of the other," Elizabeth said as the warmth in the room made her irritability increase. "And what did you mean by saying Wickham was frightened away? You can see in his bearing that Wickham *must* be a brave fellow. Just as you can see in the bearing of Mr Darcy that he has a too high opinion of his abilities, a resentful temper, a sardonic eye, an unrelenting, prideful stiffness in his back…"

Elizabeth felt the nudge of Charlotte's sharp elbow in her ribs. Her mind had been so preoccupied with angrily devising critiques of Mr Darcy that she had been unconsciously fidgeting her new fan about. The end of it had been alternately tapping at the spot just below her lips and gliding along her heated right cheek. Into her vision stepped Mr Darcy. Elizabeth stared at him, shocked.

It had been well over a week since their last encounter. His cheeks were less sunken, his skin had lost its former wan cast, and his face had a ruddy hue of good health. The dark circles under his eyes had completely disappeared. Elizabeth realised—now that he had the additional radiance of health and contentment—he was even more handsome than when she had first encountered him during the card reading at Netherfield.

"Miss Bennet."

"Mr Darcy."

"Will you do me the honour of dancing with me?"

Elizabeth stood silent for a moment. There was the smallest hint of a self-assured smirk playing on the edges of his mouth. She narrowed her eyes, still silent. Only a small cough from Charlotte brought her back to her senses.

"I, well, that is…yes. I am engaged to my cousin for the first…"

"Then the second?"

She could only manage a brief nod.

He bowed and moved away.

"I will never forgive myself!" she moaned. "I promised myself that I would never dance with him. Why on earth did he ask *me* to dance?"

"Can you blame him? While you were relating to me everything you hate about Mr Darcy, you were staring straight at him and flirting with that beautiful new fan of yours!"

"Charlotte! What can you mean?"

"Tapping below the lips with your fan…that means that you wish to kiss. And drawing it across your cheek as you were means that—well, how do I put this delicately—you hold him in high regard." She cleared her throat. "*Very* high regard."

Elizabeth looked down at her new fan, beautiful and undamaged, like a traitor lying in her palm. Just a few days prior, the rivet in her old fan had sprung out and the silk had finally ripped as the entire thing had fallen to shreds on the floor. She had not wished to spend the money on a new fan, but it was a necessity. If she were perfectly frank with herself, the new fan had been such a pleasure that she had unconsciously been toying with it all evening. Her old fan would have stayed clutched in her fist for the entire ball for fear it would fall to pieces. She stared up at Charlotte, aghast.

"You do not think that he believes I was—No, it is too fantastical! I would not dream of such nonsense."

"I have never actually seen you flirting with your fan before, so I do believe you when you say it was done unintentionally. But I doubt Mr Darcy saw it that way." Charlotte giggled lightly.

"A man so given to vicious judgements upon my person can hardly be flattered by some swoops of my fan. No. You are wrong."

"But my dear Eliza, you must acknowledge that—besides Mr Bingley's sisters—you are the only other woman in the room he has asked to stand up with him. It is quite the distinction."

"He only intends it as a means of upbraiding me and not as a badge of happy consequence. Perhaps Miss Bingley instructed him to dance with me so that they may have more follies to criticise me of."

"Have it either way, but the truth of the matter is that it is only you he singles out. Do not let your passing fancy for Wickham allow you to slight a man of Mr Darcy's importance and standing."

Elizabeth opened her mouth to respond definitively to that piece of advice. But at that moment, the music was beginning for the first dance and Mr Collins oozed up beside her.

"My fair cousin, I believe that the honour of this very first dance on this splendid evening had been most solemnly, kindly, and sincerely promised to me by you. So, if I may be so very bold, I have arrived by your side to claim that which—"

"Yes, yes. Come," Elizabeth blurted out as she resolutely took his arm and practically led him onto the floor. She was almost grateful to Mr Collins for his timely appearance. Anything to take her mind off what had just occurred. It was only when the music began and the steps of the dance became slightly more intricate that she became aware of the many missteps of her cousin. Her embarrassments multiplied. A passing glance of Mr Darcy only increased her chagrin.

Now I know he is most definitely smiling! It is too much to bear. What must he think of me?

Her cheeks were positively on fire once the dance had ended. Mr Collins gratefully scurried away to secure her some refreshments. Before he returned, the music struck up again and Mr Darcy approached Elizabeth. They walked onto the floor and began to dance. Elizabeth's eyes stayed locked on Mr Darcy as they passed close to each other. The hint of a breeze brushed across her lips, like a phantom of a kiss, each time their bodies glided past one another.

A slight bobbing of a black-clad figure in the crowd caught her eye. Mr Collins looked at her plaintively as he held her glass of punch in the air over his head, waving it about. A small splash of the punch crested over the lip of the cup and landed on the shoulder of a very irate, white-haired dowager. The old lady, rightfully indignant, popped him on the head with her fan as he cowered away from her. Mr Collins dodged the continued wrath of the old lady's fan and came closer to the dancing couples.

"Miss Elizabeth!" he cried out. Several people around turned and stared at him, curious and amused. "I have your punch! Shall I hold it for you or—"

Elizabeth turned her head, ignoring Mr Collins as best she could. Desperate for a distraction, she began to speak to Mr Darcy.

"I believe a little conversation must be attempted, Mr Darcy. It would not do to pass the entire time together in morose silence."

Her partner pulled his eyes away from the prancing Mr Collins, who was claiming to those nearest him that he had been promised a second dance with Miss Elizabeth and was making enquiries as to the identity of the tall fellow she was now engaged with.

Eager to keep attention away from the spectacle of her cousin and on herself, Elizabeth said, "I always talk as a rule when dancing, for it makes the time pass so much more quickly."

"But what if you are desirous of your partner's company and do not wish it to come to an end?" Mr Darcy replied, his attention focused most sincerely on her. "Would you then advise complete silence so that the time will seem to pass more slowly? For if you are enjoying the company of your partner, anything to lengthen the time together, even the illusion of time passing more slowly, would be beneficial."

"As a passionate enthusiast of sketching characters, I could never conduct myself in that manner." Elizabeth smiled as she spoke, hoping to dissemble the turbulent emotions within her breast. Mr Darcy responded by smiling warmly back at her, which added another layer of confusion to her heart. "It gives me such joy to attempt to compose a portrait of the nature of others that I could never commit myself to total silence while dancing. Conversation is the best path to knowing the character of another."

"Really? But many facts may be obtained through quiet observation, do you not agree? If I recall correctly, you expressed yourself quite well during your stay at Netherfield on the benefits of studying another person's actions. Much can be discerned from little trifles. Such as how someone drinks from a wine glass, sits in a chair, or how a lady may move her fan about her person."

They parted after that last remark, giving Elizabeth the opportunity to let seething resentment rise to the top of her feelings. She pursed her lips together and lifted her chin at Mr Darcy, refusing to encourage further teasing.

"If I may be so bold, Miss Elizabeth, what is your take upon my character?" he continued.

She stood silent as they gazed at each other during a pause in the steps. This undeniably handsome, intelligent man before her truly did have her perplexed. During his card reading, he had struck her as polite, considerate, and deeply wounded from some unknown cause. Her heart had soared during the encounter and, if she had been pressed to tell of it, Elizabeth would have sworn that she had fallen suddenly and violently in love with him. Then came the several instances of rudeness to herself and those she loved. And his unjust treatment of Wickham. For a moment, Elizabeth felt that all her experience in reading people had been torn to shreds and cast out onto a strong wind—scattered and useless. She bit her lip and then responded, "Truthfully, I hear such conflicting accounts of you that I am unsure what to conclude."

Darkness creased his brow. "I am certain some of those accounts have come from new acquaintances of yours."

"We have had the fortune of meeting some of the officers of the militia. As you witnessed last week in Meryton, we were making a new acquaintance. Many of the officers are in attendance this evening. It is a shame that *all* could not be present."

He actually scowled at this. Elizabeth's brows raised in surprise.

"Mr Wickham," Mr Darcy said, "has the good fortune to be able to easily form new acquaintances. Whether he can retain a person's good opinion over time is much more uncertain."

She rolled her eyes upward when she turned and was unobserved by Mr Darcy.

My abilities of discernment cannot have failed me so utterly in the case of Mr Wickham. Though this infuriating man before me is a hard one to know, I am certain of myself with Wickham.

She smiled slightly and only gave the briefest of nods in acknowledgement of his last statement. By this time, they had worked their way to the other side of the room. Mrs Bennet was sitting with several of the other neighbourhood matrons and had a merry sheen to her cheek as she took another large swallow of punch. Mr Darcy's visage became positively grim as snatches of her mother's conversation floated in their direction.

"Five thousand a year…make Jane an offer…a wealthy son-in-law…of course Jane would be the first to marry, but who would ever want Lizzy? Fortunately, Mr Collins may be persuaded to take her off our hands…"

If Elizabeth could have shrunk to the form of a mouse and scurried between the dancing feet and out of the room, she would have. Mr Darcy distractedly looked about the room, seeming to forget about her for a few moments. His gaze locked on a spot in the distance. Elizabeth turned to see that he had found Jane and Mr Bingley standing close together by the potted plants. Miss Bingley joined the couple. Mr Darcy visibly relaxed and turned his gaze back to her.

"I would ask that you do not attempt to sketch my character at the present moment. It would reflect poorly on both of us."

Frustrated and embarrassed, Elizabeth replied with asperity. "You are not a monarch, sir—" He startled as though he had been forcefully struck, but she persisted. "—who-who can direct in what way a subject may or may not indulge in their thinking. Besides, if I do not take your likeness now, I may not have another opportunity."

Mr Darcy blinked rapidly several times. The music ended and they stared severely at each other as the couples around them melted into the surrounding crowd with happy smiles on their faces.

"Did you just refer to me as…a king?"

Elizabeth forced herself through sheer strength of will to neither blink nor grimace. The image of the King of Swords, proud and unapproachable, sitting on his throne flashed up in her mind's eye. Her heart skipped a beat as she kept her gaze on the handsome face before her.

Am I truly so foolish as to risk exposure by this man? He is too shrewd by far. I must watch my words around him with much more circumspection.

"It was merely a humorous observation. I imagine any man of substantial means must see themselves as ruler of all they survey."

Mr Darcy shook his head. "Of course. It was merely one of your quick-witted jests. I did not mean anything by that. I-I would by no means suspend any pleasure of yours." He bowed quickly. "Miss Elizabeth."

She dropped a small curtsey. "Mr Darcy."

A furious blend of confused mortification swirled in her heart as she left the ballroom and walked out onto the terrace. The cool breeze on her cheeks did little to assuage her discomfort.

There is no possible way that the evening can degrade any further. To be teased by Mr Darcy and Charlotte, embarrassed by my relations, and deprived of the company of the one man I wished to see.

With a smack of fury, Elizabeth brought her new fan down hard upon the stone railing of the terrace. A sharp crunch was heard. She moaned in frustration as she carefully opened the new piece of finery, only to discover that she had cracked the two end pieces. The delicate wooden ends sagged to one side and the fan bent in half. Frustrated tears pricked at the corners of her eyes. With a huff of anger, she tossed the broken fan into the bushes below and turned to go back inside.

I will make the best of the evening. I will not allow myself to become humiliated by anything else my family does. Absolutely nothing they do or say will mortify me further.

Chapter 10

Without Any Intention of Coming Back

Darcy was waiting at the front of Netherfield to see Bingley off. It was fortuitous that his friend had received a summons from his solicitor in London that his presence was needed to attend to some matters to do with his finances. Although both men were tired from the ball the previous evening, they had met for breakfast.

Before Bingley mounted his horse, Darcy finally broached the subject that Bingley had been anxiously hinting at all morning.

"I think it is good that you will have a few nights away from Netherfield. It will give you a chance to examine the nature of your intentions towards Miss Jane Bennet as well as the state of Miss Bennet's regard for you."

"Yes? You know, I was intending on riding over to Longbourn this morning to see if I could have a bit more conversation with her. It is dashed unfortunate that I must be in town. Unlucky, but I will be back before next week, I assure you."

"You should take advantage of this opportunity to reflect. If you wish to have my opinion—"

"Yes?" Bingley leaned towards Darcy, eager to hear his friend's insights. "That is, if you wish to advise me, that would be wonderful. It is not as if I may purchase a pamphlet on how to ask a girl for her hand in marriage, is it? And neither of us has the benefit of a father to ask for guidance. So I would very much like your view on such matters."

Darcy started back. He had not truly anticipated that Bingley was on the precipice of proposing. He knew that his friend was quite taken by Jane Bennet. He had seen him in love before and had not realised how quickly this had evolved into something much more serious.

"Bingley, I think—before you pursue a deeper understanding between yourself and Miss Bennet—you should closely examine your past encounters. Can you say, honestly, that she seems to prefer your company to the company of any other? Have you seen the passion of love in her eyes? Is she visibly moved to be near you, to see you, to converse with you?"

This series of questions evidently dampened Bingley's hopeful mood. His shoulders slouched and a worried crease came to his forehead.

"I do not mean to dictate your feelings to you, but as someone who has been pursued by the ladies of the *ton* since before I was eighteen years old, I feel it my onus as your friend to bring your attention to these points. I would never forgive myself if you were persuaded into a marriage where all of the warm regard was on your side and not equally returned."

"Are you saying that you believe Miss Bennet to be a fortune hunter? With no real respect for me? No passion of finer feelings in her breast that would be the primary cause of her agreeing to be my wife?"

Darcy straightened his spine and clasped his hands behind his back. "I would not go so far as to accuse her of pursuing you for purely mercenary purposes." *I most certainly cannot say the same of her mother*, Darcy thought, but did not voice. "I must speak from my own experience. You are younger than I and, as you pointed out, have no father or close male relative to advise you upon this matter. I am being perfectly honest in saying that you must deeply examine your heart to discover whether you think she returns your sentiments fully and completely. If you cannot, with absolute certainty, say that she does, I do not think it advisable to make her an offer. It may be a precipitate act that you come to regret. I would hope that if I were on the cusp of a decision that *you* deemed potentially unwise, you would be so generous as to share your concerns with me. I do not dare to say that I believe it to be an incorrect course of action, merely that you consider it further."

The ever-present twinkle in Bingley's eye dimmed. "It is unlikely that I would ever have to step in and advise you to think more deeply on a subject," Bingley muttered. "But I do vow to speak up, if, in the future, I think you would benefit from my counsel."

Bingley dropped his gaze to the ground before him for several moments, not looking Darcy in the eye. Finally, he glanced up and extended his hand. They shook and then Bingley slung up into his saddle.

"You have given much to ponder, Darcy. I know I am not as serious-minded as you. It is well that I have a friend such as you to give me pause to consider a thing from all sides. I am much obliged."

Bingley switched his horse lightly with his riding crop and took off at a canter through the gates of Netherfield. Darcy frowned and shuffled one boot in the gravel beneath him. Something about that conversation did not sit correctly in his chest, like a chewy bit of beef that may have begun to go off during a stretch of warm weather.

But I truly do have his best interests at heart. Can he claim any one instance when Jane Bennet gave him assurances, either by word, deed or look, that she loved him best above all others? No. I am sure he cannot. Her countenance has been smooth and unyielding to any deep, passionate sentiment. Never have I witnessed a moment of unguarded affection in her gaze. I am correct in what I have said.

Then a smile crept up to his face, slow and unfolding.

Not like Elizabeth. The way she used her fan last night. How bright red her cheeks were when we danced. Even her breathing, when we were near, showed that she too was feeling the desire to have me so close that our flesh—

Darcy shook his head and turned to the front door of Netherfield. Glancing up, he saw that Miss Bingley was closely observing him from a window. He looked away quickly, giving no indication that he had perceived her. Very casually, he turned his tread from the house and towards the stables. Suddenly, the idea of being in company with only Miss Bingley and the Hursts for the next few days—alone and isolated in this country house, with Miss Bingley stalking his every move and mood—made his stomach tighten painfully. Darcy rubbed his belly to make the stab of anxiety cease, to no effect.

Perhaps it would be best if we followed Charles to London. There we could truly point out to him that there is little evidence of Jane Bennet being in love with him. And now that I have finally had my dance with Elizabeth, there is nothing to prevent me from beginning to erase her from my thoughts. It is unfortunate that her family is so beneath me and that they embarrass at every turn with their impropriety. The way Miss Mary Bennet assaulted our ears with that song last night. And how her cousin, Mr Collins, practically bowled me over in an effort to force an introduction upon me. If it were just a matter of her low connexions, that could be eventually dismissed, for many are willing to have a short memory when a great estate has made a connexion of marriage. But the combination of those low connexions as well as their complete lack of scruples in regards to how to conduct themselves properly in society... No, it is too much. Elizabeth will be hurt, no doubt, but that cannot be helped. The more time and distance between the Bennet ladies and us, the better.

Feeling quite proud of his morning of wonderfully sensible wisdom that he had dispensed to both himself and his friend, Darcy entered the stables and called for his horse to be saddled for a ride. When he returned, he would tell the rest of the party of his intention to journey to London tomorrow.

As he wheeled his horse around to leave the grounds through the front gate, he saw one of the gardeners scratching his head over an object in his hand as he walked back towards the house. For some reason, Darcy's curiosity piqued and he trotted up to the young man.

"What is that in your hand?"

The young fellow spun around and gulped, staring up at Darcy with eyes wide.

"I found it, sir. In the shrubberies by the terrace. It must be left over from last night."

Darcy held out his hand. The boy placed the thing into it. Darcy held up Elizabeth's fan, opened it and saw, with amusement, that it collapsed over. He grinned as he folded it back up and nodded to the boy. "It is all right. I know the owner of this and will see that it is returned."

"Yes, sir."

Darcy wheeled his horse about and passed through the gates of Netherfield. The fan was clasped in his hand as he spurred the horse into a canter. His admirable plan of ridding himself of any thought of Miss Elizabeth Bennet was off to a rocky start. It had been his intention to have that one dance with her to terminate what had been a foolish indulgence of a whim. Then the chapter of their acquaintance could be permanently closed. He had allowed himself to think of her and watch her closely for the last several weeks without checking himself. To indulge in conversation with her that strayed into deeper waters than the common polite chatter that only skimmed the surface of most social gatherings. To imagine holding her tight, kissing her, trailing his finger along her cheek to sweep down and out along those shoulders of hers...

He gave his horse an unnecessary tap from his riding crop. The eager beast never needed much encouragement to lengthen his stride and seemed to take some offence by the way he lurched into a gallop.

I allowed myself the indulgence of this admiration because, when my thoughts were consumed by Elizabeth, my spirits were no longer depressed by my failure to protect Georgiana. But this minor passion has served its purpose and now must be dismissed. I am fully recovered and ready to return to London society and attend to whatever needs Georgiana has.

He pulled his horse back from a gallop and into a trot as he took stock of where he was. Darcy was surprised to note that he was near the outskirts of the Longbourn estate. He *should* return this fan to Elizabeth. After all, he was so close. Perhaps she would be available to speak with him for a time. Maybe he would be asked to stay for a cup of tea.

It would be delightful to see the arch of her neck as she poured tea into a cup. The bend of her wrist as she passes it to me. Perhaps the tips of our fingers will brush together.

Darcy quelled those thoughts. Frowning, he turned up his palm to look at the wilted fan that was clutched alongside the reins. It was beyond use. And now the added stress of being pressed into the leather of the reins had given it a distinctly soiled appearance.

She can have no further use for the fan. I am being an utter fool. I must put a stop to this at once.

He turned his horse into a thick stand of woods that ran along a creek to make a wide loop back to Netherfield at a slow pace. At the bank of the creek, he raised his hand to throw the fan into the water. His horse snorted and tossed his head. Darcy's hand paused. His fingers were unwilling to release it.

With a groan of frustration, still clutching the broken fan in his hand, Darcy nudged his horse back into a calm, stately walk towards Netherfield.

Chapter 11

Find Such a Woman

Elizabeth was in complete misery. The sleepy morning after the ball had been even more wretched than the previous evening. Humiliations of her family's making, the disappointment over the absence of Wickham, and the strained dance with Mr Darcy had made the entire ball unsettling and dissatisfying. Although it had been a trying night, the morning after was so much worse than anything she could have envisioned.

Elizabeth had received a most unwelcome, interminable proposal of marriage from Mr Collins. As she patiently listened to the wearisome monologue, it was all she could do not to laugh at the performance. For it was much like an inferior stage play, by an actor with no real understanding of the words or sentiments he was attempting to express. It was a pantomime of a man making love to a woman, performed by an awkward, insincere player to a reluctant fellow actor.

And then, after Elizabeth had politely and gently declined the honour of marrying him, Mr Collins had the audacity to explain back to *her* exactly why *she* had declined his proposal. As if she were too stupid to understand her own thoughts, actions, and words.

Insufferable, insipid man!

Any sympathy she might have felt for his disappointment had rapidly dissipated at this outrage. Then her mother had arrived on the scene. And so began a train of threats, entreaties, and ultimatums that echoed through Longbourn till Elizabeth could take no more. Mrs Bennet was certain that if Elizabeth did not marry Mr Collins that she would drop dead and would not Lizzy feel like an ungrateful child then? Elizabeth had ventured out for a long walk. When she had returned, Mrs Bennet had simply picked up where she had ceased. Elizabeth pleaded feeling unwell and retreated to her room where she locked the door and plugged her ears to the wood-piercing shouts of her mother. Unable to cope any longer and knowing that any response other than an agreement to wed Mr Collins would bring no peace, she fled through the priest's hole to the little stone cottage in the woods.

Elizabeth sighed loudly at the remembrance as she gazed out of the window of the cottage. She leaned back in the ancient chair made of curved wood and twined vines. A light doze overtook her as her head slipped softly down to rest gently on one shoulder.

She heard a soft cough. Her eyes cracked open. As if through a fog, the dim image of Mr Darcy was before her. She smiled. Then, with shock, she recalled that he sat at the window of the stone cottage.

"Mr Darcy!" she croaked, sitting up straight and coughing loudly.

He frowned. "Yes. You recall my name from our previous meeting. This is the correct place. I had to make a few enquiries among the servants of Netherfield to be certain."

Elizabeth's hand shot up to her face. The veil was drawn down.

Relief washed over her. That is why he appeared before her as if in a dream of shadow and mist. She cleared her throat to make her words sound raspy and tired.

"Of course. I do not forget. Ever."

"Naturally. I would imagine in your line of work, a good memory is essential." He leaned forward to peer more deeply into the dark room. "I assume you also sell love charms? One was placed under my pillow. Do I have you to thank for making it?"

Elizabeth could not help but chuckle at this revelation. She leaned back farther in her chair so she could be certain her face was completely obscured from his view. "The charm was indeed made by my hand. Did it work?"

"Hardly. It had almost the opposite effect. I do not think you should sell those anymore, unless you wish to hear that they fanned flames of disdain."

Poor Miss Bingley! If only she knew.

"I am sorry, sir. I am sure that the lady in question was well-intentioned."

Elizabeth noticed that Mr Darcy seemed to clutch something close to his side. With a start, she realised it was her fan. He leaned over and began to tap it absentmindedly upon the sill that ran under the window bars.

"Madam, I sought you out to obtain some clarification."

"So, you are not here to purchase a charm of your own?"

"Um, no. When you read my cards, the very last one, what was it?"

Elizabeth remembered clearly every moment from that brief encounter. The accompanying sensations returned as well. How her heart had leapt the moment she saw him. How sad he had looked. How he had been kind when it was unnecessary, unexpected, and unwitnessed. How she had felt so warmly towards him before she knew anything of his wealth and property.

"The last card was the Seven of Cups. The card of many possibilities."

"Yes, that was the one."

Mr Darcy glanced around at the trees, seeming to try to organise his thoughts. His focus returned to the fan in his hand. He opened it slowly, it straightened up tall, then it flopped over. A small frown emerged on his lips.

"And, if you would not mind, if you have the time, could you remind me of what the cups meant?"

"Of course, sir," Elizabeth rasped out breathlessly as she gazed at the fan and then up into his pensive face. "The cups are different paths that are open to you. Paths that will succeed if chosen. The paths of wealth, lust, ambition, revenge, power, illusion, and…happiness. It means that, if you dream of what you desire, you can make it a reality. A very different life than the one you live now."

"But how will I know? How will I know what the path to happiness is? What if it is before me and I do not know it?"

The air felt charged. What was he asking of her? Elizabeth could sense her heart beating so strongly, it must be visible for him to see. Her fan that had been in his hand now lay quietly on the slab of wood. For the briefest of moments, an urge to take advantage of the situation slid over her. All she had to do was to encourage him to pursue a local girl that he already knew to attain happiness. Then she need never worry over money matters again. Her family would be forever certain of security. Elizabeth possessed the imagination to see all possibilities before her, but she had the goodness to pursue only the most honourable.

I must be completely honest with him. I will not lie to this man. It is the right thing to do, and he will sense deception in anything but the absolute truth.

"People think the cards tell them their future," Elizabeth said. "That is not true. The cards act as a mirror. They can only tell you what is already within you. Nothing more or less. It will be for you to decide which path to risk for happiness."

Mr Darcy nodded. "I see. So I must rely upon my own judgement to discern the correct way forward."

She imagined that lonely king upon the throne, his only companions being his logic and reason. "Yes. Your judgement is a very important tool. But even the strongest of tools can break and ultimately fail us. In moments of uncertainty, you must also call upon the heart to guide you. If you examine your heart closely, you will know how to proceed."

With a slight sneer of disdain, Mr Darcy quietly asked, "But what if the heart is so foolish, so weak, so unused to exertion that it cannot be trusted?"

"Then you must begin to call upon it. The heart cannot advise you if you never consult it or trust it. It will become stronger with use. Your heart can be your strongest, most-worthy ally—if you permit it."

Mr Darcy sat silently for several moments. His eyes closed and he appeared as if he was a judge sitting in deliberation of some weighty matter. Elizabeth found herself wishing this moment would not end. Here was the Mr Darcy of their first encounter. Unguarded, relaxed, fascinating. He was exactly the sort of man whom she could easily love above all others for the rest of her life.

With his eyes still squeezed shut, as if pained by what he was saying, Mr Darcy muttered out, "But I cannot— How can I make such a bold leap— I would risk—" His mouth snapped shut and he opened his eyes and stared straight up into the branches overhead. Any answer he may have been hoping for was not forthcoming from the silent sky.

Suddenly, he stood and placed a coin of too much value upon the sill.

"Thank you for your time. I wish you the best, madam." Mr Darcy turned and walked towards his horse.

Elizabeth sat motionless, looking at the sad fan lying on the sill next to the coin. Her hand had just begun to snake out to take up the fan when Mr Darcy stopped just before his horse and returned.

"I almost left this."

He took up the fan and turned back to his horse.

He may be on his way to Longbourn to return my broken fan!

He was just gone from sight when Elizabeth sprang up, covered the window, and tore off the black robes she wore. Never had she more furiously scrambled through the long passageway back to Longbourn. She arrived back in her room, panting and exhausted. She lay on her bed for a moment, feeling that her heart would burst out of her chest. Once her heavy breathing subsided, she cracked open her bedroom door and crept downstairs. Her mother was not there to assault her with demands and pleadings. Elizabeth moved to the door of the parlour and cracked it open. Only Jane was within.

"Jane, where is everyone?"

"Oh Lizzy! How are you? Come and sit, you look flushed and worried."

"Is Mama within?"

"No, she has just gone to visit with our aunt Philips. Kitty and Lydia have walked to Meryton with Mr Collins. Mary reads in her room. Father stays in his study with orders that he does not wish to be disturbed."

Elizabeth flopped down in a chair, grateful that her mother and Mr Collins were not within. Jane reached out a hand to press to her forearm.

"Are you well?"

She could only nod in response to her sister's concern. "Has anyone else come to visit?"

Elizabeth now saw a hint of disappointment cross Jane's face as she lowered her head back over her needlework. "No. No one has come here today."

"Ah. I see. Were you expecting a visit from—from someone?"

"No, nothing definite was mentioned. I thought that perhaps…but the day is not over yet. And you? Were you expecting a visit from someone?"

Elizabeth hardly knew how to reply to that question, it had been such an unusual hour. Was Mr Darcy going to return her broken fan? Did he even realise that it belonged to Elizabeth? Her heart sank at the thought that she had destroyed such a piece of finery in a fit of anger and confusion. The outburst had given her no relief. The anger was gone. But the confusion was still firmly in place.

"I was not expecting a visitor. No, I was not." She picked up a novel from the lending library that she had been reading. "I think I shall enjoy this small moment of peace before Mama returns and reignites her assault."

"Elizabeth, you were correct to refuse Mr Collins if you believe that he could not have made you happy, nor you him."

"Thank you, dear Jane. Let us hope that the next proposal to take place under this roof will be for a match of love and happiness."

"Yes. That would be wonderful. Truly."

The rest of the afternoon passed with an air of languid anxiety. It seemed to Elizabeth that Jane was not fully attending to her needlework. Any sound outside drew her focus suddenly. That she anticipated a visit from Mr Bingley was apparent.

The novel hung heavy in Elizabeth's hand. The heroine was tremulously indecisive, attempting to choose whether she should draw back a castle tapestry that swayed as a storm raged outside. Elizabeth could not help but sigh in frustration, feeling her own life provided just as many instances of suspense as the book before her.

Eventually, everyone returned from their various escapades. Charlotte visited as well with the intent of discussing the ball. But it was difficult to converse about anything in a rational manner with Mrs Bennet and Mr Collins canvassing the evils of a rejected proposal of marriage. Charlotte, who must have sensed some of what had occurred, very kindly drew Mr Collins into conversation as much as she could.

Finally, Elizabeth could hardly stand it any longer. Excusing herself, she returned to the safety of her room and the firm bolt on the door. Exhausted, she flung herself on the bed and mourned over the perverseness of the entire situation.

The one man we all desire to see here today, Mr Bingley, is nowhere to be seen! Could there be a man who was more in love? What does he wait for? He must know my sister will accept a proposal. And Mr Collins! Except for Mama, we all wish him to leave. And he insists he will stay until Saturday. How could anyone be so disobliging? Obtuse blockhead of a man. And Mr Darcy... Why he— I wish— How could he...

She struggled to wade through the mire of her thoughts on that particular man.

I thought for certain he would ride over to return my fan. Perhaps he does not realise it is mine. I am convinced that he would not so closely note how my particular fan differs from the fans of other ladies. It was a trifling nonsense. I make something out of nothing. He danced with me as a diverting way to pass the time in a place he so obviously disdains. Perhaps it will even become an amusing antidote that he can relate to his acquaintances. Something to laugh over. The silly country girl thinking she was particularly fine with her new fan, having a dance with a handsome man of consequence who would typically never deign to look twice at her. It is too much...

The heaviness of all of her concerns became wearisome. Elizabeth drifted off into a fitful sleep.

Chapter 12

Serious Attachments

Mr Darcy has done his bit admirably. Charles will never think again upon the name of Miss Jane Bennet transforming into Mrs Charles Bingley. I could see by his face as he rode away yesterday morning. That is done and closed. Now, all that is left is to cleanse ourselves of the dirt of these environs and return to properly civilised society in London.

Caroline Bingley smiled with satisfaction as she sat at her desk. It was very early in the morning, but all of the remaining party were so eager to take their leave of Netherfield that they had agreed upon a particularly early starting time for their journey back to London. They would feel the cobblestones of the streets under the carriage well before the noon hour. All of her trunks were packed, the carriage was being prepared, and all that they waited for was for Mr Darcy to return from one of his rides.

Why he felt the urge to ride out into the countryside when we will be travelling to London is beyond me! What can he be thinking of? Well, the only good thing about our time here at Netherfield has been a marked improvement in his looks. Mr Darcy appeared tired and low upon his arrival. Now, all of his former handsomeness has returned with even more vigour, if that is possible.

Caroline dipped her pen and began to write a letter to Jane Bennet.

My dear friend

My brother Charles left for London yesterday, and we have decided that we must join him. The entire party will have left Netherfield by the time you receive this letter. I do not pretend to regret anything I shall leave in Hertfordshire, except your society, dear friend—

Caroline smiled at this. The *dear friend* was a lie, to be sure, but one never knew how far a woman with exceptional beauty—such as Jane Bennet possessed—could travel up the ranks of society. Should Jane end up the wife of an earl one day, it was better to leave things on a good footing than not. These little false flatteries cost Caroline nothing, and they could keep their relationship in such a standing that Caroline could easily re-engage with Jane if the country girl ever married far above her sphere.

Caroline continued with her hollow hopes and pretend longings for a reunion with Jane at some vague point in the future. Her pen supplied a limitless scroll of flattery, fibs, and veiled warnings. She made sure to close the letter with the thinly concealed assertion that her brother was madly in love with Miss Georgiana Darcy and that they expected a union between them very shortly.

And if Jane herself is too dense to understand the meaning of this last bit, I am sure that she will read it aloud to that shrew of a sister, Elizabeth. She is a sharp one and will explain to Jane the meaning of my praise of Georgiana.

Caroline sealed the letter and went downstairs to await the return of Mr Darcy. Tapping the letter in her hand—for she did not want to give it to a servant to be delivered until they were actually stepping into the carriage—she paced back and forth in the front hall. Caroline smiled at the image of Mrs Bennet, learning of the Netherfield party's imminent departure, herding the entire brood into their carriage and dashing over in record time to thrust her daughters in their path. If the matron did conduct herself in such a ridiculous fashion, she would find Netherfield empty of her quarry.

No, better to give this letter just moments before the carriage is in motion and on its way to London. Mrs Bennet could arrive and attempt to weasel out of us some sort of commitment to return to Netherfield, she is such a pushing, unrefined sort.

With a slight start, Caroline realised that if she were Mrs Bennet, that is exactly what she would have done. The idea that she could be so similar in character to Mrs Bennet made her momentarily blush. She shook her head and looked out of the open front door.

Where in the world can Mr Darcy be?

Caroline smiled at the thought that he was looking so well these days. She could not be certain, but ever since her maid had placed that love charm under his pillow, Mr Darcy seemed like a changed man. He was as handsome and virile as she could ever recall seeing him before.

He must truly be in love with me. I suppose that silly little charm actually worked!

Darcy reined in his horse at the top of a rise. He had solemnly promised himself that he would leave this morning without a thought of Miss Elizabeth Bennet. Without pining for one last glance. But upon rising this morning, earlier than anyone else in the household, he had convinced himself there could be little harm in a short ride. The journey back to London was not a long one. His horse was more than fit for the quick jaunt to this spot and then on to London.

The morning mists still hung low in the valley below. He could just make out the smoke teasing its way up from the chimney of Longbourn. As the sun continued its climb and the mists burned off, the sunlight bounced off several of the windows and beamed brightly up at Darcy.

I wonder which window is Elizabeth's? Is she still asleep, her hair fanned out around her? Or does she rise early, like me? She is an excellent walker, as Mrs Hurst pointed out. Does she walk in the morning? Or does she only walk so far when a sister is in need of nursing?

The sun had shifted and the magical glow of Longbourn disappeared. It was now just a mildly neglected manor house of a country gentleman. With the change, Darcy's more sensible side began to exert itself.

Miss Elizabeth Bennet served her purpose. A witty, comely young woman to be sure, but not anyone to be taken seriously. She distracted me from my recent sorrows. Georgiana sounded like she is blooming and happy again in her last letter. Her time with Mrs Annesley, her new companion, has gone a far way towards healing her heart. I can look back on the incident with Wickham as a terrible scare. Nothing more or less. It was a lesson to be more vigilant.

Darcy turned his horse and gave him a light squeeze with his thighs. He was now anxious to leave as soon as possible. Any impulse to linger there must be ignored. He spurred his beast into a gallop and rode hard until he came back into the gates of Netherfield.

At the base of the rise, Elizabeth had watched the man on the horse with anxiety. The sun rising behind him made it difficult to see who it was.

It must be Mr Bingley! At last. He has come to propose to dear Jane. Silly man thinks that the house is not up yet and lingers there watching from a distance. And he is correct. I am the only early riser at Longbourn.

Several more minutes passed as she hid behind the trunk of a massive oak. Her desire to step out from behind the tree was great. Elizabeth wanted to go up and speak to him. To give him a smile of encouragement. To invite him to join her family for breakfast. But she did not move. This was not her affair to meddle in. Mr Bingley must show the courage it took to enter their house and request a private talk with Jane and then her father.

Her heart ached terribly. Elizabeth began to shiver from staying still for too long in the cool mist of the morning. But she dared not tear her eyes off the rider.

Then, to her puzzlement, he turned and rode in the opposite direction, fast and hard as if a pack of wolves bayed at the heels of his horse. Her heart dropped as her teeth chattered. Determined to discover more, Elizabeth walked and ran part of the way towards Netherfield. Once she was just a half of a mile away, she paused, breathless and tired, holding the drenched hems of her skirts up to just below her knees. In the distance, she saw the carriage exit the pillars of the park with one rider leading the way.

Elizabeth exclaimed, "Where are you going?"

In a fit of confused anger, she even ran a few paces towards them. They were so hopelessly far in the distance, it was futile.

London! They must be on their way to London. But why would they leave so suddenly? It seemed that Jane was certain that Mr Bingley would visit.

But then, with a shake of her head at her romantic foolishness, she recalled there had only been one rider with the carriage.

It must have been Mr Darcy who accompanied Miss Bingley and the Hursts back to London. For if Mr Bingley had accompanied them, there would have been two riders out in front of the carriage. I know well that Mr Hurst spoke at length about how he was no horseman and greatly preferred to lounge in a carriage during a journey. No, Mr Bingley must still be at Netherfield. I feel as silly as the girl from the novel. Imagine—me chasing that rider all the way back to Netherfield. Did I really think I was going to run down that carriage and horse?

Elizabeth could not help but laugh at herself.

It is a good thing I did NOT catch that rider. It would have been very awkward to explain myself to him or to the occupants of the carriage.

Elizabeth smiled and began a circumspect walk back to Longbourn, happy in the knowledge that Mr Bingley would appear sometime today. Hopefully, with the intention of making sweet Jane an offer.

The rest of the day unfolded in the most unsatisfactory way possible. There was no vision of Mr Bingley riding up to Longbourn to request a private interview with Jane. No happy explosion of effusive screeches from Mrs Bennet. No secluded meeting with Mr Bennet to attain the desired approval upon the future match.

Elizabeth had overcome her disappointment at Mr Darcy not appearing with her tattered fan in hand. Despite her constantly vacillating regard for the man, she had looked forward to seeing him. Whether he drove her to vexation or partiality, both were accompanied by the invigoration of warmth and excitement that Elizabeth anticipated more than she cared to admit. Besides the company of her father and Charlotte Lucas, it was rare for her to have a conversation in which she was not the superior in understanding. With a determination that was admirable, if not doomed to failure, she resolved to think of Mr Darcy no more.

A walk later in the day with her sisters to Meryton provided a chance to receive a confusing explanation from Mr Wickham as to why he had been absent from the ball at Netherfield.

"I found that as the time drew near, that I had better not meet with Mr Darcy...scenes might arise unpleasant to more than myself."

Even Elizabeth could not paint this in the most pleasing light. It was the exact opposite of his claims just a few days before that he would brave the wrath of Mr Darcy to attend the ball.

As they walked home, Elizabeth became more and more cross with the men of her acquaintance.

All of them are at cross-purposes. Mr Bingley does not attend when he should. Mr Collins attends far too well and too often, even when he is clearly not wanted. Wickham was not the brave knight willing to face down the demon dragon Darcy to risk a dance with me at the ball. And Mr Darcy! Why does he... I could really just—

Her heart beat more rapidly as she attempted to compose her opinion. But there was no clarity, no resolution, no peace. In one instance, Mr Darcy was the gentle, troubled soul with whom she sat and counselled with her cards. When her veil was pulled down and her voice disguised, she wished nothing more than to lay a warm hand on his arm, look into his eyes, and smile reassuringly. Her heart swelled at the very thought of such a dimly lit scene of intimacy.

Then, meeting with him when she was dressed and presented to the world as Miss Elizabeth Bennet, he was the most irksome, contrary, insulting man who could ever be conjured.

It is as if he is a ghoul that can change as he pleases. Except his handsome face never shifts, it is constant.

Her cross mood only increased when Jane received a letter from Caroline Bingley declaring that all had abandoned Netherfield in favour of London and with no desire to ever see the Hertfordshire landscapes again. The false flattery and double meanings of the writer that fairly dripped from the parchment was revolting to every sense of honour and sincerity that Elizabeth possessed. She tried her very best to cheer her sister and point out the distortions that she knew in her heart to be untrue. But it was heavy work. Jane had obviously been anticipating a visit from Mr Bingley. A visit and perhaps an offer.

Elizabeth sighed as they prepared to go to dinner at the Lucases' for the evening.

At least this visit to Lucas Lodge will serve as a distraction for Mr Collins. Charlotte does not seem to mind engaging him in conversation. How fortunate I am to have such a friend as Charlotte. Hopefully the next few days will bring some peace and quiet. And our cousin is set to leave soon. What else can possibly go wrong?

Chapter 13

In the Middle Before Beginning

Darcy had intended that his time in London would serve to cleanse himself, body and spirit, of any thoughts of a certain Hertfordshire lady who had the deliciously uncomfortable habit of watching him with eyes that bedevilled. He had to acknowledge that the deep despondency that he was suffering from when he first arrived at Netherfield had evaporated. But in its place was an uneasiness that never gave him peace. This disquietude was not causing him to constantly reprimand himself about his failings as a protector and brother, rather it was making him act as an animal caged, on edge and prowling. Even his cousin, Colonel Fitzwilliam, noted the alteration.

"The theatre! Darcy, do you not attend to anything I say anymore?"

Colonel Fitzwilliam was sitting in one of the chairs in the study of Darcy's London home, his leg slung over the armrest as he fiddled with his snuff box. He inhaled deeply and rubbed his nose with the cuff of his jacket.

"What?" Darcy asked, blinking at his cousin as if he had forgotten about his very presence in the room.

"You are in higher spirits than when you left to visit your friend Bingley at his estate. And for that I am grateful. However, since your return to London, you seem to always be on the move and lost in your own thoughts. A person in your company may talk themselves blue in the face till they are heard by you. I say, did something occur in Hertfordshire that you should tell me of?"

"Of course not. I was attending to every word you spoke. The theatre tonight? I do not think I will accompany you. The thought of sitting, hemmed in on all sides in the dark, for several hours makes me..."

"Itchy? Dithery? So, the day has finally arrived. I expected there to be trumpets from the heavens or at least fat little cherubs buzzing my head as I walked down the street."

"What are you talking about? Are you mad?"

"What is her name? And—more to the point—where will you spend the wedding night?"

Darcy stiffened. "I have no idea what you are rambling on about." He pulled his pocket watch from his vest. "And if you do not hurry, you will miss the first act."

Fitzwilliam jumped up and began to pour himself a drink.

"No, no, no! If you think that any playwright, from this century or any previous era, has written anything that can compare to Mr Darcy of Pemberley finally being shot through by cupid's arrow, you are deluded. You have listened to my tales of well-endowed and well-dowered ladies breaking my heart. I think the least I can do is return the favour."

With a brimming glass, he flopped back down into his chair as Darcy moved to stare out another window.

"Nothing out there can save you from the truth of my words. You may as well turn and spill it. I am a comforting shoulder, a sympathetic ear, loving arms ready to offer you the warm embrace of solace, a—"

"Oh, do be quiet!"

"She must be pretty indeed," he murmured into his glass before a quick sip. "A thoroughly unsettled Darcy. My, my. Miracles do happen. Is she a future countess? A wealthy heiress? A beauty who shall be sung about by the bards through the ages?"

Darcy, his patience and will beginning to wear thin, mumbled, "She is none of those things. Although she is quite pretty in an unconventional sort of way."

Silence filled the room, thick with words that did not suit a proper description for the Bennet girl who haunted his dreams and waking thoughts. "She is—she *was* a pleasant distraction that filled my time."

"A pleasant distraction?" Fitzwilliam drained the last sip from his glass. "More than that, I imagine. You are no longer the brooding, sad sack that left here a few weeks ago. She must be a fearsome thing indeed to have accomplished what the finest ladies of the *ton* have failed at these ten years at least."

"I am the same as before that—that unfortunate incident occurred."

"That will be a relief to Georgiana, I imagine."

"What do you mean?"

"You must have noticed that she condemned herself more strongly when she was constantly reminded by your low spirits of what had occurred with Wickham. I can tell by her letters that she has recovered well. She has brightened considerably. And now I see that you have removed the hair shirt as well. The self-flagellation that you two insisted on putting yourselves through—it was exhausting to witness. I am so glad that the time of penance has ended. And I have this lady to thank? This Hertfordshire beauty must be remarkable. To whom shall I address my gratitude? A Miss..."

Darcy sat in the chair opposite Fitzwilliam. He crossed his arms and legs, unwilling to further his cousin's speculation.

"Your icy stare no longer works upon me, Darcy. Come now. I must know more. If you will not inform me, then I must resort to my own sort of investigation."

Fitzwilliam stood and made towards the door as if ready to leave the study.

"Where are you off to?" Darcy asked.

"I have some leisure time at present, and I am suddenly struck with a strong desire to see the countryside of Hertfordshire. I am certain if I solicit enough innkeepers, tradesmen, and tavern owners, I will be able to discover all I wish to know of how Mr Darcy passed his time there."

"You will do no such thing. Come back, you harpy, and ask your questions."

Grinning, Fitzwilliam sat in the chair once more.

"So, this paragon of womanly perfection, is she a gentlewoman?"

"Yes," Darcy responded curtly.

"So a lady of quality? One you could pursue without raising the hackles of society?"

"In some ways. She is the daughter of a gentleman, but she lacks any sort of fortune or title, and her mother is of uncertain…"

Fitzwilliam waved his hand to shoo away this middling detail that circled about his head. "If her father is a gentleman, you are on equal ground. But were she serving drinks at the local tavern, it would hardly matter, for you are the master of Pemberley! Any woman you choose would eventually be acceptable in the eyes of society. So, no need to be overly concerned on that point. The only thing that hinders the romance is most probably your scruples."

Darcy could not help but grind his teeth at this oversimplification of the situation. "But her mother and younger sisters behave in a way that can be entirely inappropriate."

Fitzwilliam templed his fingertips and pursed his lips in mock outrage. "I see. And are you proposing to the whole lot or just the one lady?"

"Proposing? Do not be absurd."

"My point being, unless you plan on sharing your bedchamber with her whole clan, I think a few unpleasant relations can be forgiven and mostly even forgotten. Especially if you see them but rarely. We all have our embarrassing relations, do we not? But on to the more salient and essential issue—how is her figure?"

"I will not deign to answer that question," Darcy replied in his most frosty voice.

"Well, judging by that reply, I think we can safely assume that she is well formed. And her mind? Does she let you get away with all of your superior nonsense?"

"What do you mean by that?"

"My dear cousin, you *do* occasionally come off as a bit high-handed. Not that I am complaining, for your discernment is better than most. Does she accept every word from your mouth as the absolute truth to be worshipped, as Caroline Bingley does? Or does she give you pause and make you think?"

After a moment of reflection, Darcy muttered, "She does. She makes me think and…smile."

Fitzwilliam threw both hands in the air. "There you have it! All the defences have been shattered. You are gone, far gone."

The familiar urge to be on the move returned to Darcy's veins. He sprang up and resumed his position at the window. "I have no intention of making an offer to her."

"Frightened you will be turned down, are you?"

Darcy turned to fix his cousin with a look of incredulity. "Do not be absurd. I am certain she would accept my offer."

"So, you *do* plan on making her an offer."

"Absolutely not."

"But, if you are secure of her feelings and you are obviously in love with her, why not?"

Darcy turned his back to the room once more. "Like I mentioned before, Miss Elizabeth Bennet was nothing more than a helpful distraction to ease me through a dark time."

"Miss Elizabeth Bennet, eh? Well, if it is as you say, then this pretty, shapely, smart, good-humoured, lively young woman who causes you to prowl around like a confined bull in springtime is not worth your attention. I am certain that someday you will come across another who is her superior. Perhaps. *If* you are incredibly fortunate."

Darcy turned. His cousin rose and ran a hand through his luxuriant, light locks. "Indeed, she sounds so awful that I hope that I will have the chance to meet her someday soon. It will be highly amusing, I think. Now, I am off to the theatre."

"Thank God."

"I will leave you to your thoughts of how terribly lucky you are to never have to see that young lady ever again. Sounds like you had a close shave in Hertfordshire."

"Just go!"

His cousin closed the door as he left. A moment later the door cracked open and Colonel Fitzwilliam popped his head back in. "Do you think she has a weakness for men in uniform? I could be prevailed upon to overlook a lack of dowry for one such as you described."

A pillow from the chair he had just been occupying flung across the room and hit the door as Colonel Fitzwilliam closed it with a bang and a laugh.

Darcy pulled his jacket down forcefully to bring it back into proper order. He turned back to his place at the window. For a long time that evening, he stood watching the street below, trying to repeat to himself the myriad sensible reasons that he should forget all about Elizabeth Bennet. Carriages passed. A slight drizzle began in a half-hearted attempt to spoil the night for those out and about. A servant came in to stoke the fire and glance with timid curiosity at Darcy. And still the reasons for never making Elizabeth an offer of marriage circled through his thoughts. The more frequently they were repeated, the less power they had over his heart, mind, and body. By the time he walked away from the window, his entire being ached to see Elizabeth again.

Darcy busied himself relentlessly through the remaining winter weeks. He regularly engaged himself in social activities such as balls and routs, to the surprise of his friends and relations. He attended to some improvements of Darcy House. The possibilities of some new investments came his way, and he explored them with even more interest than he had previously.

Although there was much to call on his attention, nothing was enough to banish the thoughts of Elizabeth from his mind. The small evasions and misdirections he employed to ensure that Bingley never learned of the presence of Miss Jane Bennet—who was currently visiting relatives in London for the winter—did not help in any way to progress his own endeavours to forget. But, he stayed the course with relentless stubbornness. The thought that Jane Bennet or Elizabeth Bennet could be taken seriously as potential partners for either his friend or himself was still preposterous to him.

Even through his stolid wall of stubbornness, Darcy could not help but notice how frequently he ended every interesting conversation, every potential investment opportunity, every enquiry from Georgiana as to his opinion on the colour of a gown with the thought of, *I wonder what Elizabeth would say?*

To his astonishment, he could never guess what she would say, she was that much of a beguiling mystery to his senses. It made the longing for her conversation that much more of a torture. But that did not stop him from wondering about her opinion on matters big and small. His wondering would almost certainly lead to a minute smile and a distant look in his eye.

"Why is it, Darcy, that you inevitably appear as vacant as a puppet these days? Have you given any serious consideration to what I have just told you?"

Darcy startled. He put his glass down, painfully aware that he had been staring into the flame of a candle.

"Pardon, uncle? I seem to have lost the thread of the conversation."

His cousin Fitzwilliam shook his head with a smile. Darcy shot him a warning look to hold his tongue.

"Lady Susanna Almstock has hinted to your aunt how agreeable she finds your company."

"Lady Susanna?"

Darcy pulled his focus fully into the present moment. He was sitting at his uncle's table, enjoying a drink before joining the ladies.

"You have danced with her twice, you know. I think you have raised her expectations."

Darcy frowned, racking his brain to put a face to the name. But it was futile. He had no recollection of whom he had danced with. It caused him no little alarm to realise that his inability to attend to what was right in front of his face might lead to gossip.

"If I danced with her more than once, it was unintentional, I assure you. I would hope that it would please my relations to see me more in company. But I have no interest in pursuing a courtship at this time."

With a groan of frustration, the Earl of Matlock reached up and absently straightened his white wig. Fitzwilliam widened his eyes at Darcy, a knowing look upon his face.

"Lady Susanna has an enormous dowry. It would be a marriage that would catapult the Darcy estate to the wealthiest in England. Wealth and a title!"

"Indeed," Darcy replied dryly. "I am very content with the state of the Darcy finances. I am making an effort to widen the areas of investment at this time. Just the other day, I had the privilege to examine some of the newest innovations in regards to the steam engine. It is only a matter of time before travel across the ocean will be powered by steam and—"

"Darcy, be serious. I am speaking of a marriage that would make these little speculations of yours unnecessary. And you want to sit there and weave some fairy tale of smoke and magic taking ships across the sea."

"Even if I were the wealthiest man in England, I find it in the interests of the nation and the progression of science a proper thing to take an interest in. The one thing I do not have an interest in, however, is Lady Susanna Almstock. Nor do I feel the compulsion to court any woman or discover a future bride. I will marry when I am ready."

The tension in the air between the earl and Darcy was thick. Both men refused to look away first. What finally distracted them was a shuffling of papers on the dining table. Fitzwilliam was casually looking through a letter that had apparently been tucked away in his jacket, examining one page, then the next in a mock show of disinterestedness.

"What are you looking at?" the earl exclaimed with irritation.

"Oh, I apologise, Father. You two were so entangled, I thought it best to review this recent missive I had from my aunt, Lady Catherine. I just received it this morning."

Eager to remove the attention from himself, Darcy exclaimed, "How interesting. What does she have to say?"

"Oh, the usual. Anne having low spirits—really, who can blame her?—not enough rain for the spring crops, a smoky chimney in the music room that no one ever uses, a strong suspicion that a local tradesman is supposedly wrong dealing her, the several visits of a Miss Maria Lucas and a Miss Elizabeth Bennet—"

A tumble of glass on the table caused everyone to look at Darcy. A ruby balloon of port spread across the white cloth as Darcy sprung up and tapped at it with his napkin.

"Leave it, Darcy! Now you have spoilt a napkin as well!"

"I apologise. What were you saying, cousin?"

With eyebrows raised and fingers lightly resting on his chest, Fitzwilliam responded, "Moi?"

"Yes, you. You were retelling some news from that letter."

"Oh, yes. About the smoky chimney?"

Darcy resisted the urge to toss the platter of fruit at his cousin's head. As the fingertips of his right hand drummed on the table, he said, "Not the smoky chimney. The bit after that."

"Oh! You must be referring to the shady tradesman. Too bad, that. Although, the fellow should be careful before Lady Catherine dons her magistrate's cap and throws him into the stocks with nothing but bread and water."

"The visitors. You know very well that I was—" Darcy glanced at his uncle's startled look and tried to relax back in his chair, projecting boredom as best he could.

"I see now what part of the letter you are asking about! That bit about Miss Maria Lucas and—oooh, let me see, her name is in here somewhere...just a moment..."

Darcy continued to drum his fingers impatiently on the table. Fitzwilliam made a show of scouring the lines closely with the paper held mere inches before the tip of his nose.

"Ah, here it is, silly fool that I am, I lost my place. A Miss Elizabeth Bennet. She is visiting her friend, Mrs Charlotte Collins, lately married to the Hunsford parson. And, this shall interest you exceedingly, Darcy, all three ladies hail from Hertfordshire! The very place where you visited your friend Bingley in the autumn. Did you not happen to make their acquaintance while you were there? No? Yes?"

"I may have met them. It is possible," Darcy managed to utter through a daze.

"Apparently, Miss Lucas and Miss *Elizabeth Bennet*"—he glanced up at Darcy with a distinct twinkle in his eye—"have been at Rosings Park for almost a fortnight and plan to be there for several weeks more."

Darcy froze, welded bodily to the chair, unable to move or speak.

"You know, Darcy, it has been almost a year since I have been to visit our dear aunt and cousin. I do enjoy taking a tour of the park at Rosings at least once a year, just to see that all is being maintained in the proper order for Lady Catherine. But"—he shrugged—"I have no way to travel there. It is too bad, really, too, too unfortunate."

"You know you can always borrow a horse from my stable...the horses are freely yours to use whenever you need to," the earl said.

"That is unnecessary, uncle," Darcy interrupted. "I, too, am overdue for a visit to Lady Catherine."

"And Anne! Do not forget about Anne," Fitzwilliam chimed in.

"And Anne. So, if you will permit me, I will take my cousin there myself for a visit."

"That is kind of you, Darcy!" the earl said with a beaming smile on his face. "You may find, during this visit, that the company of Anne grows on you. That would be a great match as well."

"Perhaps."

Fitzwilliam clapped his hands together, rubbing them in anticipation. "Excellent! Darcy, you really are kindness itself. It is well that you have no interest in any of the London ladies. There will be no broken hearts at our departure. Truly, it is good that you have no interest in courtship at all at the present moment. Not even a hint of wooing. Lovemaking of any sort is not on the horizon for us. How fortunate. We can simply enjoy the springtime countryside with no worries or entanglements."

The gentlemen stood to leave. The earl walked ahead of the two younger men. Darcy grabbed his cousin by the elbow and hissed, "I should throttle you."

"Come now, Darcy. You have your fun speculating about investments and newfangled heating stoves for Darcy House. Your poorer relations must find amusement where they can. It was all in jest."

As much as he wanted to stay infuriated at Fitzwilliam, Darcy could only feel the heat of knowing that he would soon be close to Elizabeth. His happiness was such that he grinned as he strode out after the others.

Fitzwilliam turned and enquired, "When should we depart? Next week?"

"I was thinking tomorrow morning would work well. Early. I like to travel very early."

Fitzwilliam whistled, then said, "You do have it bad, yes?"

Chapter 14

An Attentive Neighbour

Elizabeth fondled the deck of her cards through the thin fabric of her reticule as the carriage bounced down the roads to Hunsford. The thought of leaving her cards in the stone cottage without her being there made her uneasy. She was looking forward to seeing Charlotte more than she had anticipated. The sudden proposal and rapid marriage of Mr Collins to her friend had caught everyone entirely by surprise, probably Elizabeth most of all.

Elizabeth acknowledged herself as having been a bit lonely this past winter. With both Charlotte and Jane absent from the small social circle of Meryton society, it had been heavy work for Elizabeth to find a partner for sensible conversation. Of course, her father was good company for a topic that strayed from the typical talk of Longbourn, but he was reluctant to leave his study. If Elizabeth wanted to converse with him, she typically had to stay within the confines of his sanctuary.

With a recollection of the company around her, Elizabeth looked across the carriage at Sir William Lucas and Maria. Both had drifted off to sleep, leaving her the only one to enjoy the scenery and think of all that lay ahead. She had to admit that she was terribly curious to discover what was truth and what was fiction in the various descriptions she had heard of Lady Catherine and her daughter, Anne. An honest portrait had probably been conveyed in Charlotte's letters. Although even that had most likely been filtered through a lens of increasing the pleasant and dimming the unpleasant for the sake of Charlotte's equanimity. The descriptions from Charlotte's husband, Mr Collins, were useless. The idea that he could give any rational account of his patroness was unlikely in the extreme. His effusions bordered on the farcical. They were so smothered in praise of his patroness. The descriptions from Mr Wickham might be fairly accurate. His information that everyone expected a declaration of an engagement between Miss Anne de Bourgh and Mr Darcy at any time fuelled a sharp curiosity in Elizabeth to see the woman whom Mr Darcy thought of as perfect in every way.

For what does Mr Wickham have to either gain or lose by painting an untruthful portrait of the residents of Rosings Park? He may not be the most steady young man, but his information regarding Lady Catherine and Anne must be accurate. As well as his retelling of his history with Mr Darcy and his sister, Georgiana. If only George Wickham were a man of financial substance who may marry where he is most inclined…

Elizabeth allowed herself to indulge in fantasies of being wed to Wickham. But even as her mind created scenarios of herself attending to their home and arranging a happy life together in a manor house similar to Longbourn, her spirit became quickly bored by the prospect. Something did not fit correctly, like a shoe that has been outgrown by a foot. She drifted into a doze of her own as her head leaned gently on the side of the carriage.

Bemused, Elizabeth stood in a line of ladies, each holding a large, opulent chalice. Their backs were to a wall. The women on either side of her had white veils over their faces. Elizabeth realised her own face was covered as well. They were lined against a wall of a great room with high ceilings and stone arches, such as one would find in a castle of old.

"Where are we?" she asked a young woman standing next to her.

"Silence," the woman snapped back. "We do not ask questions. We are here only to serve the King and obey his edicts. Speculation is forbidden."

"No questions? That hardly seems fun, does it? If life has no questions, then how are we to better know ourselves and the world around us? Was it not Aristotle who said, 'The ignorant man pronounces, the wise man questions and reflects.' I am not certain I would ever be named as the wisest, but I do make an effort to ask questions and reflect."

"Then you will not be chosen by him."

"Well, the King sounds like a stick in the muck if all he wants is obedience and silence, so I will count it as no great loss for myself."

Just then the great wooden door creaked open and in walked a man in armour that gleamed as if lit from within. His sword hung sheathed at his side. He began to walk with deliberate tread, down the line of chalice-bearing women, passing each slowly as if contemplating their merits and the quality of what they offered in their golden cups. The face of the man was obscured by the sides of the helmet he wore. Despite finding the entire situation beyond absurd, Elizabeth held her breath and waited, her focus forward. His approaching footsteps rang loud on the flagstone floor. Her heart beat faster with each footfall as he drew closer to where she stood.

For the first time, Elizabeth peeked down from under her veil at the cup before her. It appeared to be a rich sort of wine that swirled, thick and dark red. A reflection of her own eyes shone back up at her from the surface of the opaque drink. She could not resist. Her throat felt suddenly dry and desperate, craving the coating of that cool-looking refreshment. Without heeding who observed her, Elizabeth threw back her veil and took a long, deep drink from the golden chalice in her hand. Instantly, her spirit and body felt invigorated and coursed with vivacity. She let out a loud and long sigh of contentment and lowered the golden cup.

Before her stood the man in armour—startled and mildly scandalised. His handsome face was framed by a burnished helmet, looking as regal as any monarch through the ages.

"Miss Elizabeth!"

"Mr Darcy!"

Gasps and shocked murmurs echoed around the chamber from the other women in the long line. Elizabeth's heart leapt as the corners of her mouth pulled up and a warm happiness spread through her body.

Smiling so broadly that her cheeks ached—for the look upon Mr Darcy's face was such a humorous blend of shock and amusement—Elizabeth raised her chalice. "Care for a drink, Mr Darcy?"

Finally allowing the smile that sparkled in his eyes to reach his mouth, Mr Darcy took the cup with a grin and began to raise it up to his waiting lips.

A severe jolt caused Elizabeth's eyes to spring open. Blinking, she looked around, hoping not to miss the sight of Mr Darcy drinking deeply from the chalice of gold. But the interior of the Lucas carriage was all she saw.

With a frustrated breath out, she sank back into her seat.

"Miss Eliza! I am so very happy that you have awoken. For I believe we are just beginning to witness the outer boundaries of Rosings Park. But, as my son-in-law has informed me, it is such a very grand estate that I think we will be travelling for some time yet before we reach the parsonage."

"All of this is Rosings!" Maria exclaimed with breathless awe.

"I believe so, Maria." Sir William pulled a folded piece of paper out of his vest pocket and unfolded it before her. "This map was rendered by Mr Collins and sent in his last letter to me. He did not wish us to miss a single moment of enjoyment of the magnificence of the estate. I believe we are here."

He pointed a finger at the paper that Maria was bent over in rapturous curiosity. "Oh, how wonderful!"

"It is very impressive, my dear. I do not think your sister could have connected herself to a more powerful family. Her future is bright indeed."

Seeming to recollect the presence of Elizabeth—the unlucky woman who had rejected a proposal of marriage from Mr Collins just two days before the young suitor developed his undying love for Charlotte—Sir William leaned over and offered the map to Elizabeth. His face had a shade of contrite self-consciousness to it.

"Would you like to see the map?"

"Well, I— Yes, I suppose so. Thank you. How thoughtful of Mr Collins to send this sketch in anticipation of your visit."

She took the paper more out of courtesy than actual curiosity. Her eyes stayed but a moment on the map before the scenery outside drew her attention.

What will she be like? Despite all the rudeness that Mr Darcy has heaped on me, I hope that his intended bride, Miss Anne de Bourgh, is a pleasant woman. One who will be able to liven him up and make him laugh. I think if he could just not take himself quite so seriously, not feel the need to pass judgement on everyone he encounters, he could be—what? A good sort of husband?

That thought made her frown. The image of Mr Darcy standing before her in full armour, regal, but ready to smile as well, made her cheeks warm.

"May I see it? If you are done?" Maria enquired.

"See what?"

"The map. I wish to track the turns and creeks we pass over."

"Of course, I apologise. I forgot myself momentarily." Elizabeth handed the map to Maria's eager hand.

Their reception at the parsonage was all that Elizabeth had imagined it would be. The stark contrast between the calm measured tones of Charlotte to the embellished raptures of her husband was so diverting that, in more than one instance, Elizabeth had to conceal a smile by dropping her gaze downward. After their initial greeting, a tour—mostly led by Mr Collins—of the house was begun.

How can Charlotte bear this treatment daily? To have every small thing explained and re-explained as if she did not have the wit of a squirrel. Come what may, I would rather face the uncertainties of a future unknown than suffer through this torment. It would have been my fate had I accepted Mr Collins's proposal.

"Are you chilled, cousin?"

Elizabeth realised that she had involuntarily shuddered at the vision of her narrowly averted Hunsford destiny.

"Nothing of consequence, I assure you. I thank you for your concern, you are most kind, sir."

With a look of smug certainty, Mr Collins continued his tour. Elizabeth could not help but smile to herself as she was asked to put her entire head in a cupboard to inspect and approve of its worthiness.

She was quite certain that Mr Collins's insistence at close inspection was an attempt by him to increase whatever regret over her rejection of his proposal she may feel by thoroughly exposing every single advantage that she was missing. Elizabeth began to be annoyed by this spectacle when a very bawdy thought entered her head.

I wonder if he shall make me witness nighttime relations between himself and Charlotte? Explaining loudly how very advantageous certain positions are so that my jealousies will multiply?

Elizabeth barked out suddenly with a laugh and banged her head. She withdrew from the cupboard. Everyone gazed at her in surprise. She covered her mouth with her hand and coughed loudly.

"A bit of dust caught in my throat. Do forgive me."

"My dear," Charlotte said, more familiar with Elizabeth's nature, "perhaps you could take Father and Maria around the fields? Elizabeth may need to rest her lungs."

This was agreed upon and the party split. Elizabeth could have hugged Charlotte, she was that grateful to escape a continuation of fatuous blabber from her cousin.

Chapter 15

A Triumph Sadly Lessened

What in Heaven's name is Darcy on about? He behaves like a dolt in breeches too tight and a jacket too short. His skills in genteel conversation have never been extraordinary, but it is as if every notion of how to speak to a beautiful woman has completely left his head. A bumbling sixteen-year-old would make a better show of conversing with ladies than he.

Colonel Fitzwilliam pulled his gaze away from the dark, imposing figure of Darcy staring out of the window of the parsonage parlour and back to the entrancing face of Miss Elizabeth Bennet. Approval of her excellent eyes, lithe figure, and rosy cheeks swelled his heart with casual admiration. The dark curls framing her face had the most delightful way of bouncing as she became animated while speaking on a subject that caught her interest. And her mind was just what a man of taste, education, and wit should seek out in a partner.

She is just the sort of woman that Darcy ought to pursue as a wife. It will cheer him to no end to have her humour and mind brighten the dark, quiet evenings at Pemberley. And to be able to reach out in the middle of the night and pull her eager, firm figure in close…

His eyes had unconsciously dipped down, and he sighed as he fully appreciated her varied attributes. A curse for his perpetual limbo of uncertain finances that was the burden of most second sons of wealthy families crossed his mind. It was hardly fair.

But, we would not suit each other in the long run, Miss Bennet and I. We are both too merry in our character. Two such dispositions would exasperate each other eventually.

"And you saw my cousin frequently during his stay in Hertfordshire?" Fitzwilliam asked with a casual glance towards Darcy. He pursed his lips in frustration at seeing that Darcy was not grasping the helpful line he had just tossed to him so that he may enter into the conversation.

"Why, yes," Miss Bennet responded, "we did have occasion to meet while Mr Darcy was in Hertfordshire. Although, I think that some of the party at Netherfield enjoyed their own company more than the surrounding society."

The colonel raised his eyebrows at the obvious little barb poked at his cousin. He turned to see if Darcy would rouse himself to respond. Fitzwilliam was amused that he had found another who was not so intimidated by Darcy's taciturn, stoic turn of mind as to be awed into silence. An occasional bout of good-humoured needling was just the thing to keep Darcy from straying too far into a morass of ennui. His opinion of Elizabeth Bennet increased even more.

As if emerging from a fog, Darcy slowly turned and said, "I hope you left your family in good health, Miss Bennet."

Eager to see how she responded to the stilted overture, Fitzwilliam glanced back at the fortunate young woman. Her face had become more guarded, stony in its cast.

"Yes, thank you. All were well. We stopped over in London for a night on our way here. I had the opportunity to see my sister Jane. My eldest sister has been in London these three months. Have you never happened to see her there?"

"I have not had that good fortune."

To Fitzwilliam's amazement, Darcy turned from Miss Bennet and continued his vigil at the window. She turned back to Fitzwilliam with pressed lips, resolute and accepting.

"You see, I do not think that Hertfordshire society so delighted Mr Darcy that it would cause him to seek it out further."

"That is not— I do not think that is *completely* true. I am certain that Hertfordshire society made a stronger impression on my cousin than you imagine."

"Oh! As to a strong impression on Mr Darcy, I have no doubt as to *that*. Whether it was an impression that was favourable, I am certain that I cannot say. I am just mentioning that I do not predict that he will seek to further any of those acquaintances."

With a chuckle, Fitzwilliam opened his mouth to say more, but happened to catch a warning glance from Darcy. He changed the subject immediately to a more innocuous topic. He and Miss Bennet entered into a debate as to whether the weather for Easter-day would be warmer or cooler than would be desirable.

This is the most peculiar sort of courtship that I have ever witnessed. Why does Darcy stand there, unable to flatter or flirt with this toothsome woman? Were she in my sights, I would have her blushing and giggling shamelessly. He is behaving like a troglodyte. I know he is reserved, but this is too much. She will begin to think that he does not care for her at all.

"And when she was baiting you? Telling all the world that you did not care for Hertfordshire society? What was your response? A playful contradiction? Some blatant flattery? No! Silence. Well, bravo, Darcy. *Bravo*. What woman would not be swept off her feet by being treated thus?"

Fitzwilliam swatted at an irksome fly. It was warmer than he liked, and this ride with Darcy to the easternmost edge of Rosings was taking longer than he thought it would. He could not help but continually harp on Darcy's questionable behavior at the parsonage the day before.

"I do not expect you to understand how I conduct myself around women. I must be careful so that unrealistic expectations are not raised. As I said before, Eliza—" Darcy paused, sighed, and squeezed his eyes shut before continuing. "Miss Elizabeth Bennet is a pleasant distraction that has helped me through a dark time. Nothing more."

Fitzwilliam laughed loudly up into the treetops at this. A few birds took flight, not waiting to hear more of the exchange.

"Excuse me, cousin. I have had more than my fair share of 'pleasant distractions' over the years. I do not think that I ever rushed to encounter one quite as you did when I informed you of the contents of that letter. You veritably set the London roads ablaze with your hurry to come to Kent!"

Darcy pulled his horse up to a halt. Fitzwilliam did the same.

"And just what are you implying?"

"Implying, is it? Well then, I am *implying* that you are utterly lost in the deepest of loves with Miss Elizabeth Bennet. And I would also like to *imply* that if you continue your ridiculous campaign of treating her poorly just to attempt to convince yourself and the world how much you *do not* love her, you will be in a fair way towards making her despise you."

Darcy tapped the hind of his horse and walked on. "Do not be ridiculous."

"You may have ample experience in ignoring women, but I am better schooled in how to engage their favour. And, in case you wish to hear my opinion, you are doing a terrible job of fanning the flames of passion in her breast."

"You are mistaken. I am most definitely not deeply in love with her. I can keep out of her company as much as I wish. You have seen how pleasant she is. Lively, attractive, quick-witted... The point being that I can take her company or leave it. We were overdue for a call here at Rosings, as you are well aware. That is the main reason for our presence in Kent. Miss Bennet's being here is a happy coincidence."

"Yes, yes! Thank you for clearing that up. I apologise for my wrong assumptions. You are clearly in tight control of your heart. In fact, I will be completely convinced *if* you avoid her company for a week. That would fully convince me of just how safe and untouched your heart really is."

Fitzwilliam could almost hear Darcy grinding his teeth.

Good. Being so close to her and yet avoiding her company will let Darcy know exactly how he feels. And that will give me a chance to call upon her and get to know her for myself.

"It is of little consequence whether I see her or not," Darcy said in a tone that was unnaturally calm and level. "I will be glad to accept your challenge. A full week will be nothing, I assure you."

"Mmm. Excellent."

True to his word, Darcy spent the next week actively avoiding the parsonage. Colonel Fitzwilliam did the exact opposite and had one of the most pleasant weeks of his recollection. He called frequently, thoroughly enjoying the vivacious company of Miss Bennet, the sensible conversation of Mrs Collins, and the infatuated glances of a blushing Miss Lucas.

Every time he encountered Darcy after his visit to the parsonage, Fitzwilliam had the distinct impression that his cousin was fishing for information in that high-buttoned, distinctly honourable manner of his. This would gradually manifest into a prowling sort of unease where Darcy could hardly stay seated or attend to what was being said or occurring in the room. His conversation was curt and short. Nothing seemed to engage him for long.

Fitzwilliam thought of pointing this out to his cousin, but withdrew from involving himself to such an extent, knowing he would be met by more false outrage from Darcy.

The wall around Darcy's heart is so high and thick, for him to realise it has been breached by the most unlikely of women, it must be a shock. I will tease him no further. For such a protected thing as his heart must be tender and vulnerable when it finally sees the light of day. Too bad, for it was a jolly bit of fun to poke at him when I had the chance. I just hope he gets on with attempting to woo her. She will need some more warming up before she is ready to accept Darcy, that much is clear. Perhaps I should aid him in his quest. Maybe if I told her some stories that displayed his noble, caring nature. Talk him up a bit. Such as how he helped a friend out of a most inconvenient marriage to a conniving fortune hunter. That is a good one. Yes. I will slip it into conversation at the first opportunity.

Chapter 16

The Pretty Follies That Themselves Commit

Over the next few weeks, Elizabeth had the misfortune to encounter Mr Darcy several times while out on her rambles. It confounded her to no end. She was explicit in where she anticipated walking and made certain to tell those present. And yet, there he was, again and again. He was a confusion of contradictions to her mind.

The very first week after the unexpected arrival of Mr Darcy and Colonel Fitzwilliam, one had been most attentive and the other completely absent. Elizabeth had enjoyed the visits from Colonel Fitzwilliam. The withdrawal of Mr Darcy seemed to her to tell that the mere idea of her company was revolting to every sense of propriety that he possessed. She was intolerable to him. He could not be more clear in his opinion of her. Elizabeth privately mourned the loss of the man she had felt so warmly about during his visits to the fortune-teller.

But then his persistent interruptions of her walks disturbed every negative feeling she had of him. He was more attentive in company now than he had been. But could any amount of easy conversation erase the many times he had been neglectful of her and scornful of her family? It was so puzzling, she could not decide how all the pieces fit together to make one cohesive picture of the man.

Elizabeth sat at the desk in the parlour of the parsonage, looking through several letters from Jane. She had begged off from visiting Rosings that day. Her foul mood had brought on an aching head, and she desired nothing more than to sit, reflect, and write a letter to Jane. Her accidental meeting with Colonel Fitzwilliam yesterday had finally solidified Mr Darcy in her mind as the most proud, officious, cruel, overbearing man that was ever her misfortune to be acquainted with. There was no more lingering doubt as to his true character. Every impulse of warm feelings towards Mr Darcy must be smothered after learning what she had. There were truly not enough words to convey the heated anger she was feeling towards that particular gentleman.

Elizabeth shook her head as her grip on the pen tightened. Her hand began to ache from her frustration at the mere thought of Mr Darcy. Breathing deeply, Elizabeth attempted to clear her mind and return her awareness to the blank paper before her, waiting to receive her musings to Jane.

Dear Jane

I was so pleased to hear of the outings that you and our aunt took. I am certain that going to the theatre is one of the best ways to cure any— I hope your spirits are well! I expect that you must be enjoying—

Frustrated, Elizabeth crumpled up the sheet. It was so unlike her to be without the words to express herself.

But what can I write? It is terribly unfortunate that Mr Darcy stuck his nose in and disrupted the course of all your future happiness? Sorry the status of our family cost you a marriage of love and mutual respect to an amiable man of good fortune?

She sighed and started anew on a fresh sheet of paper. But images of yesterday and the humiliating walk with Colonel Fitzwilliam could not be ignored. The colonel had openly revealed how Mr Darcy had separated Mr Bingley from her sister Jane. He had not named any names when telling the tale of Mr Darcy's monstrous interference, but Elizabeth knew very well who the injured parties were. It was unlikely that Mr Darcy went around the country frequently meddling in and breaking up courtships. Elizabeth also thought it improbable that Mr Darcy could have two such malleable friends who would heed his advice and abandon the courtship of a lady with a possibly objectionable family. It was apparent that the colonel had meant to emphasise how good a friend Mr Darcy was to Mr Bingley for the hindrance of the natural progression of the courtship, but it was a crushing revelation to Elizabeth. She had always suspected some underhanded doings to cause Mr Bingley to abandon Netherfield and, as a consequence, Jane, but nothing like this. And she had attributed most of it to Mr Bingley's sisters, not Mr Darcy.

After she spoilt yet another sheet of paper, Elizabeth threw the pen down, crossed her arms, and sat back in the chair. She picked up the letters from Jane again. A card slid out and landed on the floor. Bending over, she reached out with careful fingertips to grasp it by the edges. It was one she had picked out of her deck just that morning. The King of Swords.

There he is, upon his throne. Oh, how could I have been so deceived? I will never allow my heart to escape my control so suddenly again. Finding myself so totally and shockingly in love was a truly miserable experience. One that I will never repeat. Particularly not with such a hateful man.

With a flush of heat, she recalled several of the dreams that had tormented her since arriving in Hunsford. Always with Mr Darcy in his suit of armour, meeting with her in various settings. Always feelings of warm happiness rushed through her during these dreams only to splinter and fade when she woke and remembered his true nature.

If only those dreams would leave me in peace. It is too terrible that we are unable to talk some steady sense into our world of dreams. It runs amok with no consideration to the reality that must be faced when we awake.

She was gently tapping the King of Swords against her chin, staring out the window, when a commotion from the direction of the front door caused her to straighten in her chair. She pushed her letters from Jane and the card hastily under some other papers and stood quickly. Mr Darcy entered, in a state of visible agitation.

Elizabeth grimaced inwardly at the cruelty of fate for sending this visitor to her at this particular moment. Any other would be preferable. Even Mr Collins.

They stood, eyeing each other from across the room.

"Mr Darcy, would you care to be seated?"

They sat. Silence ensued. He stood suddenly as if shot from a cannon and lapped the room once, twice, and then halted before her.

"In vain I have struggled. It will not do. My feelings will not be repressed. You must allow me to tell you how ardently I admire and love you."

Elizabeth was stunned beyond all knowledge. For a moment, before her rationale could fully process what had just been spoken to her, she felt her heart flutter happily.

Perhaps there is a chance that I could love him again! I think that the ardour I felt upon first seeing him, in the library at Netherfield, could be rekindled. It still lives within me…it still smoulders and was never truly extinguished. It only needs encouragement to reignite. I am certain he can recompense those he has injured with the help of my guidance. I could help him in making amends to Jane and Wickham. His words are so beautiful with such a pulse of passion, everything that I could ever have dreamed of—

Elizabeth opened her mouth to respond, to give him some piece of the encouragement he sought. One word was all it would take. But Mr Darcy had resumed his pacing, his eyes fixed on the floor as he moved back and forth in front of her. And then he spoke.

"I fully realise this would be a vast leap in social standing for you and your family. I can only hope that the rest of the Bennets do not cause the Darcy name to be a source of merriment for the London gossips. Scorn and ridicule from others, especially those in an inferior social position, is something that I have always sought to avoid. But, it will have to be risked so that we can wed. It is terribly unfortunate, but your family will be a cruel reality that must be endured. I have laboured so intensely to scour all regard for you from my heart. But it was folly. Despite all I have done to forget you, to ignore your hold on me, to eliminate any image of you as my partner in life, I have failed. But, perhaps we can mitigate some of the evils of your relations. If we limit your exposure to your family after we wed—"

He went on for quite some time in this vein, seemingly oblivious to the fact that she had not responded. She assumed that her silence was being interpreted by him as a blissful consent to all he said. Abashed and angry, Elizabeth listened to each and every degrading insult that he laid at her feet as if he was bringing sweet, fragrant blooms of a rare rose to her. With each word that fell from his lips, her disgusted rage increased. When he finally paused, tall in his confidence of her complete acquiescence to his proposal, she responded.

"In such cases as these, it is, I believe, the established mode to express a sense of obligation for the sentiments avowed, however unequally they may be returned. But I cannot. You have insulted and injured me and my family in every conceivable way."

Elizabeth continued with her own tally of Mr Darcy's crimes of slights and injustices towards herself, her family—especially Jane—Mr Bingley, and poor Mr Wickham. Added to these misdeeds was the insulting manner of his proposal. It was a heavy load of transgressions to pile upon anyone's shoulders. Momentarily, Mr Darcy did indeed wilt from the pressure. But his ingrained sense of superiority seemed to rally him. He stood taller, as a flush of anger overcame his obvious bewilderment.

He began to stalk the room again under the torrent of her accusations. He stopped before the writing desk.

"You have said quite enough, madam. I perfectly comprehend your feelings and have now only to be ashamed of what my own have been. Forgive me for having taken up so much of your—" His words fell off. Mr Darcy's eyes fixed on a point on the desk.

There, on the surface of the desk, was the tip of a sword, on a card, sticking out from beneath the hastily organised papers. Elizabeth gasped deeply as Mr Darcy leaned in, bringing his eyes closer to the pile of letters. Seemingly spellbound and unable to stay his hand from the impropriety of it, he placed the tip of his finger on the point of the sword and slid the card out from under the papers. Picking it up, he raised the card close to his face. He sniffed the edge of it.

"Smoke and…mint?"

"Do not touch my letters, sir!" Elizabeth jumped to her feet. "I forbid you!" she cried in a desperate attempt to distract him from the card he held. Mr Darcy gazed at her and then the card held up before him, his eyes begging for some sort of explanation as his brows drew up in injured bafflement.

The King of Swords. Stoic and solitary, held up before his chest, just over his heart. Mr Darcy's eyes were filled with hurt and confusion.

"What is the meaning of this? Are you the… No, it cannot be…" he whispered.

All fire of indignation wafted out of Elizabeth, leaving her weak and unsteady. She gripped the back of a chair, attempting to keep a swoon at bay. Her mouth opened and formed words, but no sound came out.

"Why is this card in your possession? Was it—was it you? In the library at Netherfield? In the stone cottage in the woods?"

A slow dawning of realisation bloomed in his face. The lines of confusion smoothed out to be replaced by outraged comprehension.

"Have you been...mocking me? Playing at being a card reader? Getting people to confess to you that which they keep hidden? Making my private thoughts your playthings?"

"No! No, I swear to you, Mr Darcy. I promise you most solemnly that there was no ill-intent." She took a step forward, holding her hand out towards him, hoping to assuage the hurt of the insulting deception.

He stepped closer to her, but with a growing rage. "Was this all some sort of twisted plot to ensnare me into proposing? Are you no better than all the scheming women of London, all conniving to trap me in a loveless marriage? You, who I thought was different from them, are worse! You are many times more manifold in your devious plotting than they!"

Braving his anger, she took another step closer, pleading in her heart and voice. "Please, Mr Darcy, if you will but listen. I never intended any sort of manipulation of you or your friends. If I can but explain why—"

But he was horrified. Suddenly desperate to make an escape, he stepped back, recoiling his arm from her.

"Stay away from me. Playing with hearts, amusing yourself by tormenting others... Keep back!"

Mr Darcy turned, stumbled, and fell over a chair in his haste. Scooting himself back from Elizabeth as if she were a succubus trying to wrench his soul out of his chest, he threw the card at her. He leapt to his feet and burst through the door and out of the parsonage.

Elizabeth ran to the window, seeing Mr Darcy walk, then break into a run, back in the direction of Rosings Park. She placed her hand on the pane of chill glass. "No! Please!" she whispered at his retreating form.

Elizabeth sank to her knees and picked the card up off the floor as silent tears cascaded down her cheeks. The noble king looked out at her, unmoved. She covered her face with her hands and began to sob.

Chapter 17

What a Letter Is This!

Humiliated, confused, and hurt, Darcy made his way back to the front steps of Rosings. His sight blurred as he pressed through the front doors. He wiped at his eyes and ran halfway up the grand stairs.

"Darcy," his cousin called out.

Darcy paused and looked down at Fitzwilliam. His panting breath hitched in his chest. Recalling himself, he straightened up tall and tugged his jacket downwards. The action calmed him immediately. Controlled order began to claw its way back up through his awareness.

"Yes?" he asked, his voice quavering.

"Are you unwell? Where have you been? Lady Catherine is beside herself. Anne almost asked after you. Almost."

Darcy shook his head, looking down to rapidly blink back tears. "I am well. I have some…letters to attend to. Please explain."

Without waiting for any further questions or jests from his cousin, Darcy bounded the rest of the way up to his room. Crump was within, tending to his wardrobe.

"I wish to be alone to write some letters. You may send dinner for me up here. Otherwise, I do *not* wish to be disturbed. Even by Lady Catherine herself."

"Understood, sir." Crump bowed and departed.

Darcy paced the room, suddenly regretful that he had not walked farther around the park to expend this fury of emotion within him. He replayed the scene over and over in his head. He could see the solitary monarch on his throne, staring up at him from that silly card. But then he recalled the card of The Hanged Man, helpless and bound, hanging by one ankle from the tree, trapped and unable to set himself free.

That is how I felt when I first went to Netherfield. Dangerously low-spirited, helpless, feeling myself to be a complete failure in my guardianship of Georgiana and as master of Pemberley. And then I met Elizabeth. Even with her face hidden by that comical veil, in the library of Netherfield. Although I thought her to be an old woman who told fortunes, things began to brighten from that moment forward, I cannot deny that.

Darcy immediately put a halt to that thought. Every word of their exchange from this afternoon echoed in his mind. Her many accusations of his misdeeds towards Jane Bennet, Bingley, and his old childhood companion, Wickham. His concealing of Jane Bennet in London from Bingley. His treatment of 'poor Wickham'. His arrogance at every turn while he had been in Hertfordshire. His lack of gentleman-like behaviour in the very manner of his proposal.

Darcy groaned and sank his face into his hands as he sat at his desk. Some of the truth of her words was beginning to peek through the storm cloud of his mind.

But even if these charges are all true, nothing forgives the very real crime of her falsity as the old fortune-teller. What can she be playing at? If it had all been a ruse to entrap me into proposing, why did she refuse me? If it was all for a rich husband, she would have accepted me immediately. No woman is so certain of a man's heart as to abuse them so cruelly to their face after they have just laid their soul bare. If it were all a ploy, how could that have served her ends?

None of it made any rational sense. Confusion at her deception made the hurt of her refusal even sharper as he knew not how to feel or proceed. He had no control over his life, just as the upside-down fellow on the card had appeared. The only thing he had control of was his response to the charges Miss Elizabeth had laid at his feet. There, at least, he could defend himself. He picked up his pen and began to write a letter.

To Miss Elizabeth Bennet

Be not alarmed, Madam, on receiving this letter...

Hours passed. In a long letter, Darcy methodically pointed out his reasons for his actions to build a solid, strong defence for himself. He recounted his belief in Jane's indifference to his friend and how he had acted to attempt to separate them. He laid bare the true history of Wickham and how that man's underhanded actions had hurt his younger sister and left Darcy bereft of all happiness afterward. And finally, he attempted to retell in somewhat gentler terms than he had earlier that day how exactly he felt about the behaviour of the Bennet family. He put to her the very real concerns a man of significant fortune may have about connecting himself with such a family. But, as often happened when thoughts are written to paper, they lose some of their power. When he looked at those paragraphs, he began to truly see how misled he was by this thinking. He remembered his cousin asking if he was planning on marrying the entire family or just Elizabeth.

Bleary-eyed and no less miserable than when he began, Darcy glanced out the window and saw the early hints of dawn outline the trees of Rosings forest. Weary and still confounded, he sealed the long letter and flung himself on the bed, hoping that exhaustion of heart and body would help him fall to sleep.

Darcy knew well Miss Elizabeth's favourite walks. But something drew him to the palings of Rosings and a grove of trees to one side. There was no reason for this, for he had yet to witness her take a stroll here, but his feet followed this direction and the rest of his being was too weary to argue. He stalked the grove, looking in all directions for a sign of Miss Elizabeth.

Why should I care what her opinion of me is? Why should I feel impelled to explain my actions to her? I cannot say. I should be furious. But if her intent had been to ensnare me, she would have eagerly agreed to my proposal—no matter how many legitimate concerns I had raised and no matter how poorly I may have expressed myself. However, Elizabeth refused me, so, logically, trapping me in marriage could not have ever been her intent. And why was she so upset by my reservations? Everything I said was truthful and honest, though perhaps I could have been more tactful, as Fitzwilliam advised. Frankness is an admirable quality that a man of honour should possess, is it not?

After an hour, he considered returning to the manor house and leaving for London immediately. He felt himself to be a pathetic spectacle, prowling around, waiting to explain himself to a woman who apparently despised him and had actively deceived him. His back fell against a tree trunk as he tried to rub weariness and self-doubt out of his eyes.

But was I above employing questionable arts to conceal the presence of Miss Jane Bennet in London? No, I was not. Should I really judge her so quickly when I acted so dishonourably?

Frustrated—for Darcy knew the answer to his own question quite well—he pushed away from the trunk of the oak. At that same moment, a twig snapped and he saw Elizabeth before him, looking just as stunned as he felt.

"Miss Elizabeth! Please stay a moment," he said as he stepped towards her.

"Mr Darcy! Please, allow me to give you something," she said at the exact same moment as she stepped towards him.

They were both shocked into an awkward silence, finding themselves far closer to each other than either had intended. Darcy felt the heat rise to his cheeks as he stepped back, suddenly anxious to know what she could possibly have to give him.

"Here!" she blurted as she handed a letter towards him. "Will you please do me the honour of reading this letter?"

He took the letter and stared at it as though he had never before received a correspondence in his life. After a long moment, Darcy looked up to see Miss Elizabeth walking rapidly away. He bounded over a log and reached out to touch her shoulder. She spun around.

Again, they both found themselves closer than they had expected and stepped away from each other simultaneously.

"Miss Elizabeth, I, too, wrote this." Darcy held his letter before him, pausing. The thick letter stayed there, hanging between them, in his hand. Then, feeling silly, he reached out and took her hand and pressed the pages into it. He snatched his palm away from her and took several more steps back.

"If you would do me the honour... What I mean to say is—if you could perhaps look over what I have written. There on those pages. I would be most obliged. I mean, grateful. Yes."

Feeling the desperation of fumbled words coursing through his chest, Darcy turned and walked away quickly on shaky legs. After a minute, he passionately wanted to turn around to see if she was still there on the hill, observing him. He silently cursed himself for having chosen a path that led across an open, small meadow with no tree to conceal him momentarily. He continued his upright voyage across the ocean of grass until he reached the verge of the far woods. After entering the shade of the trees, he stole behind a trunk and strained his eyes back in the direction from whence he came.

She was still on the hill, sitting on the log that he had leapt over. Her brow furrowed as she rapidly scanned the lines of the letter he had written. Relief washed over him.

She will not destroy it immediately. Will she acknowledge how she has misjudged me? Well, no matter. It is over and done. I will no longer care what Miss Elizabeth thinks of me.

Darcy turned, tugged his jacket down and resumed his course to Rosings. The letter she had written to him was pressed against his heart in his jacket. But he was not ready to open it. If it contained more hateful speech directed at him, he was not strong enough to read it yet.

I will tell Fitzwilliam that we are leaving today. Now. I will return to London and have one too many glasses of brandy and begin to put all of this behind me. It is done. At least I have the knowledge that she has a true sketch of my character. Perhaps I am not as despicable as she thought. Nothing was done out of spite or vengeance. I had my reasons for treating Wickham poorly and for trying to separate Bingley from her sister. Although, in the latter case, there may be the slightest possibility that I was wrong. Maybe.

Darcy and Colonel Fitzwilliam left later that morning. The silent drive was undisturbed by the normally verbose Fitzwilliam.

"I wish," Darcy suddenly exclaimed loudly, "to get properly foxed this evening. So much so that I will not be able to say my name without a slur. Do you think you would like to accompany me in that venture?"

Fitzwilliam shot Darcy a startled look. Shock turned to sympathy. "It went that badly, did it?"

"I have no idea to what you are alluding," Darcy replied frostily. "A man can drink more brandy than is good for him, can he not? I rarely ever do, but let us make tonight the exception."

"I told you to try just a hint of flirt and flatter," Fitzwilliam muttered. "But did you heed my advice? No. In what way did you ply her with compliments? Did you mention those bewitching eyes of hers? How about her silky hair? Her sparkling wit that invigorates, but does not insult? There is so much to admire about the girl, I am certain it was hard to mention just a few of her attributes."

Darcy remained stony. "You do not know of what you speak."

"You did say something along those lines, did you not?"

"It may have slipped my mind."

"Oh Lord."

"I was honest and open in regards to my real concerns about connecting my family to hers."

"I have heard that ladies love that sort of thing, to be sure. Did you say anything that even bordered on romantic?"

"I told her how ardently I admired her and loved her."

Fitzwilliam was silent for a moment. "That, actually, was not bad. Not bad at all. I may remember that for a proposal of my own someday. But I really think things would have gone better if you had left out the tally of reasons that you thought you should not marry her."

Darcy angrily asked, "And did *you* mention anything of my dealings with my friend Bingley and Miss Elizabeth's sister Jane Bennet?"

Fitzwilliam raised his brows. "It *was* Bingley? And Jane Bennet? Is that one of Miss Elizabeth's sisters? Are those the two you attempted to separate? You could have been more explicit. How can it be my fault? If I had known the facts, I would have made no mention of the entire affair. Really, when you examine it, it is entirely your fault for being so reticent. Besides, I was attempting to raise you in Miss Elizabeth's estimation."

"Your attempt to give rise to esteem for me in her had the opposite effect. Her opinion of me could be no lower, thanks to your loose tongue and recklessness."

"Even though I did not know the names of the players in your drama, I only related the truth of what you had mentioned to me. If her opinion of you is lower as a result, perhaps you should examine your actions more closely and ask yourself if you behaved in a way that was worthy of you."

"It matters not. I spoke in such a way when I was alone with her that I do not think I will ever gain her regard back, if it was ever there to begin with. Besides, I learned some things about Miss Elizabeth that call into question whether it would be wise for me to think upon her seriously ever again."

"Really? Do tell."

"You must be in jest. If it were a matter that I wished everyone to know of, I would be happy to relate it to you."

"But I would be the soul of indiscretion!"

"I think you mean to say that you would be the soul of discretion," Darcy said, dryly.

"That is what I said, was it not?" Fitzwilliam smiled broadly.

"I know you are attempting to cheer me. And I appreciate it, truly I do. But I think I have made a thorough mess of things. Even if you had not opened that mouth of yours and told Elizabeth of my dealings with Bingley and Jane Bennet, it is doubtful she would have accepted me after such a proposal. I truly love her...I can imagine no other by my side for the rest of my days. She is my heart, my breath, the reason to rise out of bed in the morning. I dream of her every night and cannot stop my mind from pursuing her every day."

"If only you had said that to her and not me, things may have gone a little better."

"What am I to do?" Darcy asked.

"I do not have the answer, but I suspect we should attempt to find the solution at the bottom of one of your fine bottles of brandy."

"That, sir, is some bold and admirable advice."

The next morning, Darcy's head was a mire of knotted ropes and fog. He drank deeply from the pitcher of water by his bed and moaned. He had a vague recollection of being carried up to his room the evening before, slung over the shoulder of Colonel Fitzwilliam as one would transport an irksome sack of potatoes. He definitely recalled singing—poorly and loudly—bawdy songs of love that he had learned during his school days.

Crump entered and began to open the drapes.

"For the love of God, Crump, I beg you, leave the drapes closed. It is bright enough in here."

"Yes, sir."

"Were any of the servants up late last night? I was not...feeling well. I have no wish to be talked about while I was in that state."

"No, sir. I believe everyone had retired for the evening. We *saw* nothing. As to what was *heard*..."

Darcy could only groan in response.

"I would not concern yourself too deeply, sir. From what is told of other grand houses in London, Darcy House is one of the most unremarkable to work in, which is somewhat surprising as it is run by an unmarried, young gentleman. It has the reputation of the servants being treated with respect and fairness. If anything, your vocalisations of last evening may have raised you somewhat in the esteem of the young men of the staff."

"Wonderful," Darcy muttered in a surly whisper.

Crump picked up Darcy's jacket and began to brush it straight with his hand. A letter fell to the ground with a papery smack.

"Would you hand that to me?" Darcy said as he sat up straight.

"Of course, sir."

The gentle handwriting of Miss Elizabeth Bennet was on the folded page. Darcy's fingers ran over the script with a soft, loving caress.

To F D

"I think I should like a few moments alone, Crump. If you could return with just some tea and plain toast in about ten minutes, that would be suitable."

"Yes, sir."

Darcy snapped the seal and began to read.

Dear Sir,

Scorn me if you must, but let it be done for reasons that are just and true. The idea of you moving through the world with disdain for me based on false notions is too much to bear. Once I have given you all the reasons for my deceptions, if you still choose to hold me in contempt, it will be done honestly. I have never sought to manipulate you in any way. If that occurred, it was unconsciously done. No one is accountable for my actions except for myself. What I have to relate may be difficult for a man of your station to comprehend, but, without embellishment or unnecessary dramatics, I will lay my history before you. As I contemplate where to begin, I suspect that perhaps you were correct. The difference in our stations in life is vast. Maybe too far to bridge. On this one point, during your proposal, perhaps you were in the right.

Darcy had to pause and cover his eyes. The language of his marriage offer to Elizabeth came floating back to him on a wave that made his stomach lurch.

What possessed me to be so insulting to her? What did I hope to gain? This was not a business proposition, but a calling of my heart to hers. God, I am a fool.

He kept his head bowed until the surge of bile threatening to push farther upward settled. His hand fell from his eyes, and he raised the letter again.

To all outward appearances, our family is doing well enough to maintain our station in life. The reality is far from this picture. My father has allowed our finances to sink further and further during his lifetime. I wish nothing more than to list reasons that may pardon him from responsibility for this fact. But I cannot. Mr Bennet has a mind that would be better suited to a position at a university, or as a tutor to a wealthy family with no children of his own to provide for. As the manager of an estate with many agricultural ventures, he has not excelled; nor has he sought to better his understanding of these responsibilities. I am sorry to say this of someone I love, but it is the truth.

Several years ago, Mrs Hill, our housekeeper, approached me with the true state of the books for the purchase of groceries for Longbourn. I was shocked. My mother, with whom you are acquainted, has the skills to budget, but not the perseverance. She prefers to attend to other matters. Hill suggested that I take up a venture that has served my family before. Hill taught me how to cast the cards and their meanings. Those cards had once belonged to my great-grandmother. After I had discovered the priest's hole that led from my bedroom to a tunnel, she began her instruction in the use of the deck. The tunnel leads to the stone cottage in the woods that stands on a nearby estate that has long been embroiled in legal difficulties and therefore is abandoned. The property was originally part of our estate, but has not been so for many decades. I can only assume that it was there to provide an escape for previous generations of my family that may have been Catholic, and this was a way for them to flee Longbourn during times of persecution. You are too intelligent to doubt the rest. I received payment in many forms that has helped to sustain my family for the past two years. Sometimes it was little more than a few dozen eggs from a tradesman. Occasionally, it will be a substantial payment such as I received from the party at Netherfield. Between the charm Miss Bingley bought—which was no more than mint and salt—and the evening I spent casting cards at Netherfield, I made enough to help supplement the groceries through the winter. I even bought myself new gloves and a fan, which I accidentally spoilt in a fit of frustration after we danced at—but that is not germane to what I am attempting to relate. I know that the master of Pemberley and multiple estates can hardly be expected to understand the desperation of facing a winter with no way of knowing whether the table will be filled. But that was the reality of our situation. No amount of my skipping meals and going to bed with an empty stomach would help fill the *plates better. My actions had no other interest than to provide for my family by means other than a loveless marriage—such as to my cousin Mr Collins, who did me the honour of making me an offer before his interest was drawn elsewhere—or taking a position as a governess. I believed that if Jane were to marry—but, please excuse me, that is unlikely to occur. I hope, after reading the above, you will pardon me from the crime of using arts to ensnare you or compromise you in some way. That was never my intent, I swear to you solemnly. The times we met—when I was in disguise as the fortune-teller—I was impressed by your kindness and openness. You seemed to be in some sort of distress, and I desired nothing more than to provide you with some form of comfort, in the only way I was able. I hope that, whatever was disturbing your equanimity, you have found a solution or a way to be at peace with it. If I may venture, I also would hope that you may extend some small portion of that kindness to me now and say nothing to anyone else of what I have told in these pages. And, if you can find it in your heart, please forgive me.*

E B

Darcy hung his head into his hands once more and allowed another wave of nausea to wash over him. Crump brought in a tray of tea and toast and sagely left without remark. He sat for some time, trying to reconcile his sensations of hurt, anger, and embarrassment. But the one feeling that demanded to be acknowledged above all the other unpleasant sensations was the force of his continued love for Elizabeth. No matter how poorly he had thought of her in the last day and night, that one truth had never wavered for an instant. If anything, her frank letter—exposing the compromising information of the state of her family finances and her reasons for the fortune-teller charade—only increased his respect and admiration for her.

Such resilience and cleverness. To have to resort to such measures after having a father who could not attend to his duties in a proper way. It would be difficult to name who is the more damaging of her parents. Such a mother. Such a father. And yet, she—and Jane, it would seem— have risen above their beginnings to become something more. Women to be admired and respected. And I have made a complete muddle of it with Elizabeth!

Darcy flopped back on his bed and flung his forearm over his eyes. The letter, so intimate and heart-wrenching, laid on his chest with his palm pressed to it. The paper rustled lightly with each breath he took. Once the frustration that was aimed at Elizabeth's parents had cooled somewhat, he turned to his old habit of examining his own actions and motives to see if anything he had done was wanting. Darcy was not pleased with what he found.

If I had been more attentive and present for Georgiana, that foul bounder Wickham would never have been able to persuade her to elope. I was too reserved in my affections and guidance. And now, thinking I was being a most excellent friend to Bingley, I have convinced him that Jane Bennet had no real affection for him when she truly did. If Jane loved him deeply, Bingley would have been able to tolerate an embarrassing family with a laugh and a shrug, as is his way. Never was my inclination to be of service more misguided. How was I so wrong in my thinking in both instances? As a result of my reserve and muddled high-handedness, the one woman who has ever held my heart within her power despises me.

Darcy allowed himself a few more moments of wretched musings before he swallowed hard and pushed up to a seated position. Feeling even more bedraggled than when he first woke, he swayed for a moment before standing and stepping forward to his desk. He retrieved a key from the top drawer and crossed the room to a large walnut wardrobe. On the floor of the tall cabinet was a German-made strong box of solid, black iron. He ran a hand along the top of it. The round rivet tops rumbled under the skin of his palm. Straps of woven, black iron criss-crossed the lid. With a sigh, Darcy inserted the key and opened it.

He pushed aside the several stacks of pound notes, deeds to properties, and a few boxes of the jewels that had belonged to his mother. Under all of this wealth and exquisite finery, Darcy saw the object he was looking for—the broken fan that had fallen from Elizabeth's hand the night of the ball at Netherfield. Gingerly, he lifted it and placed her letter under it. Arranging the rest of the contents back on top, he closed the heavy lid and sat back on the floor. Darcy stared at the cold metal box, sitting at the base of the wardrobe, looking like a sort of beetle king. With a sad, wry smile, he relocked the strongbox and stood up.

He walked to the tray and took a bite of his toast and a small sip of his tea. Feeling less unsteady on his legs, Darcy went to the curtains and resolutely opened them. The blast of light made him wince, but he did not retreat from it.

Chapter 18

A Dear, Sweet Girl

Jane did not understand why Lizzy had insisted she take her place with Aunt and Uncle Gardiner on the trip north. Jane had already enjoyed so many months of time away from Longbourn during her stay with them in London that winter, she would have gladly remained in Hertfordshire to help watch after their young cousins. But her sister had been so insistent that it was she who must stay and help their father attend to some estate matters. Lizzy also claimed that she could not bear to miss the final warm days of late summer away from Longbourn. Jane had stated that she could not escape the nagging sensation that Lizzy was hiding things from her. It made little sense that her sister's adventurous spirit would not have relished this journey to parts of the country that she had never seen before.

Jane watched the passing landscape with calm enjoyment. The sway of the carriage reminded her of the sway of the horse she would occasionally ride at Longbourn. Her aunt and uncle dozed lightly as they all travelled north.

What can Lizzy mean that she must stay near Longbourn and attend to estate matters? What matters?

Jane could not guess what was on her sister's mind. It was clear that something was troubling her lately. Ever since her return from visiting the Collinses in Kent, Lizzy had been distracted by some quiet concern of her own. Jane had asked, but not pressed, for further knowledge, but had only been met with reassurances that somehow rang hollow to her ear. She had her suspicions that something was occurring with the finances and asked her sister. Lizzy had always been the one to help their father organise the money matters of Longbourn as much as she was allowed to. But even on this subject, she had been evasive and dismissed further queries with a laugh.

"Although we are so delighted to have you with us, it is too bad that Lizzy felt unequal to this trip," Mrs Gardiner said as she straightened up in her seat, blinking her doze away from her eyes. "When I first asked her, she was overjoyed at the prospect. She said the funniest thing, 'Adieu to disappointment and spleen! What are men to rocks and mountains?' She made me laugh heartily at that!"

"Yes, my sister *was* excited for this trip. She was, indeed, before she went into Kent…"

"Hmmm. Do you think something happened there that caused her to have a secret anxiety?"

"She has not confided in me, aunt. I have asked her privately if anything had occurred to vex her, but, you know Lizzy."

"Always the first to attempt to transform lemons by smothering them in sugar. Out of all of your family, she is the one who tries to rally the most and cheer the loudest."

"Yes, but at what cost? I wish she would be more open. I sense something is happening that I am unaware of."

"Do you think it was because of Wickham's departure? I know the militia left Meryton shortly before our trip."

"No, I do not believe that is it. She enjoyed Mr Wickham's company, but when she returned from Kent, Lizzy told me of past occurrences that led me to conclude that Wickham was not always an honourable man. Even if he leads a life of virtue from now on, someone like Lizzy would not be able to give him her full trust. Indeed, I think none of us should be confident in Mr Wickham."

"Really? That is shocking! I do not like to think ill of the fellow, for we had so many pleasant conversations about Lambton and the surrounding environs when I was visiting before. One of the reasons we chose to travel this way is because of the remembrances stirred up by my chats with Wickham. It brought so many pleasant memories to mind."

"It is too bad. I am not at liberty to expand on the details, but I do not think he is a man to be trusted. I do not know why there has been a change in Lizzy. Truly, beyond the information about Wickham, I can think of nothing that should be a burden to her."

"It is puzzling!"

"I agree."

The two ladies continued their tete-a-tete, attempting to root out a clue as to Lizzy's recent low spirits. But neither had any success.

After several lovely days in Derbyshire, Mrs Gardiner insisted that the party visit the famous Pemberley. Jane raised some reservation over the possibility of encountering Mr Darcy and touring his house without a formal invitation. More pressing in her concern was the possibility that Mr Bingley might be visiting if the family was in residence. But these worries were smoothed over by her aunt's sensible opinion that it would be no different than the other houses they had toured. She also noted that the Bennet family's acquaintance with Mr Darcy had been so slight that there was no need to feel uneasy.

"Besides, the chambermaid here at the inn assured us that the family was not at home," Mrs Gardiner exclaimed. "If Mr Darcy and none of his friends are in residence, there can be no awkwardness in us receiving a tour from the housekeeper and having a short stroll around the grounds. Would you not agree?"

Jane nodded and dropped her gaze down to fidget with her cup of tea. She was grateful that her aunt and uncle immediately launched into a conversation concerning the future schooling of their eldest boy. Both were quite passionate about their particular viewpoint. It was the only time Jane could recall seeing them in anything approaching a conflict.

"Just because you went off to school at that age does not mean that Hugh should, my dear."

"Be reasonable, my dearest," Mr Gardiner countered. "He is of an age that it will do him good to have time away from us. Just as I had as a child. I can tell you, getting out of that house and having some distance from my two sisters was—well, let us just say that it was a jolly good thing to occur."

"But our house is such a happy place. There is nothing equal to a happy home to foster good health. Any tutor he needs can be retained."

The two continued and did not notice just how hot Jane's cheeks became. Even the idea that Bingley might be at Pemberley one day in the near future was enough to discompose her.

But he is not there. I worry over nothing. If I am never to see him again, I will have to learn to be content with that. I must.

Only one tear dropped from her lower lashes. It was such a quiet thing that no one noticed. Jane covered the small wet spot upon her sleeve with her palm and looked up again, forcing a mild smile to her face.

"It is such a lovely day, viewing Pemberley will be delightful."

The tour of the house was just as pleasant as it was anticipated to be. It was particularly interesting to see the large portrait of Mr Darcy on the wall in the gallery. Jane tilted her head slightly to one side, feeling that the artist had captured a certain warmth to his countenance that was elusive, yet becoming. She was glad to have received the information from Lizzy that had painted Darcy in a kinder light as a caring brother, even if it came at the price of a poor opinion of George Wickham.

I have always suspected that there must be some good in him. Charles—I mean, Mr Bingley could not have been so very deceived as to become close friends with a man who was as cruel as Wickham portrayed Mr Darcy to be. If only there was a little more openness about Mr Darcy, I am certain his nature would be better understood.

Jane smiled at the irony of her giving counsel to another to be more open. She was aware that she could be perceived as being too reserved and unknowable. But Jane thought it would be wrong to force herself into the image of someone she was not. It was a form of lying to the world, a form of sneaking your true self around under the cloak of an entirely different character.

After a brief tour of the garden, Jane and Mrs Gardiner were feeling ready to return to Lambton.

"One more quick stop, ladies, if you do not mind. The lake is something I simply must visit. Perhaps I will see a few fish jump in the air," Mr Gardiner exclaimed. "Of course, my dear, we are not too fatigued for that, are we?"

"No, not at all," replied Jane. "I know how much fishing interests you."

Jane strolled along the lawn above the lake. It was a grassy open area that showed the lake off at its most impressive. She was just approaching the heavy cover of some trees to stand in the shade and out of the heat of the sun for a moment when the snap of a twig caused her to start. There, emerging from the shade of the trees, was Mr Darcy, smiling with his hair, shirt, and breeches soaking wet.

"Mr Darcy?" Jane cried.

"Miss Bennet!" Mr Darcy exclaimed.

A branch was shoved out of the way behind Mr Darcy, and Mr Bingley, also with soaked clothes, emerged.

"Mr Bingley?"

"Miss Bennet!" The three stood stock-still, silent, and shocked for almost a full minute. Mr Darcy looked at his friend, back to Jane, and then back to his friend. Jane and Mr Bingley were staring, unabashed, at each other. Mr Bingley's wide eyes and open mouth left no doubt as to how deeply he felt the surprise of coming upon Jane so unexpectedly. For just a moment, Jane felt a swell of cloudy darkness creep in from the corners of her eyes.

I will not swoon. I will not swoon. I will not swoon.

Mr Darcy cleared his throat.

"Miss Bennet, how wonderful to see you. What a pleasant surprise. Are you staying in the neighbourhood?"

Jane finally forced her mouth to work and ordered sound to be produced in her throat. "I...Yes. My aunt and uncle Gardiner. We—that is, they—I mean, *she* spent much of her childhood in Lambton. We are staying at the inn there."

"How interesting. Is that not interesting? Bingley?"

Mr Bingley continued to stare, dumbfounded. With an almost indiscernible groan, Mr Darcy pressed on. "You must forgive us for our sudden, damp appearance. We were riding on ahead of our party, and the heat was unbearable. So we took a quick dip in a small pond on the other side of the forest. Is that not so, Bingley?"

Mr Bingley nodded.

"I apologise, sir. We were told none of the family were at home," Jane whispered, averting her eyes from their undignified appearance.

"Do not concern yourself with that," Mr Darcy continued in an easy, friendly manner, "We are early. None at the house expected us until tomorrow. Is your family well, Miss Bennet? Your parents?"

"Yes."

"And your sisters, they are well?"

"Yes."

"And are they *all* still at home?" Mr Darcy asked with an edge creeping into his voice.

"All but one."

"Oh."

Mr Darcy seemed to slump at this and stared at the ground. Not wishing the conversation to sink into nothingness, Jane said, "My youngest sister has gone to stay in Brighton."

"Oh, your youngest sister. Miss Lydia, I think? Yes. Miss Lydia. That is wonderful. She is the *only* sister not currently at Longbourn. Is that correct?"

By this time, Jane's small store of courage—already taxed from making this trip and the shock of seeing Mr Bingley's rakishly handsome face and damp, clinging shirt—was completely gone. She could only nod in response.

"May we call on you?" Mr Darcy asked, "Mr Bingley and myself? At the Inn at Lambton? Tomorrow morning, perhaps?"

Jane, from the corner of her eye, thought she saw Mr Darcy shove an elbow into Mr Bingley's side.

"Ah! Yes! May we? Please?" Mr Bingley barked in a voice slightly too loud.

"And my sister, Georgiana, as well? May I bring her as well?"

Jane, now thoroughly confused and embarrassed, could only respond with a barely audible, "Yes. Of course."

The Gardiners had walked up and Jane managed to whisper out a brief introduction. Mr Bingley, appearing to be more at ease in a crowd, became more of his old self. He was even telling Mr Gardiner an amusing story of their earlier swim and a curious fish who thought his ankle was a bit of bait upon a hook. Her aunt and uncle laughed loudly, but it was all Jane could do not to run from the spot and hide herself away. Shocked mortification left her unable to raise her eyes or join in the conversation at all. At last, the small party broke up.

The Gardiners spoke softly to each other on the ride back to Lambton. Jane was grateful they had no questions for her, for she did not think she could rationally respond to any query without bursting into tears.

Several days passed in which so much occurred that Jane, who was normally a steady, reliable correspondent, had not written to Lizzy. Their time had been so much taken up with social calls that a moment to spare to sit quietly and put pen to paper rarely presented itself. Mrs Gardiner had so many old acquaintances to catch up with and new ones to visit with that they barely took a meal at the inn.

Jane and the Gardiners had received and paid calls to Mr and Miss Darcy and their guests. It was shocking to Jane how rapidly her heart fell back into the old habit of adoring Mr Bingley. Every time they met, it was so delightful to witness the eager openness in his countenance as he attempted to engage Jane in conversation.

Mr Bingley's sisters did not gain such immediate entrance back into Jane's heart. Once it was discovered by Jane that Mr Bingley had no idea that she had been in London for months—though his sisters had obviously known quite well that she had—Jane struggled to forgive them of the deception. It was apparent, even to her sanguine, magnanimous spirit, that they had plotted against Mr Bingley and herself. Although she continued to be pleasant and engaged with the sisters, there was none of the easy intercourse that had existed previously.

I will forgive them, for I believe they thought I was conniving to capture Mr Bingley in some sort of mercenary marriage, but I shall never trust them again.

One fine morning just after they had dined at Pemberley the night before, Jane planned to accompany the Gardiners on a social call. As she rose to retrieve her bonnet and shawl, Mrs Gardiner placed a hand on her forearm.

"My dear Jane! You are not accompanying us, are you? For I expect that Lizzy is eagerly awaiting a letter from you. Perhaps you should stay and attend to that. I particularly wanted her to hear all about that interesting turban that Miss Bingley was wearing last evening. It was so peculiarly wound about her head with such a flourish of lace and feather on top. Please tell her all about it and that I think it would look becoming on her."

Puzzled, Jane asked, "You wish me to remain here?"

"If you do not mind staying and seeing to a letter to Lizzy, that would be wonderful."

"I have been negligent. It is true. I am curious why I have not heard from her."

"When one is travelling, these things can be misdirected so easily. I am sure her letters will catch up to us soon."

After her aunt and uncle left, Jane began a letter to her sister.

Dearest Lizzy,

You will be amazed to learn what has happened since our arrival in Lambton. A most surprising encounter occurred between myself, Mr Darcy, and Mr Bingley. They arrived at Pemberley just after we had taken a tour with the housekeeper, Mrs Reynolds. Oh, how I wish you had taken this trip instead of me! I almost fainted dead away upon seeing Mr Bingley again. He has been most kind and attentive during our visits to Pemberley, but you need not worry about me. Although I do truly enjoy his company, I know that he must not feel for me as I once did for him. Else, why would he have avoided Netherfield for so very long? His sisters are here as well. Let me assure you that I am not as deceived by their attentions as I once was. I will not carry animosity against them, but I cannot permit the level of intimacy that we once enjoyed. I do not understand how they can sit and converse with no sense of shame or contrition over their treatment of me while I was staying in London. Mr Bingley knew absolutely nothing of my presence in the city for all those months! He was startled to learn of it. But I will not ruminate any longer upon that subject. I have had the great pleasure of meeting Miss Georgiana Darcy. Lizzy, you would be proud of me, I think. Once I saw that she was shy and reserved—not at all superior and disagreeable as Mr

Wickham had led us to believe—I have endeavoured to behave as you would. Every time we meet, I attempt conversation that draws her out. She has become noticeably more lively and comfortable. I even convinced her to play the pianoforte while in company. I have never heard anyone perform with so much ability. And Mr Darcy! What a pleasure it has been to see him at ease in his home. The difference has been remarkable. Any attention that could be paid to us has been done by him immediately. Twice he has had our uncle Gardiner over for fishing in the streams and lakes of the great estate. He is all affability. I suspect, upon knowing him better, that he was in low spirits during his time in Hertfordshire when we were first introduced. I wish you could encounter him as he is now, Lizzy. It is striking, to be sure. He is the perfect gentleman, at ease in company, and an exceptionally attentive older brother to Georgiana. There is still that air of reserve and dignity about him, but I have never thought those qualities to be deficiencies in his character.

Our aunt wanted me most particularly to mention a style of turban that Miss Bingley wore the other night. She says that it would look handsome upon you. I am not as certain, but she was most insistent. It was a fine burgundy material that had a glossy cast to it. Silk, I think. The bottom was trimmed in a lace that reminded me very much of that one bonnet that Lydia wore—

Jane broke off her writing. The maid was escorting someone up the stairs to their parlour. Jane hid the letter under some other papers and stood. The door opened.

"Mr Bingley," Jane uttered, her brows rising in surprise.

"Miss Bennet," he said as he bowed.

"I am sorry that my aunt and uncle are not here to receive you. They have stepped out to call upon a friend. I was just catching up on my letters. We have been much engaged since coming into Lambton, and I have been neglectful in writing to Longbourn."

"I interrupted you, I am sorry. However, there is something I wish to—that is, I think we could have a discussion about…" Mr Bingley twisted his hands together before him.

Jane felt an enormous flush of anxious heat spread along the flesh of her chest. Turning her gaze down to the carpet just before Mr Bingley's boots, she whispered, "Would you care to sit down?"

"Sitting down. Yes! What a capital suggestion. How thoughtful of you."

They sat opposite each other, just before the fireplace. Several minutes passed as they sat in silence. Jane wanted to speak, but found she could not. There was too much in her heart that she could not find the proper words for. When she would sneak a glance up at Mr Bingley, his brows were contracted and his gaze darted all around the room, anywhere but upon her. Suddenly, Mr Bingley sprang up out of his chair.

"Should I call for some tea?" Jane ventured, startled by his sudden movement.

"Tea?" Mr Bingley laughed nervously as he moved towards the fireplace. "I should think that we can find better ways to pass the time. No tea is needed, I assure you. That is, unless you wish to have some! I beg your pardon, I did not mean to answer for you. Forgive my rudeness."

"I was not offended, sir. You are not rude in the least."

"Ah, very good. You may be wondering why I called today, alone. Well, Miss Bennet. *Jane.*" Mr Bingley paused, clearing his throat, and slid a hand up on the mantel without heeding where it was placed. A small vase of blue and white slowly slid from the mantel and shattered on the hearth. The noise caused both Jane and Mr Bingley to start. They looked at the shards and then at each other.

"I broke the vase," he cried out.

"Yes, it would appear that you did."

At that moment, Mr Darcy entered and bowed. Mr Bingley looked at him wide-eyed. "I broke the vase," he exclaimed forlornly.

"Vase? What vase?"

Mr Bingley gestured towards the shards.

"Why were you fiddling around with the vase?"

"I was not fiddling, it fell."

At that moment, the Gardiners entered. Both had a look of happy expectancy on their faces.

Mr Darcy turned to Mr Gardiner and said, "Bingley broke a vase."

"Vase? What vase?"

Mr Darcy gestured towards the broken pieces on the floor. Mr Gardiner and Mr Darcy began to speak softly to each other on a subject that Jane could not quite catch the thread of. Her uncle seemed amused, and Mr Darcy appeared exasperated.

With a rising blush of mortification, Jane began to suspect that she had been asked to stay here and write a letter by design. That Mr Bingley had been sent here alone for the reason of paying his addresses. And that he had been so nervous that the poor vase had fallen victim to his agitation.

The next morning went in a similar vein as the previous. Jane was encouraged by her aunt to stay and finish the letter that she had begun on the previous day. She protested mildly to this repetition of an unusual command from her aunt, but relented after Mrs Gardiner gave her some words of encouragement.

Feeling restless, Jane paced the room several times before she sat down to resume her letter.

Forgive me, Lizzy. I had a visitor yesterday and had to leave off writing. Mr Bingley paid a call. I was alone. It was difficult to know what he wanted to speak to me about. He seemed ready to unburden himself about something, but then he broke a vase. It was all very strange. But let me continue to describe the headdress of Miss Bingley. Aunt Gardiner is insistent that I remain again this morning and finish my description of Caroline's headdress. It is almost as if they want me to remain here for a reason. But that cannot be the case; I do not think that can be the case. I let my imagination get the better of me on occasion. So, in continuation of the description I had begun yesterday, a brooch of seed pearls and silver was at the centre of the turban. It was larger than a—

Just as on the previous day, Jane heard someone travelling up the creaky staircase. With a fluttering heart, she slid the letter under the blank sheets and stood. The chambermaid entered.

"Excuse me, miss. Two letters come for you."

"Thank you."

Jane took the letters and sat in front of the fireplace. The first one had been misdirected. It was from Lizzy.

Dear Jane

You are sorely missed here in the Kingdom of Longbourn. There is no replacement for your wise counsel and steady heart. But our little cousins provide enough of a diversion for me every day that I hardly have time to notice. Do you remember the apple tree that I fell from when I was about 10 years old? Well, it finally has someone as eager to climb it as I always was. Hugh insists that it is his frigate and that he is the brave English captain. I, of course, am the French forces attempting to invade. The apples are his cannonballs, and I assure you they can pack quite a punch. Since I am the

French fleet—sometimes speedy frigates, sometimes a ship of the line—I do attempt to route him out on a regular basis, but to no avail. I hope our aunt is pleased by his improvement in speaking French, for I absolutely insist that if he is to hurl insults and threaten me with the worst sort of retaliations, that he speak only in French, otherwise I will scoff and laugh. Only when he speaks fluently do I quail and order a retreat. Hattie sits on a bench nearby, unsure of which side to join, so she is usually a Spanish or American vessel. The other day, Hugh sunk me completely and I lay in the grass so long that they both ran to check on me. But I had laid a trap, my weapons were a thorough tickling of the both of them. I think I can count that as a victory for my fleet. I do attempt to keep a few of the children out of the house every day so that Mama's nerves can have peace. I am not sure how she managed the five of us, she professes to be so ill-suited to the sound of rambunctious, happy children. Kitty has been surprisingly helpful during this time. Though she does not run and play with them as I do, she is quite happy to read aloud or stack blocks with the smaller ones. I am sorry to say that her time separate from Lydia has made a marked improvement in her. It is not Lydia's fault that her nature is such that she seeks to always be the centre of attention, that is simply who she is. But I believe Lydia's domineering ways have stifled Kitty's uncertain nature even further. Her intimacy with Maria Lucas grows deeper, and I am encouraged by her increase of daily reading. I hope that, when Lydia returns, Kitty is able to retain some of her spirit that has blossomed of late.

After a space, the script changed noticeably in style. Lizzy was writing hurriedly with little care for appearance.

Jane, a dispatch arrived in the middle of the night containing wretched news. Lydia has run off from Brighton to elope with George Wickham! They have gone to Scotland—at least that is what was said in her hurried letter to Harriet Forster—and Lydia has abandoned all friends and protection. Mama is in a constant state of hysterics and faintness. Papa has gone off to

London to try and trace their journey to Scotland. I hope I have much better news soon. What can Wickham hope to gain by the seduction of our sister? She has no money. I hope they will be found to be wed, but based on what we now know of the miscreant, I believe he is capable of the lowest sort of degradations imaginable. I ought to have told the entire neighbourhood of his character! Why did I not? I am miserable at the thought that all of this could have been prevented by myself! I had warned father of Lydia's wild behaviour and the dangers of Brighton for one such as she, but, as you see, it did little good. My hope for a happy outcome of all this is little to none. I will write again as soon as may be.

Yours affectionately,
Elizabeth

Jane sat, incredulous, reading through the letter again to be certain that she had properly understood its contents. She placed it quietly on the table after two more readings, thinking of all that she had read. Her eyes wandered over to the unopened, second letter. It lay calmly folded in on itself, ready to wreak absolute havoc or raise her heart in joy at the either good or bad news it contained. Trembling, her hand reached for it.

Jane

You and aunt and uncle must return to Longbourn immediately. We need the assistance of our uncle urgently. I am so sorry to say that I have nothing good to tell. Colonel Forster traced the pair as far as Clapham, but no farther. Nothing has been found of them. They were seen on the road to London. A fellow officer expressed his belief that Wickham had no intention of marrying Lydia. Papa is still in London, attempting to trace them. But it is almost certain that they did not go to Scotland from London.

Such a man! Is it to be believed? And Lydia! She has ruined her own prospects of future happiness and perhaps the prospects of all four of her sisters. I am misery itself, Jane. Mama is hindering any efforts to improve the situation through her constant hysterics. We suspect Kitty had some inkling of the attachment, but was sworn to secrecy. Poor girl, she feels wretched about the entire business. Jane, please come home at once.

I cannot believe that a man such as Wickham will not expect to be paid an enormous sum of money, if he can even be prevailed upon to marry Lydia. Our family finances are worse than what is commonly known. I have kept it to myself, but I have been making a little money for the family through a side venture to supplement the food for our table. That is the sole reason I deferred from joining our aunt and uncle on their trip north. After my absence to visit Kent, I did not think the family finances could bear another trip of mine. I am able to make enough to help with groceries and small items for the house, but it will not nearly be equal to make up any sort of ransom that Wickham will be sure to demand. What will we do? In the last month, I have sent out several enquiries to America to attempt to secure a position as a governess to a wealthy family or perhaps a teacher in a school there. But, as we are now at war again with America, I will not be able to answer any responses to my enquiries. Perhaps the Canadas? It is so far, but we are already beginning to be desperate and will be far more so if we must pay a small fortune to salvage Lydia's reputation and the reputation of our family. And that is only if Wickham will allow us to pay him off in small sums over time. I cannot hope he has enough goodness in his heart to allow us that small grace, but I am attempting to not surrender to heartache and despair.

I am sorry. I unburden myself far too much in this letter. It is not fair to you, dear Jane. I hardly know what to write. It has been hard without your steady presence here to calm us. Perhaps it should be me there in Derbyshire and you here, helping our mother and calming Kitty. Mary is worse than useless. All she does is preach sermons to unhearing ears and go into great detail about Lydia's irretrievably sullied reputation. Although I know all she says is with good intentions, it wearies me to no end. This entire affair has *served to give her a broader platform on which to scold through sermons. It is hardly any use to preach when the one person who desperately needed the guidance is no longer even here. Please convince the Gardiners to bring you back to Longbourn as soon as may be.*

Your loving sister,

Elizabeth

Tears splashed down, one after the other, as Jane placed the second letter next to the first. She was silent for several minutes, unable to make her body move. The familiar creaking of the staircase outside the parlour began to make its way into her awareness.

"Miss Bennet, I came to see if you had any additional vases that needed breaking," Mr Bingley said from the doorway.

Jane looked up to see the beaming face of Mr Bingley staring at her. His happiness was instantly replaced by worry when he saw her tear-streaked cheeks.

"My dearest Jane! Whatever is the matter?" he asked as he rushed to her and took both of her hands in his. He knelt before her, looking up into her face, the picture of loving worry.

"Please, speak, my angel! I will fetch the apothecary at once!"

"No, stay," she whispered. "It is some terrible news from Longbourn. My youngest sister, Lydia, has run off with Mr George Wickham. It was hoped that they went to Scotland to wed. But now, as no evidence can be found of them, it is thought that— What I mean to say is that— perhaps no marriage has occurred and—"

Here, she glanced back up at the wide eyes of Mr Bingley, so full of genuine worry and warmth. It was too much for her fortitude. She collapsed into his arms and sobbed.

Jane took little heed of what occurred next. She was aware that, just like yesterday, Mr Darcy joined them. He and Mr Bingley spoke in low voices.

Mr Gardiner was fetched. She saw Mr Darcy raise the two letters and scan them quickly, dark ire spreading across his features. When her aunt and uncle returned, the two gentlemen left. Jane told her aunt to read the letters and that they must prepare for a return. As she apologised repeatedly at the unfortunate shortening of their trip, Jane noticed that her aunt held but one letter in her hand.

"Where is the other letter?"

"Other letter?" Mrs Gardiner asked as she glanced around the room. "This was the only letter on the table, my dear. You must have been mistaken. No surprise given the nature of this news."

Jane frowned and tried to recall the last hour through her stuffy, aching head that suffered after releasing so many tears. She could have sworn she had received two letters, but the other was nowhere to be found.

Chapter 19

The Bitterest Kind of Distress

Elizabeth almost cried out in relief when the Gardiners' carriage was spotted coming up the drive of Longbourn. Never had she been more keenly aware of how very much she and Jane depended on each other for support and comfort in difficult times.

Once the shock of the news of Lydia's elopement had settled, the entire burden of keeping the family in some semblance of order had fallen upon Elizabeth. Mr Bennet was gone to London in what seemed to be an increasingly futile effort to locate Wickham and Lydia. Mrs Bennet stayed in her room and played at being sick, though her appetite remained healthy and her loud voice when she insisted she was suffering from a case of the vapours made the claim of her poor health questionable. Mary behaved as if nothing had changed and was only irritated when an alteration to her schedule was made by some crisis of the business at hand. Kitty, once she overcame the perception of herself as a pariah of some sort for keeping the knowledge of Lydia's preference for Wickham a secret, was able to assist Elizabeth occasionally. With all of this to manage—in addition to the sly social calls of friends and neighbours hoping to glean some new crumb of gossip—and with the responsibilities of managing the estate in her father's absence and the care of the Gardiner children, Elizabeth felt herself on the verge of a complete collapse by the time Jane returned.

Jane emerged from the carriage and Elizabeth threw her arms around her neck, heedless of anyone else for the moment.

"Oh Jane, how grateful I am to see you!"

"I am glad to be home. It is terrible that you have had to bear all of this on your own!"

Elizabeth whispered under her breath, "Who else should bear this burden? It was my foolishly poor decision to keep Mr Wickham's true nature to myself. I have never been more misguided by my judgement in my life."

But then Elizabeth could not help but recall her misjudgements of Mr Darcy as well. Without intending to be so open at such a moment, she covered her face with her hands and let out a small moan. Jane placed her hand on Elizabeth's back and steered her away from the others. She grasped Elizabeth's wrists and gently pulled her arms down.

"Lizzy, you are not to blame. No more than anyone else who has been tricked by Wickham's pleasing countenance. A man who could have possibly been so malevolent towards Georgiana Darcy, who is the sweetest of girls, or Mr Darcy—"

"You have seen Georgiana Darcy?" cried Elizabeth. "How have you met her? Where?"

"Pardon me, I had forgotten that I never had the opportunity to send you a letter." Jane blushed at this question. Elizabeth thought a very small smile reached her lips as Jane seemed to recall something pleasing.

"Mr Bingley, Miss Georgiana Darcy, and Mr Darcy arrived at Pemberley while we were staying at the Inn at Lambton. We encountered Mr Darcy and Mr Bingley for the first time while we were taking a tour of the house at Pemberley. We had been informed by several people that none of the family—or their acquaintance—were thought to be there. Lizzy, it was most shocking. I came upon Mr Bingley so suddenly, I hardly knew what to do..." Jane trailed off to a soft whisper.

Elizabeth placed a hand on her sister's forearm and squeezed gently. "It sounds as though we both have much to tell. But I am afraid it will have to wait until later. Mama has been frantically asking about you since the moment she awoke."

Jane nodded, obviously grateful that Elizabeth pressed her no further.

Their mother needed to retell every little detail of the tragedy with animation and relish. Jane sat quietly and offered the occasional murmur of solace to Mrs Bennet. Between their mother's starkly divergent fits of anguish and hopeful speculation, Jane and Elizabeth would sneak glances at each other. Both sisters were clearly aware that the other had so much in her heart to tell once privacy could ensure that no one else heard. The last thing either of them wanted was for Mrs Bennet to even suspect that Jane had seen Mr Bingley. Elizabeth was completely uncertain how their mother would respond to a development such as that. It might truly cause Mrs Bennet a genuine fit. Elizabeth rose to go downstairs and advise her aunt and uncle to say nothing of seeing Mr Bingley for the moment.

Between the chaos of the Gardiners packing up their children and leaving to return home to London and the unpacking of Jane, it was several days before the two eldest sisters could get away to have a chat of their own in private.

They decided to take a long walk, as experience had taught them that Longbourn was too small to ensure that secrets were not overheard. Mary had no taste for exercise that day as clouds threatened rain. Kitty was feeling low in spirits and nursing the beginnings of a head cold. So, Jane and Elizabeth finally had a tranquil stretch of time to themselves.

Jane told Elizabeth of everything that had happened during her stay in Lambton. Elizabeth was silent for a moment.

"And do you suspect that Mr Bingley had reasons to wish to speak to you privately? Do you think he was going to make you an offer?"

"Oh, Lizzy, I do not know. It was all so unusual. His coming to visit two mornings in a row when I was alone, my aunt insisting I stay back from visiting and write to you about that hideous turban of Caroline Bingley's..."

Jane covered her mouth with her hand and looked at Elizabeth with wide eyes. "What a wicked thing for me to say! Whatever her past actions were to me, she did not deserve that."

Elizabeth could not help but laugh aloud, long and hard. Before long, Jane was laughing as well. They were so overcome that they had to sit on a log for several minutes.

Wiping tears of mirth from the corners of her eyes, Elizabeth asked, "Was it too awful? The turban?"

"Perhaps there are styles in London that I am not privy to. I believe it is considered very elegant in the smart circles and looks lovely on certain ladies. But, if I am to be completely honest, it did not become her at all."

"I am glad you were unable to send me that letter. You may have come home to me sporting a grand turban of my own."

"It may look better on you than it did on her. But, Lizzy, tell me, did you send me two letters or just the one? For the life of me, I cannot seem to recall, for I was so set to by the upsetting information."

"I sent two letters. The first began with information about our cousins and the game in the apple tree, then telling of this awful business with Lydia. Then the second letter begging you to come home."

"That is odd. One of your letters must have been misplaced. The first one, with the funny stories of you and the apple tree." Jane's eyes were puzzled, but then they lit up, as if realising something of great import. "Of course," she murmured.

"What is it?"

"Nothing. It is nothing. A silly thought of mine. And your scheme to take a position as governess across the Atlantic?"

"Honestly, Jane, I do not see any other recourse. Even if Wickham and Lydia are discovered and made to marry, it will most likely cost us an enormous sum of money. And if they are not discovered, or we are unable to force Wickham to marry Lydia, well, my pride forbids me from staying here and possibly meeting with our acquaintances as a governess. The humiliation of such encounters and their piteous concern that hides their gleeful gossiping, I could not bear it!" Elizabeth said with finality. The image of seeing Mr Darcy across a room, standing next to some turbaned high society lady wife, as she herself was an impoverished governess, was too much to bear. It caused her throat to close and her breath to quicken. "I would rather be on the other side of the world than risk it. I can send some of my pay home. I have heard that English governesses from good families can fetch a large salary."

Jane looked horrified. "But when would we see you again? What if this war with America drags on for years and our separation is longer than anticipated? There must be a better way."

"If there is another way, then I cannot see it. Uncle Gardiner could hardly afford to help us pay a man such as Wickham anything beyond a few hundred pounds. I am uncertain we could scrape together more than a thousand to bribe him into marrying Lydia. And he would be a fool not to ask for at least five thousand."

"Five thousand! How is half such a sum to be found?"

"I do not know. Come, let us walk. Melancholy cannot resist seeping in like damp from a log when we sit too long. Movement will chase away these gloomy speculations."

They rose and continued their stroll.

"I think I should mention," Jane ventured, "that we were misled by Wickham's description of Georgiana Darcy. She was a pleasant, shy girl whose company I found delightful."

"Another lie from Wickham. How shocking," Elizabeth said with no attempt to disguise her pique.

"And Mr Darcy..."

"Yes?" Elizabeth asked with an eagerness that surprised even herself.

"I know you will be upset by this, but I must be frank with you on this point. I found Mr Darcy to be an entirely pleasant sort of man. He was gracious and kindness itself during our time at Lambton. Any courtesy he could extend to myself and the Gardiners was done. I think he is one of those people who is not at their best in unfamiliar company, especially when away from home. He was the perfect gentleman. Our uncle had two invitations to fish at the lakes at Pemberley with Mr Darcy and said nothing of finding him prideful or unpleasant. And you know our uncle is quite cutting in his way when he perceives folly or superciliousness in others."

They walked in silence for several moments before Elizabeth slowly said, "I think I can believe what you say, Jane. I have had moments with Mr Darcy, too few by far, that were pleasing. They were quiet instances when there were not many others around. He was a very different sort of man from the one we saw at the Meryton assembly and the Netherfield ball. I think I would venture to agree with you; his true nature becomes more apparent in moments of tranquillity."

Elizabeth felt sudden agitation at the memory of how often she had retold the tale of Mr Darcy's rudeness and supposed mistreatment of

Wickham. "I am ashamed of myself. I denigrated Mr Darcy so willingly to any who would listen. It would appear that I misjudged him terribly."

"No, Lizzy. Mr Darcy had moments of discourtesy, you were not mistaken on that count. What he said of you at the assembly is not something to be easily forgotten. But, unless I am very much mistaken, he must have been in particularly low spirits when he first arrived here in Hertfordshire. Do you think it was that business with Wickham attempting an elopement with his sister Georgiana that made him so unpleasant? For he seemed to brighten during his time at Netherfield."

"If I must guess, I believe he blamed himself for what happened to his sister. If he is half as severe upon himself as he is in his judgement of others, I can imagine that he could make himself very unhappy indeed." Elizabeth could not help but recollect The Hanged Man card. *For such a proud man, he must have felt terribly helpless, perhaps for the first time in his life. It is little wonder that he was so callous to others. It was a way to defend himself from more injury.*

"Lizzy," Jane said suddenly, stopping in the path before her. She grasped Elizabeth's hands and squeezed them. "Promise me that you will not accept an offer for a governess position for a few months at least."

"Why? If our father and uncle fail to discover Wickham and Lydia, we will still need more money than the estate produces now to survive. Marriages for the remaining Bennet sisters may prove more difficult with our youngest sister having made such a spectacle of herself."

"What of your—what did you call it?—your side venture? Do you wish to tell me of it? Perhaps I may be of assistance and we may make additional money."

Blushing, Elizabeth pulled her hands away and shook her head. "I do not think that would be possible. Even if Lydia and Wickham are found and made to marry, what if Papa passes away soon? We will still need more money than what we will have."

"Please, I beg of you, promise to wait a while?"

Elizabeth sighed and looked up at the passing clouds. *If only I could truly see the future. If I actually had a way to know what was ahead for me.* Finally, she brought her gaze back to the lovely face of her sister. "Do you know something that I do not?"

Jane smiled and looked away. "I do not wish to say what is only a very vague feeling. But I think that if we are patient, things may change in ways we cannot predict."

Elizabeth saw the warm glow in Jane's eyes, full of sisterly affection and admiration. The thought of sailing to the other side of the world and never seeing those kind, blue eyes again filled Elizabeth with an unanticipated wave of dread. She took Jane's hand in her own and pulled her gently so that they recommenced their stroll.

"For you, Jane, I promise. I will wait until the end of the year before I come to any final resolution as to whether I should stay or go. However, I will not stand by for years and observe as our family falls further and further into debt while I possess the intelligence and a spirit ready for any adventure. But for now, until the end of the year, I promise, I will not leave you."

Elizabeth was rewarded by Jane's soft smile radiating towards her. That was enough to settle her anxieties and restore some of her contentment.

"Come, we have been gone so long, perhaps there will be a letter from Papa that awaits us. One with glad tidings."

Chapter 20

Bingley, Master of Subterfuge

"Well? How do I look? Shall Napoleon be quaking in his boots if he saw me approach?"

Darcy shook his head with a grin and looked as though he were attempting to repress a laugh. Bingley stood before Darcy and Colonel Fitzwilliam, turning, so that they could see him dressed as an officer of the militia. Colonel Fitzwilliam clapped his hands and nodded in approval.

"If you ever have need of a profession, Bingley, I think you look dashing as a military man."

"Do you really think so?" Bingley replied, smiling. "I am not quite sure that I would be a decent officer. I think I would be far more interested in making peace and having a drink together than defeating enemy armies."

"I shall bring that up as a possible strategy next time any superior officer asks my opinion about what we should do next in battle. I do not believe getting the opposing forces drunk and jolly is tried half as often as it should be."

"If you were suited to any profession, I think that being a businessman or politician would be more to your liking and abilities," Darcy said.

"Those stoves you are having installed in your London house for heating in winter sound like an interesting speculation."

"I believe they will become quite popular in the near future," Darcy replied.

"But, I must confess that I have always had a secret desire to try my hand at running for an MP once I was settled down at an estate. Netherfield would suit that perfectly. I think I would get a great many votes to be a Member of Parliament. But, I think I need a wife first…"

"Which will be difficult if we do not proceed quickly."

"Right. Are you certain that this Mrs Younge would recognise the both of you?"

Darcy's face darkened. "That foul woman would not only recognise either Colonel Fitzwilliam or myself, she would relish negotiating with us for days over an enormous sum of money before she would reveal the location of Wickham and Lydia. And during that time, the chances are high that she would inform Wickham—no doubt receiving even more payment in the process—that we are searching for him and he would abscond. This is the best scheme, I think. Anything else would cause our quarry to bolt and probably leave me poorer in the bargain."

"What a ghastly woman. I will be brave and think of my dear Jane every moment."

"That is the spirit. Now let us hire a carriage and be on our way."

The three gentlemen left Darcy's townhouse. The need to avoid detection was the reason for hiring transport as opposed to using one of Darcy's carriages. Darcy and Colonel Fitzwilliam both had on simpler clothes borrowed from servants of similar build. Crump had been able to procure the outfits for them so as to avoid undue speculations from the servants' hall. Their carriage travelled for quite some time until they reached another quarter of London. Fitzwilliam and Darcy departed a block from the final destination.

Before shutting the door, Darcy asked, "Are you certain you remember everything we told you? Mrs Younge is not bright, but she is devilishly slippery."

"The lady must be if she was able to convince both you and Colonel Fitzwilliam that she was all goodness and sunshine while truly being a she-demon. The pair of you are the sharpest fellows I know. Do not concern yourself, I remember everything. The stakes for my future happiness are too high for me to make a misstep."

Bingley continued on his way and alighted from the carriage in front of a building of several storeys. The rest of the neighbourhood, though not wealthy, had a cheery demeanour, excepting for this house. It had the air of a malevolent creature attempting to pass itself off as harmless. Bingley had to repress a shiver as he glanced up at the windows and leaning chimney. He glanced back over his shoulder at the corner where Colonel Fitzwilliam and Darcy were loitering. He looked away quickly, straightened his shoulders, and stood taller as a military man should.

Bingley walked up the steps and rapped on the door. Darcy had hired a man to watch the house for a day. The hired fellow had not reported much activity, but that did not mean there would not be a gang of ruffians waiting within. As he heard footsteps approach the door, Bingley steeled himself with the remembrance of Jane sobbing in his arms at the Inn in Lambton.

She is far and away worth any peril I face. I would do anything that might help ease her suffering.

The door creaked open. A woman's face peeked through the crack and asked with asperity, "What do you want?"

"Ah, good evening. Pardon me for intruding, but I am searching for a friend of mine. Perhaps you could direct me to him? His name is Wickham. George Wickham."

"Never heard of him."

"Ah, that is unfortunate. I thought that Mrs Younge resided here. Wickham told me if I ever needed to find him that I should enquire with her first."

"Too sad for you."

She began to shut the door.

"The reverse is true, madam. It is really too sad for him, I should say." Bingley laughed. "For I have a heavy purse for him."

The door instantly paused in its closing. Bingley reached under his cloak and pulled out a purse of coins. "I finally have the money owed to him from a night of cards that did not go my way. Wickham was in rare form and outdid us all. Oh well, if you do not know him…"

"Did you say *George* Wickham? Oh yes! Bless me, he and I go back. As fine a fellow as one is ever likely to encounter. He is a very close acquaintance of mine, I assure you, sir. Almost as a son to me, he is. I will not have a friend of dear Wickham left out on the stoop. Come in, come in!"

The middle-aged woman opened the door to Bingley and waved him into the house. She directed him to a small parlour to the right and begged him to take a seat. Bingley glanced around, trying to appear at ease. The woman he assumed to be Mrs Younge had a respectable appearance in her dress and had seamlessly switched to a much more elegant accent the moment she had seen the purse that Bingley had shown her. He examined the room. It was neat and clean, but there was something that he could not quite put his finger on that unsettled him. At last he realised that there were no personal touches of paintings, unfinished needlework, silhouettes, books, or cosy rugs. Nothing that denoted that a person with a history lived here. It was as though the house itself was a shell that could be shed by her at a moment's notice.

"So, you are Mrs Younge? The friend of Wickham?"

"Of course I am. It is so pleasant to meet another military man. George has been such a generous, kind friend to me. Did he mention how much he has helped me in the past?"

"Well, no, I cannot say that he has." Bingley sat on the very edge of the small sofa. He was beginning to feel as if the walls were closer than they had been when he had first entered. He ran a finger under the edge of his collar in an attempt to loosen it and swallowed loudly.

"How inconsiderate of me! I have neglected to offer you some refreshments. I will be back momentarily."

"Do not trouble yourself, I beg of you. If you could just direct me to where I might find good old Wickham—such a splendid fellow he is, that one—I shall be much obliged."

But she had already left the room. Bingley wiped a bead of sweat from his brow and thought about running out and never looking back. But then, as a ghost who loves one dearly might, an image of Jane Bennet seemed to materialise before him in the middle of the stuffy room. Mrs Younge re-entered.

"Wine! Very quality drink. I just opened it. Here."

She handed him a glass and sat uncomfortably close to him on the little sofa. Bingley tried to scoot away, but found that he had been left little room for any sort of retreat from the figure of Mrs Younge. He recalled Darcy's words to him just an hour before. *'And for God's sake, Bingley, do not drink anything that she offers you. There is a good chance it may be drugged if she has had a glimpse of your change purse. I do not relish the thought of finding you dumped in a field, miles into the country. Jane Bennet would never forgive me.*

He took the glass from her in his one hand and with his other reached to his side for his satchel of coins.

"Perhaps it would be best for me to leave this on the table while we refresh ourselves, it is awfully heavy!"

Bingley lurched forward to place the coin purse on the table before them and deliberately fumbled the bag to the floor. "Oh, dashed clumsy of me, do forgive me."

As he leaned over to pick it up, he kicked it farther under the sofa.

"Oh, I think some coins came out. Allow me, dear." Mrs Younge placed her glass on the table, knelt down, and began to scrounge for the bag and coins. Bingley switched glasses in one deft motion and then assisted her. Once some of the fallen coins had been returned to the bag—for Bingley had no doubt that several had made their way into the crevice of Mrs Younge's amply displayed bosom—they sat back up.

"So kind of you to help," Bingley said as he raised his glass. "I salute you."

Mrs Younge giggled and batted her eyes like a lady half her age. "Such gallant manners. I am flattered." She picked up her glass and took such a long drink from it that half the wine was gone by the time she brought it back down. Her free hand rested lightly on Bingley's knee and began a slow slide upward while it curved to the inside of his thigh.

"Now, where were we?" she asked with another coquettish giggle.

Restraining every impulse to flee, Bingley leaned over, placed a finger under her chin and asked in a low husky voice, "Wickham. You were telling me where he is?"

She laughed again as her eyes shut halfway. "At the Corner Crown Inn. Just a few blocks south of here on Lightly Way Road. With that loud, bothersome chit. A loose, country brat who thinks she is going to wed the man. But they skipped the vows and went straight to the connubial bliss. And the promise of wedding vows has been completely forgotten, stupid girl! Speaking of which, I think that you would conduct yourself rather well in that respect. We may also skip the connubial and move straight to the bliss part, if you catch my meaning. Such a handsome, dashing officer. Now"—her head lolled to one side as she leaned in till her mouth was but a few inches from Bingley's—"how about a kiss, sir?"

Mrs Younge swayed and then collapsed, face first, into Bingley's lap with a light groan. Her glass tumbled to the floor and the few remaining sips spread out onto the carpet. Bingley slid out from under the insensible Mrs Younge and rearranged her up on the sofa. He grabbed the purse of coins and bounded out of the house and down the steps. He did not dare to look back until he was safely on the corner and standing before Darcy and Colonel Fitzwilliam.

"How did you do, man?"

Panting, Bingley could not help but shiver slightly as he pointed to the south. "An inn that way. The Corner Crown Inn. She tried to drug me! I switched glasses and she passed out. But not before she attempted a grab at my tallywhacker."

Fitzwilliam repressed a grin as he glanced wide-eyed at Darcy, then back to Bingley. "Too bad old fellow, better luck next time."

"No, thank you, I will decline the honour," Bingley exclaimed. Darcy looked scornfully back at the house. "Conniving, wicked woman. At least we know where to find the pair of them. Let us hope she at least managed to tell the truth before she lost awareness. Bingley, if you would be so kind, hire a carriage up to the Gardiners' house and inform them of all we know. Fitzwilliam and I will deal with Wickham ourselves. Mr Gardiner may wish to come and attempt to collect Lydia himself as she may not be willing to part from the cad into our company. The benefit of a relative to sway her may be needed. Wickham can hold a power over women, both the clever ones and those who are not nearly so bright. And, if memory serves correctly, Lydia Bennet possesses a strong spirit, but not as much wit and discernment as her sisters."

Bingley hailed a carriage and left Darcy and Fitzwilliam walking down the road together, heads bent towards each other in close conversation. He leaned back in his seat and let out a relieved sigh.

The second that this is resolved, I will be on a knee before Jane, begging her to have me. And I will be absolutely certain there are no vases, dreadful letters, or conniving sisters around to ruin the moment.

Despite the trial he had just endured in the web of Mrs Younge, Bingley could not help but smile broadly at the thought of Jane in his arms again. This time, the proposal would not be marred with tears of pained mortification to dampen his jacket.

If there are to be tears, they will spring up from joy, not distress.

Chapter 21

The Happiest, Wisest, Most Reasonable End

"I will not have it! They can go straight up to the north or to the devil for all I care," Mr Bennet bellowed in an uncustomarily raised voice. "I will not have my house sullied or my other daughters swayed by what they may perceive is the correct way to catch a husband. To admit Lydia and that—that bounder she married into Longbourn is little better than a sanguine commendation of the methods and intrigues that they both used to ensnare the other. They may be deserving of each other's company, but they are most certainly *not* deserving of ours."

"But, my dear," Mrs Bennet wailed, "consider how it will look to the neighbourhood! If you do not have your youngest daughter for a visit, they will think that we slight them and that all is not proper and decent in their union."

"Excellent, that is as it should be. You know how much some of our girls"—Mr Bennet paused and looked with gravity at Kitty—"may not have the sense to understand just how wrong Lydia was in her pursuit of Wickham. It was only by the good graces of Bingley's interference that the entire incident had a happy ending. Lord only knows how much Mr Bingley and my brother-in-law Gardiner laid out to convince that rapscallion to marry Lydia."

"But I do assure you, Papa," Kitty protested, "I do understand that Lydia was not correct in her conduct. I would not be so indiscreet in my behaviour with gentlemen. I understand that Lydia was not entirely proper."

Elizabeth looked at Jane with a modest smile, suddenly proud of Kitty for having the courage to defend herself to their father, even if the subject matter was questionable.

"Not entirely proper? Not *entirely*?" Mr Bennet countered. "You see, Mrs Bennet? That statement from Kitty only serves to demonstrate that her judgement is not reliable enough to be trusted around the likes of *Mrs Lydia Wickham*." Mr Bennet spat out the name of his only married daughter like it was a sip from a jug of milk that had taken a turn for the worse.

With a forlorn wail, Kitty ran from the room, and Jane followed to comfort her. Mrs Bennet rose to pace in front of Mr Bennet as he sat in his chair before the fireplace. His efforts to build some sort of fortification by raising an open newspaper to cover his face and deflect the attacks of his wife were not entirely successful. And though Mrs Bennet could not catch a glimpse of his expressions, this did not deter her in the least from continuing her campaign of harassment.

"And who else should pay out a sum to be Lydia's dowry but her uncle and her—her—her neighbour? It was the correct way to do it. Neither Mr Bingley nor my brother have children—"

"Mama! Aunt and Uncle Gardiner have four children of their own and may have additional little ones in the future. How can you say something so untrue?"

"Hold your tongue, Elizabeth, you did not let me finish. They do not have children of *age to marry*, so who else should pay for Lydia to have an adequate dowry?"

Elizabeth could only squeeze her eyes shut and attempt to ignore any more of her mother's ridiculous assertions. She went to the window and—not for the first time that day—wished she was far from Longbourn. The initial elation from the news of Lydia's marriage had been quickly replaced by demands from her mother to see her youngest before the newlyweds departed for a northern regiment. But here, her father held firm. He was late in his attempt to regulate his daughters, but a tardy effort was better than no effort at all. Elizabeth did not completely agree with him at this banishment of Lydia. Both Jane and Elizabeth had attempted to urge him to allow the Wickhams a short stay before their travels north, but he was not to be moved. The two eldest sisters had concerns that Lydia would be affronted by this lack of paternal affection. But, when Elizabeth reflected on what she knew Lydia's true character to be, she doubted very much that her youngest sister would be downcast by this inattention for very long. It was not in her nature to brood on a subject deeply or steadily.

I suppose that Papa is right to be concerned about what effect it will have upon Kitty to witness Lydia strut and crow on the arm of her husband. Kitty may perceive it as a stamp of approval for the method with which Lydia obtained Wickham, which is the last thing that could be wished for. Jane, Mary, and myself are out of any sphere of Lydia's influence, but the same cannot be said of Kitty.

Miserable at this endlessly circulating debate that neither of her parents would give ground on, Elizabeth kept her focus out the window to the changing clouds overhead. The first chill of the approaching autumn from the wind outside could be felt through the panes of glass that she stood so close to. Elizabeth began to think of going to her cottage in the woods and seeing if anyone approached for a reading. The tops of the trees past the beginning of their drive shook suddenly in a heavy gust from the wind.

I wonder if it truly gets as cold in the Canadas as people say it does? How much colder would it be?

Elizabeth shivered as she hugged herself tightly, arms crossed before her. In the distance, she thought she saw something round and tumbling coming up Longbourn's drive. It rolled and ran in front of the wind.

A hat, a man's hat!

Pursuing the hat at a quick clip, a laughing Mr Bingley ran up to the delinquent accessory and finally caught it up in his hand. He placed it firmly on his head, turned, and shouted something back the way he came. Another tall black hat came into view; this one was doing its duty in the correct fashion atop the head of Mr Darcy. He was riding his horse and leading another riderless horse by the reins. Mr Bingley jumped up on his steed, and they made their way towards Longbourn.

Elizabeth, not realising she had been holding her breath, inhaled loudly and clapped her hand to her mouth. Her heart felt as though it had jumped significantly upwards to relocate in her throat.

"You startled me, child! Do not gape out of the window like that. You know how raw my nerves have been these past weeks. It would behove you to begin to think of me and my wretched health before you go startling and gasping like that," Mrs Bennet exclaimed as she sat clutching her handkerchief over her nose and mouth, clearly trying to devise a new tact to take with her husband.

"Mama, I believe Mr Bingley approaches. Mr Bingley and—and Mr Darcy."

Mrs Bennet leapt up and shoved Elizabeth aside bodily, took one quick look out of the window, and then ran out of the parlour shrieking, "Jane! Jane!"

Elizabeth pulled away from the view in embarrassment, not wishing to be witnessed standing there wide-eyed and open-mouthed. She went quickly to the mirror to straighten her hair and check her teeth, for lunch had included a large serving of early autumn spinach.

"I believe," Mr Bennet stated sedately as he examined the upper corner of his newspaper, "it is almost one year to the day from when I paid my first call to Netherfield. I was promised by your mother that the effort would result in the marriage of one of my daughters. One of my daughters is indeed married—though not quite as illustriously as I was assured. However, perhaps this year will end differently. If Bingley does end up making Jane an offer, I will say that he certainly took his time about it."

"Oh, Papa, do be serious."

"Yes, Lizzy. I will be, just to please you, my dear."

Mrs Bennet herded everyone else into the parlour in front of her like she was an energetic sheep dog. It was a humorous parade—Mary, obviously cross at having her studies in her room interrupted; poor Kitty, still snuffling back tears and blinking rapidly; and Jane, looking to be in the most lovely blush of nervous happiness imaginable. They all took a seat and tried their best to affect imperturbable nonchalance. The only one who truly succeeded at this was Mr Bennet, who had no need to pretend.

Mrs Hill announced the gentlemen with a tad more flourish than was her usual manner. Mr Bingley glanced nervously at Jane and then at her parents. He settled into a seat as close to Jane as he could manage and began an energetic exchange of greetings between himself and Mrs Bennet.

Mr Darcy, after a nod from himself to her parents and a brief, curt acknowledgement of him by them, walked towards Elizabeth's chair. They were in a corner of the room, somewhat out of the common flow of the conversation. Elizabeth kept her gaze mostly on the rug just in front of Mr

Darcy's boots. She risked the occasional quick glance up to his face, trying to decipher some expression of the state of his heart.

"Miss Elizabeth."

"Mr Darcy."

"Have you been well these last few months?"

"Very well, sir. And you?"

"I cannot complain of feeling low."

"That is pleasing to hear."

There was a frantic silence between them that buzzed in Elizabeth's ears. She dared a long look up again into his eyes. His gaze was so studied and cautious, his face was so immovable, it was difficult to perceive if he was happy or sad, angry or content. Frustration rose in her chest. Before her stood the very man she had speculated about endlessly since her journey to Kent, truly ever since the first moment she saw him that strange evening at Netherfield almost a year earlier, and she could see nothing in his countenance to inform her of his feelings. It was incredibly vexing. He had none of the open, handsome easiness that she had observed in him during their readings and that Jane had spoken so warmly of after her visit to Lambton. Neither was the staunch properness of his superior pride there. The cold, surveying, lordly air that he so frequently exhibited, so etched in her memories since first witnessing his entrance at the Meryton assembly, was not to be seen either. Elizabeth could not help but feel her frustration begin to give way to an angry sense of failure on her own part.

To be able to glean absolutely nothing from this man who has haunted my thoughts and dreams relentlessly! How has he rendered all of my abilities in the arts of close observation so hopelessly useless? What an infuriating man...

Heat, not just of anger, but also an uncontrolled desire that she could not quite put a name to, began to wash over her heart and face. He was not improperly close by any stretch of the imagination, but to Elizabeth it felt as if his skin might brush hers at any moment. The warmth from his body could be sensed by her own flesh in a way that startled her. She wished for the possibility of his touch so strongly that she felt as though she was breathing with difficulty through steam and storm.

"I understand," Mr Darcy said in a calm, controlled tone, "we were not so fortunate as to have your company during the recent trip of Mr and Mrs Gardiner to the north. But I believe that my sister, Georgiana, and your sister were very pleased with each other's conversation. I enjoyed meeting the Gardiners. It is regrettable that you could not also make the trip, for Pemberley is very beautiful during the late summer. There are many fine walks that I am certain you and— That you would have enjoyed exceedingly. I know of your fondness for lonely spots in the woods."

"Thank you for the sentiment, sir. However, as you are well aware, there were matters here at Longbourn that required my attention." She looked up for one moment, felt as though she had seen a bolt of lightning, and dropped her gaze from his hard stare and set jaw. Her voice lowered to a papery whisper. "If I had made the trip with the Gardiners, I am not as certain that all of the encounters would have been agreeable ones."

"Ah, I see. So that was one of your considerations for withdrawing from the trip. The possibility of unpleasantness if there were meetings with particular individuals," he muttered. Elizabeth looked up hurriedly and thought she could detect a tilt of his head that only someone familiar with his moods would know to mean he was brooding upon a hurtful reflection. He looked away at one of the paintings on the parlour wall, an indifferently placid scene of a meadow with white puffy clouds billowing above it.

She gathered up her courage and ventured to say, "But, I think, well...that is, I *hope*, most sincerely, that our understanding of one another has deepened since the last time we met. I do not think that our initial comprehension of each other's natures was true to reality. I have been heartily saddened by my poor performance at sketching characters. You were correct, sir, in advising me at the Netherfield ball, not to attempt to take your likeness, as I would do neither of us an honour with my results."

He looked back at her briefly before looking away again. "You no longer think of me as an imperious king, attempting to manipulate those around me?"

"You do have some admirable qualities that resemble those of an honourable monarch, such as a desire to protect those dear to you. Not all of a king's actions should be credited to selfishness if we are unaware of the myriad concerns that incite him."

"I think that our understanding of each other has deepened and perhaps also our—" He paused, seeming to search for the best word as his brows furrowed. "—our respect for one another?"

Their eyes met and Elizabeth felt any anger or resentment towards him completely wither and die. Her heart fluttered uncomfortably and she opened her mouth to respond when the shrill voice of her mother broke through.

"Thank Heaven that Wickham still has some friends, though perhaps not so many as he *deserves*!"

The entire room was silent for a moment. Mr Darcy's chest expanded in a deep breath as he pressed his lips tightly together and turned to look out of a nearby window. He kept his back to the room for much of the remaining visit.

Elizabeth, though glad of that quality in her mother that made her fiercely defend those she loved, could not have imagined a more hurtfully ill-timed exclamation from her. The rest of the visit was uneventful. Elizabeth stewed in a wretched blend of mortification and confusion. She could only find solace in the fact that Mr Bingley was near to bursting in his pointed attentions to Jane. And Jane—in her quiet, blushing way—seemed to give him all the encouragement that she was able to muster.

In this and this alone, I must be content. I must be happy. Jane deserves the regard of a man of such goodness as Mr Bingley. There is no way to tease out the true feelings of Mr Darcy. I treated him so unkindly and laid so many false accusations at his doorstep that I am ashamed to recall them all. It could not be possible for him to regard me with love again, could it? To be accused by me of such vicious conduct when the opposite was true. And now, to expect him to willingly attempt to connect himself to such a family as mine? And to such a man as George Wickham as a brother-in-law? No, it is too much. It is not possible. I must be satisfied with Mr Darcy as an acquaintance to be met with only occasionally. Or, if I receive some responses to my enquiries to the Canadas, perhaps never. I cannot blame him if he never wishes to be in my presence again.

Elizabeth sighed and continued in these miseries for the rest of the visit from the two gentlemen. There was no chance of ever being happy again, in her estimation, knowing that the one man she had ever fallen so deeply in love with, then openly and thoroughly rejected based on wrong assumptions and false information, was forever out of her reach.

The next day, Elizabeth's disappointment was set in stone and made fast by the information that Mr Bingley brought to Longbourn. Mr Darcy had left for London, and Bingley had no knowledge of when he might return.

It was a solitary visit that Mr Bingley paid that morning. He alone rode up to Longbourn. Mrs Bennet was quick to marshal the forces of her extra daughters into another room so that Jane and Bingley could have a private interview. Mr Bingley lost no time in leaving all of the ceramics in the room unbroken and securing the heart of Jane Bennet to his own good heart for the rest of their lives.

It was difficult for Elizabeth to be too miserable in the face of her dearest sister being so contentedly glowing with true happiness. She knew that she could always have a future with the Bingleys here in England, but the idea of it left her uneasy.

Nothing has changed. The idea of being a helpful, spinster aunt to any future Bingley children is delightful, but seeing Mr Darcy visit? And perhaps even bring a wife?

Here she could not continue her speculation because her heart sank too low. The ecstasies of her mother and seeing the loving concern between the newly betrothed couple were almost more than she could bear.

For the next several days, Elizabeth spent her mornings at the cottage in the woods, hearing the concerns and worries of the local population. She tried her best to guide people through their troubles and only accepted payments from those she knew could very well afford to part from them.

Her afternoons were spent in being a purposefully negligent chaperone to Jane and Mr Bingley during one of their long, painfully slow walks. Elizabeth tried to lose sight of them as much as possible by hurrying ahead or lingering far behind.

On the fourth day, Elizabeth happened to be near them when Mr Bingley was recounting how Lydia had been found. She had stayed closer to the couple than normal because she was genuinely curious as to how Mr Gardiner and Mr Bingley had discovered Lydia and Wickham. Seeming to forget the presence of Elizabeth just behind them, Mr Bingley related the story from when he entered the den of Mrs Younge till when Mr Darcy and

Colonel Fitzwilliam had gone off to confront Wickham and try to secure Lydia.

"Oh, Charles, how brave you are," Jane whispered as she leaned heavily on his arm, looking up into his eyes. "You could have been in some danger."

Mr Bingley, puffing up from this praise from the lips of Jane, leaned his face towards hers, clearly delighted to receive any sort of comfort Jane wished to bestow upon him.

"You mean to tell me that Mr Darcy was there?" Elizabeth exclaimed loudly.

Mr Bingley visibly jumped away from Jane and turned around to see his future sister-in-law. "Miss Elizabeth! I quite forgot your presence back there. How foolish of me," he said, blushing.

"Mr Darcy was there the entire time?" She pressed on, unwilling to allow this revelation to be brushed off with a laugh and a shrug from Mr Bingley. "He found out the hiding place of Mrs Younge and had her observed? Mr Darcy was the one who confronted Wickham with Colonel Fitzwilliam?"

Mr Bingley looked contrite and shuffled his boot through some leaves on the path. "I say, you *are* an awfully silent walker. It must be due to your many hours of rambling in the wilds about here, eh?"

"I suppose that is true. But you, sir, have not replied to my queries."

"That is because Darcy made me promise most solemnly that no one was to be told. Although, I do not know if that was to be extended to my future wife." He flashed a small smile at Jane before grinning at Elizabeth and saying, "I shall say no more about the entire incident, no matter how relentlessly you cajole me."

"But the promise has been unintentionally broken by yourself, sir. Therefore, if my opinion would help to provide guidance, I should say that you are no longer bound by the original vow. It would be perfectly acceptable for you to tell both Jane and myself the rest of your tale."

"None of your endless, clever arguments for me, Miss Elizabeth. You and Darcy and your sharp contestations! The both of you try to drag me into deep waters and watch me flounder. It will not work this time, I assure you. I insist on keeping what little of my promise is still intact."

"But—"

"Lizzy," Jane said mildly with firm pleading in her eyes, "do not badger him. He has told you what his wishes are. We must be content with that."

Elizabeth had to truly bite the inside of her mouth to keep from pressing the issue. The rest of the walk was spent in a labyrinth of speculation that only led to more unanswered questions. She did not dare let her heart race ahead of her mind with fond wishes that perhaps Mr Darcy did not think her the worst sort of deceiver imaginable.

It would not be out of the realm of possibility that Mr Darcy's influence in this matter was purely as a disinterested friend of Mr Bingley. He does not wish to see his friend suffer. My assertion that Jane did, in point of fact, care deeply for Mr Bingley is the only reason that Mr Darcy would have put himself through such ignominy as to associate himself in any way with Wickham. To aid his friend is the only impulse that persuaded him. It is certain. To ease my mind on this point, I will write to Aunt Gardiner and beg her to explain all. Then that will put an end to it and I need never think of it again.

Elizabeth wrote to her aunt immediately upon returning to Longbourn. But even after that had been accomplished, her restlessness would not abate. Finally, she made her way to the stone hut and lit a fire in the hearth. The minty smoke seemed to calm her mind as she looked out through the bars of her window to the forest beyond. Time passed and no one came to visit her. Elizabeth knew that, between Jane and Bingley being so absorbed by each other's company, her own absence would hardly be noticed. Her mother was all consumed by wedding preparations. No one else in the house sought her out for anything. She stayed there, meditating on her past, present, and future—all three states of time were clouded in a tangle of puzzled misunderstandings, some of which were of her own creation.

Chapter 22

Lady Catherine Being of Infinite Use

D*arcy,*

She accepted! Can you believe it? I am the happiest man alive. I apologise for the lateness of this letter. I have been in such a whirl of happiness. I cannot believe it has taken me almost a fortnight to write this to you! You were absolutely correct, as usual, that Jane Bennet had loved me since almost the beginning of our acquaintance. I am too fortunate. If we had not been so interrupted by that terrible intrigue over her youngest sister and that reprobate Wickham—and the broken vase, but I suppose that was my fault—we could have been engaged for at least a month now. Cruel fate. But that is all to be forgotten. She was right impressed by my role in the recovery of her sister Lydia. I may have left out the bit about Mrs Younge making a go for my— well, the less said the better. I also may have implied there were some of her ruffians in the other room, who were armed and dangerous. But, then again, I never saw into the other room, so there very well may have been brutes awaiting her instructions to rough me up, do you not think? I admit that I may have polished up the entire account to make myself appear more noble and brave than I actually was. We do odd things for love, yes? By the by, it may have occurred that Miss Elizabeth was nearby during the retelling of this adventure and I neglected to notice her presence due to the overwhelming beauty of my angel Jane. And Miss Elizabeth may have heard some items related to you being involved and confronting Wickham and such. Do not be angry! You can judge me when you are violently in love and standing too close to your angel and cannot properly recall which way is up and what day of the week it is. Ha, that is a sight that I would very much enjoy witnessing! Darcy, hopelessly in love. However, once I recalled my vow of secrecy, I refused to tell her more, though she attempted to question me relentlessly. She was most curious about it. Miss Elizabeth said she would write to Mr and Mrs Gardiner and demand answers. I saw a thick letter in her hand later in the day, so I assume that she made good on her word. Miss Elizabeth is quite pretty when she is angry. Have you ever noticed? You know, I am not in any way attempting to matchmake, for I know how much you despise the very thought of it, but it has occurred to me—and Jane, by the way—that the two of you—by which I mean you and Elizabeth Bennet, not you and Jane—could be quite well suited to each other. It is a ridiculous thought, for I remember well how you used to mock her with my sister Caroline and slight her at any opportunity. But I do think that if you spent some time in her company, you would see that she is almost as beautiful and charming as my Jane. There is a bit too much fire in her nature for my fancy, but such qualities would do well for you. My hand aches! I have never written such a letter as long as this before. How do you do it? I hope that you will be returning to Netherfield soon. You will always be most welcome here, my friend. I hope that we can count on your presence at our wedding before Christmas. I will be glad to have it done and over, for Mrs Bennet is so very enthusiastic that it can become a trifle tiring.

Yours and so on,

Charles Bingley

Darcy smiled and shook his head at this rambling letter from his friend. But the joy was short-lived, for now he must deal with the anger of Miss Elizabeth Bennet at his involvement in the recovery of Lydia Bennet.

She must be furious at what she must see as officious interference by the man she hates most in the world. I suppose I must pile this onto the long list of transgressions and crimes I have committed. How she must despise me. I had hoped that perhaps, after the wedding of Jane and Bingley, that we could start anew. But now...

Miserable, Darcy collapsed in his chair and covered his eyes with his hand. The letter from Bingley lay pinned under his elbow on his desk. He tried to recall the scenes from his most recent visit to Longbourn. As much as he racked his mind, he could not discover if he had seen any hint of encouragement from Elizabeth. Any warm look that could be interpreted as affection and not anger. It was difficult to say, for her gaze had spent much of the time on the rug.

Perhaps if I had stayed longer, I could have seen some faint sign from her. But to be in her presence while imagining that she was in a state of revulsion of me, no man could have borne it.

He shook his head at the thought, recalling the sheer torture it had been to be so near to her, wanting nothing more than to take her hand in his and plead his case just one more time. He imagined how differently he would have approached the scenario this time.

I would dwell on all that is right and just in my affections for her and make no mention of concerns. I would tell her how much I love her. How I would— But it is too late, is it not? I had my opportunity. It is a torment for me to be in the same room with her. I was correct in leaving Netherfield once I saw that Bingley would have an easy time of it in his courtship of Jane Bennet.

He sat there for a long time, unable to bring himself into a spirit of industry and contentment needed to accomplish anything.

The sound of a carriage stopping in front of his London residence broke his miserable meditations. The front door opened and the unmistakable sound of Lady Catherine de Bourgh's voice, demanding an immediate audience with her nephew, Fitzwilliam Darcy, could be easily heard echoing off the marble floors of the front hall. A slightly red-faced Crump opened the door of Darcy's study and stood in a sort of muted fury.

"Is it my aunt? Lady Catherine?"

"Yes, sir," Crump replied in a tight tone.

"Does she demand to see me?"

"Yes, sir."

"Despite having been told that I am not receiving guests at the moment?"

"Yes, sir, precisely."

"Show her in, Crump. Better to see to it now than later."

"Yes, sir."

Darcy stood, straightened his jacket, and ran his hand through his curls. Recalling the letter he had just received and the sensitive communications it contained, he hurriedly shoved it in the top drawer of his desk. He was not so foolish as to simply hide it under other papers; he had learned his lesson on that score years ago. His aunt had no shame and would rifle through every correspondence of his that she could lay her hands upon if he were so foolish as to leave them laying around out in the open. Darcy was fairly certain that, given the chance, she would absolutely not hesitate to inspect the drawers as well, but he had no intention of leaving her unattended long enough for any such opportunity to arise.

"Nephew! Why would you even dream of keeping me waiting for so very long?"

"Lady Catherine. What a pleasant surprise," Darcy said, somewhat dryly.

"Of course it is, silly boy. May I take a seat, or shall I stand till my poor bones snap under me and I lie on your study floor in agonies?"

Darcy waved to the two chairs before the fireplace. He could not help but repress an annoyed groan at her cruel dramatics as he opened the door of the study and asked a servant to bring a tray of tea.

He settled into the chair opposite and asked, "I was not aware of your being in London. To what do I owe this unexpected pleasure?"

"Oh, nephew. I assure you, this sojourn from the comfort of Rosings has been as far from a pleasure trip as one could imagine. It is difficult to be the only one of my generation to uphold the high standards of our lineage and reputation. This has been an unimaginably trying day. Never could I have conceived of the sheer gall, the effrontery, the naked ambition of social climbing of the very worst sort, the vile degradation of all that—"

Darcy—beginning to be alarmed at whatever crimes his aunt could be alluding to—interrupted, "Is all well? Have you been attacked somehow? Where is my cousin, Anne? Is she well?"

"Still at Rosings. Safe from the shadowy, rapacious connivances of fortune-hunting men. Anne could never be expected to navigate such intrigues."

"If you can be more explicit, I have a dinner engagement that I must prepare for shortly," Darcy said, not mentioning that the dinner was to be near Cheapside with the Gardiner family. He did not think that such information would sit well with his excitable aunt. Darcy had developed a warm friendship with Mr Gardiner during their times and trials together. He had few among his acquaintances whom he could speak intelligently with on matters of investments, and Mrs Gardiner was well-read with an intelligent insight always at the ready. Visits to their home were far more enjoyable than calls to many of the finest homes in London.

With a dramatic sigh, Lady Catherine said, "I am stopping here in London merely for the evening. I have travelled all the way to Hertfordshire and back today, and I am weary to the very bones of my body."

"Hertfordshire? Is my friend Bingley well?" Darcy said, truly alarmed at what he now was beginning to piece together. "Why on earth did you travel there? As I recall, you have no relatives or acquaintances in that county."

"For that modest blessing, I am eternally grateful. It was horrible. Just horrible. I went to that small farm, Longbourn, to see that conniving chit, Miss Elizabeth Bennet."

"What?" Darcy exclaimed, almost lifting from his seat in shock.

"No need to thank me, nephew. It is my duty and I was happy to do it. You are innocent, in some ways that your cousin, Colonel Fitzwilliam, is not. He would understand how a woman like that may use arts and allurements to try and bewitch you into forgetting all you owe your family and estate."

Darcy—feeling as if every drop of blood rushed out of his face—thought that it would be a blessing of some sort if God could see fit to strike him dead with a bolt of lightning at that very moment. "Are you telling me that you went to Longbourn to—to—to *rescue* me from Miss Elizabeth Bennet?"

"Exactly. You are welcome. There can be no doubt in her mind as to how she would be viewed by myself and the rest of society. I was perfectly clear what an absolute crime it would be for her to aspire to such a match as a marriage to you, *my* nephew, and how she would be scorned and despised by any proper society."

Darcy pressed his balled-up fist to his mouth and squeezed his eyes shut, calling up every ounce of strength within him to not throw this woman out on the pavement.

"I can see that you are overcome, nephew. Your gratitude is noted."

Darcy felt dizzy. Through clenched teeth, he muttered, "And, pray, do tell, what was Miss Bennet's reaction?"

"I have never been subjected to such impertinence in all my days. And after I allowed her to play the piano at Rosings! *And* offered her the use of the piano in Mrs Jenkinson's room, as you recall. All of those benevolent distinctions are quite forgotten by her. Shocking. She did acknowledge that there was no engagement between the two of you. But I had already assumed that to be the case, though Mr Collins told me there was some gossip to that effect crawling around. She upbraided me for even asking about it. As if I do not have the right to know all of the concerns of my nephew. And then when I asked her to vow to never enter into an engagement with you, what do you think? You will never guess, for it is too ridiculous. She refused! *She* refused *me*. Miss Elizabeth Bennet told me she would never agree to promise not to enter into an engagement with you. Can you believe it? Is it not beyond all comprehension?"

Cracking his eyes open, Darcy said, "What?"

"She refused to swear to never marry you! She flatly denied me any sort of assurance that she would never become engaged to you. And then, she turned her back on me and walked away. I had to chase her down out of a tangled wilderness area—at great personal danger to myself—to try to get her to pledge to me, but again, she refused! And then she ended the interview by saying any agreement that may come about in the future between the two of you was of no concern to me. No concern for your nearest relation in the world? Really, the insolence of that young woman. Well, I can assure you, she received no compliments from me, nor any to her mother! That *really* seemed to put her in her place, for she just stared at me in utter astonishment."

Behind his balled-up fist, Darcy endeavoured to hide the modest beginnings of a smile.

"I, of course, pointed out that she was not in the same sphere as you. Any attempt to connect herself to you through marriage would be so far beyond her place in society that it would be ludicrous."

"But she is a gentleman's daughter and I am a gentleman. So far we are equals."

"That is exactly, word for word, what she said," Lady Catherine said as her eyes narrowed in suspicion. "I see that I acted just in time, nephew. The influence of that friend of yours, the Bingley person and his betrothed, has not been beneficial to your character."

"I must ask you to refrain from insulting my friend and his betrothed."

"But, their youngest sister! The youngest Bennet girl. She was married in a most scandalous fashion. And to a debauched profligate. I know it all."

"That, I seriously doubt," Darcy replied as he jumped out of his seat and began to walk the room. The noise of words from his aunt continued to swirl around him, but he could not attend.

Is it possible? Why would Elizabeth so staunchly defend her right to engage herself to me at some point in the future if she had absolutely no regard for me? Could it be that I have some small chance to win her heart? If she had absolutely no regard for me, she would have agreed to my aunt's demand just to silence her and be left in peace. I know enough of her character to believe that is exactly what she would have done if she harboured no feelings for me whatsoever.

The joy Darcy felt wash over him, till he was senseless of anything else in the world, almost bowled him over. He turned to look out the window with the broadest smile that had been on his lips for many weeks.

Then, a disturbing thought crossed his mind. Had not Elizabeth mentioned seeking a governess position overseas somewhere? In her second letter to Jane Bennet. That awful day in the Inn at Lambton.

What if she has already accepted a position? What if I have lost the opportunity because I refused to demean myself to seek her hand for a second time? What if my pride has cost me...everything?

This thought shook him deeply. But his courage rose.

Then I shall buy the fastest boat and sail the seas of the entire world till I find her. I will speak with her until every single misunderstanding and mistake in pride is vanquished. I love her. And I cannot stop loving her. I do not want to stop loving her. I am completely hers, body and soul.

"It is well that you have not allowed Georgiana into such degrading society. Can you imagine the sort of influence that a young woman such as Elizabeth or Jane Bennet might have upon her? I shudder at the thought. Now that *that* matter is completely settled, let us speak of you and my daughter, dear Anne. It has been long enough for you to have dallied about with the ladies. You and Anne must marry as soon as possible. I fear that you are entering into a period of life in which young men of means can become dissipated and no longer able to be a proper husband."

Darcy had been so lost in his own musings that he had not attended to what his aunt had been saying to him. A servant brought in the tea tray and Lady Catherine served herself. Darcy shook his head and turned to her. "I would thank you, aunt, to not insert yourself into my affairs in such a ludicrous manner. If I choose to ask Miss Elizabeth Bennet to be my wife, that is strictly between myself and her. If she says yes, there will be nothing more sinister in her decision than to pursue a course that is in the best interests of her own happiness. There will not be a trace of avarice in her acceptance. If I ask her to be my bride, it will be for the same causes. I cannot think of a less mercenary, more disinterested, unwed lady in all of my acquaintance. If she accepts me as her future husband, it will be for the sake of love alone. And I cannot imagine a better foundation for a successful marriage than warm regard and respect between partners."

Lady Catherine paused, the cup of tea halfway to her mouth, a look of utter astonishment upon her face. The steam swirled before her features, for she preferred her tea with no milk to cool it—strong and scalding, like her character. The cup before her, a cup whose pattern Darcy had seen countless times before, held him transfixed. He stared, full of startled, dawning wonder.

Elizabeth! She is the one from the card! The Seven of Cups! She is the path I am meant to take, if I am ever to know true happiness in this life. Why did I not see it before...

The sound of a brittle laugh from Lady Catherine—full of spite and vinegar—filled his ears and broke his happy thoughts.

"Do *not* joke about such a serious matter, Darcy. You would be a pariah! None of us would tolerate your society. No, that young woman is out of consideration. Anne is the one for you to wed. Or even that Miss Bingley creature would be a more respectable choice. Stop your jest, it is in very poor taste."

She sipped deeply from the cup and replaced it on her saucer.

"I expect to see you at Rosings within the fortnight. We shall settle this business between you and Anne once and for all. I will brook no more delays."

"And, just out of curiosity, have you consulted Anne about your plans for her future?"

"She will do as she is told. I will tell her what will and will not make her happy."

"You may hold such sway over Anne, but not me. You will be waiting much longer than a fortnight to see me at Rosings again. I plan on returning to Hertfordshire and making Miss Bennet an offer. Again. Perhaps *this* time she will say yes."

Lady Catherine stood, swayed, grasped the arm of the chair, and sat back down. She clutched at her throat. "You have already made her an offer? And she refused? You? Fitzwilliam Darcy of Pemberley? *My* nephew? You made Miss Bennet an offer? And it was rejected?"

"Yes. And she quite rightly refused me, for I was atrociously rude with no regard for her feelings or pride. If anything, her reasons for her refusal increased my admiration of her mind."

"Her mind? Her mind!" Lady Catherine's hysteric tones increased in volume. "What man gives a fig about the mind of the woman he proposes to? What of her dowry? Her connexions? Her titles?"

"Indeed. Those are considerations when forming an attachment, but, in the end, the regard of the two parties must be of paramount importance. And I feel quite deeply for Elizabeth Bennet. If I am very fortunate, if she feels but a small fraction for me of what I feel for her, then I hope she will consent to be my bride. Now, if you will excuse me, I have a dinner engagement for the evening and plan on leaving for Hertfordshire in the morning."

Darcy waved his hand towards the door.

"A dinner engagement?" she spluttered.

"With the Gardiners, the aunt and uncle of Miss Elizabeth Bennet."

This seemed to crumble the last vestiges of outrage that Lady Catherine could fling from her tower. She covered her eyes with her handkerchief. Darcy raised his eyes upward and sighed.

"To imagine!" she wailed out to no one in particular. "My nephew, connected to a rapacious harlot of low—"

"Enough!" Darcy bellowed. "If you have nothing kind to say, you are free to leave, madam. I have endured your vituperations for long enough. You can have nothing further to say to me. You have insulted me, my friends, and the woman I care for so thoroughly that I would be grateful if you would refrain from contacting me henceforth. Good day."

He bowed and stalked out of the room and bounded up the stairs to his room.

As Crump helped him change for dinner, he could hear the poor head footman being verbally assaulted by his aunt as she was being assisted out of the door and to her waiting carriage. Darcy sighed wearily.

"Crump."

"Yes, sir."

"Remind me to buy Rupert a good bottle of port or whatever it is he prefers."

"Yes, sir."

Lady Catherine, her voice piercing the heavy stone walls of the house, continued to hurl insults out of the window as her carriage pulled away.

"Make that two bottles."

"Very good, sir."

Chapter 23

Having Been Taught to Hope

Elizabeth held the letter from Mrs Gardiner in her hand. It contained few new facts, but the ones it did reveal were heavy in their importance. It was all true, what Mr Bingley had told to Jane and, inadvertently, to herself. It was all confirmed—what Mr Darcy, Mr Bingley, and Colonel Fitzwilliam had done to locate Lydia and bring Wickham to agree to marry her.

But added to this, Mr Darcy had insisted on paying the lion's share of the ten thousand pounds to essentially bribe Wickham into marrying her youngest sister. Mr Gardiner and Mr Bingley had absolutely insisted on contributing a small amount to the settlement, but most of it had fallen to Mr Darcy to provide, by his own determined insistence.

Ten thousand pounds... and I had believed that he would ask for five thousand at most. How foolish I am to underestimate the cruel cupidity of Wickham. Poor Lydia. I can see no path to happiness in her future, but she was determined to have him and will perhaps craft a way to be content. But why had Mr Darcy helped so enormously? And at the cost of such a degradation? He could have easily had no more dealings with Wickham. I do not understand. I cannot believe that he performed an act of such magnitude for me. After I had deceived him during our two readings and had accused him of such viciousness towards Wickham and also had turned away his proposal with so much scorn. No, he must have acted so to attempt to make amends towards Mr Bingley. Mr Darcy's conscience nagged him in regards to his deception of his friend. That is the only explanation that makes any rational sense. It makes him all the more admirable.

With many sighs of dissatisfaction, Elizabeth read through the letter from her aunt for the dozenth time, attempting to find some guidance on how Mr Darcy truly felt about her. But it was a thin porridge to attempt to sate the appetite of her curiosity. For as much as her mind lectured her on the improbability of Mr Darcy performing such a monumental act with any thought of her as a motive, her heart stubbornly warmed and quickened at the mere idea. Elizabeth folded the letter and placed it under her robes. She was again at the chilly, stone cottage, finding it her only source of comfort during these confusing times. A slight drizzle had commenced, and the first sharp coolness of autumn was attempting to make itself known. With a shiver, Elizabeth turned away from the window and placed several more sticks on the smoky fire. She sat back in her chair and stared at the flames as they consumed the dried mint and branches.

Recollections of Lady Catherine coming to see her, condemning an engagement between herself and Mr Darcy that did not even exist, seemed to rise out of the flames. Elizabeth's anger at Lady Catherine's insults had been deep and untameable. Her absolute refusal to give the lady her vow to never enter into such an engagement had doubled the indignation of the unwelcome visitor. Lady Catherine had rained down every sort of insult upon her and the Bennet family imaginable. Elizabeth could not escape the opinion that, despite her grand title and vast fortune, Lady Catherine was unhinged in the extreme. To imagine any of her own family travelling for so many hours to simply bully and berate someone was ridiculous. Despite her still wounded dignity, Elizabeth could not help but smile at how ludicrous Lady Catherine had appeared during her tirade, eyes bulging with outrage, making her face a shockingly blotchy crimson.

Say what you will of the behaviour of my relatives, but I think every grand estate and name must have some embarrassing member who causes chagrin. It is definitely not just the Bennets of Hertfordshire who cause gossip. I cannot imagine that Mr Darcy himself thinks highly of a relative like Lady Catherine, a person capable of such an unprovoked attack of rude fury. It makes his claims of my own family's deficiencies a weak insult indeed.

Elizabeth felt a weariness of unhappiness in her limbs as images of their fiery confrontation in Kent flashed before her. She picked up a book from the mantel, raised her veil, and went to sit back at the window. But her book could not hold her interest today. Restless, she pushed it aside and pulled out her deck of cards. She shuffled through it until she found the three that she was searching for. She placed them carefully in front of her on the sill.

The King of Swords, The Hanged Man, the Seven of Cups. With her cheek resting on her palm, she stared blankly at them, attempting to think of any little thing she had missed during that first reading with Mr Darcy almost a year ago at Netherfield. As she ruminated on the image of the handsome gentleman, her thoughts transformed to examining what she might have missed or misinterpreted during conversations with him. Her eyes squeezed shut as she struggled to form some sense of satisfaction or closure. But none could be discovered, even by her cleverness. Her leaden heart could conjure only one conclusion.

Perhaps he was correct in his advice at the Netherfield ball. I should not have attempted to sketch his character. My performance truly did neither of us credit. My skill at taking his likeness was abysmal, his behaviour was unfortunate, and the words I threw in his face were unforgivable.

"Anything new to tell?"

With her eyes still shut, Elizabeth replied, "No, I told everything that I believed I saw."

"That is what I thought."

With a start, Elizabeth realised that she had actually heard that voice in reality, not in her head. Her eyes flew open and there, sitting on the stump on the other side of the window, was the very real Mr Darcy.

"You! Here!"

Mr Darcy only nodded with a slight grin on his face. But his eyes were careful, expectant, and wary.

Elizabeth blushed deeply, realising her veil was up and her red cheeks were on full display.

"Mr Darcy," she said as she glanced down at the cards before her, fully aware that they were the exact cards from his reading a year ago. "I was just— That is, I—"

She moved her hand to sweep them away, but he raised his palm. "Leave them, if you do not mind. It brings back pleasant memories."

"Of course." She paused, and then, before she could think long enough to convince herself out of proceeding, continued, "Mr Darcy, I wish to thank you. For the service you performed for my family. For my sister Lydia who is unable to comprehend the magnitude of your deed. No one in my family here at Longbourn knows to whom they are indebted, except for Jane. You are kindness itself. Please accept our gratitude."

His countenance darkened. Unpleasant thoughts were clouding his brow. "Do not mention my goodness. Who but I should bring Wickham to task for some of the transgressions he has committed? If I had been more open about my past, he would never have been able to take such liberties."

"But it must have been so mortifying for you, to go to such lengths, to pay so much to such a man!"

"It was a trifle to ensure that the respectability of your family stayed intact. Too much has been sacrificed to my determination to never appear foolish to the world. Momentary embarrassment at my past dealings with Wickham being exposed and examined would have been a small price to pay if it had prevented Wickham from preying upon your youngest sister. As you well know, it was only through a fortunate whim of chance that my own sister did not fall victim to him. I was happy to oblige you and your family in any way that I could. I respect your family and believe they are not indebted to me in any way."

"You are too good, sir," Elizabeth whispered in a confused tremor.

Mr Darcy looked down momentarily, as if gathering his thoughts. Looking back up into her eyes, he said, "If you wish to thank me, you could sell me one of your charms. Like the one you sold to Miss Bingley. Then we will be even. All debts will be paid."

"A charm? For such a sum as you paid out to save the reputation of my sister and our entire family? Eight thousand pounds for a charm of mint and salt?"

"I hear they are efficient in their purpose."

With a shake of her head at this bizarre request, Elizabeth reached under the counter and pulled out one of her little bundles. She slid it under the bars to Mr Darcy. He carefully picked it up, brought it to his nose, and inhaled deeply. "Mint and...?"

"Rosemary," she whispered out.

"And how does it work?"

"You place it in your palm, then you say the name of the person—of the person you wish—" Her words ceased, her mind denying whose name would be on his lips when he spoke.

"The person you wish would return your love?" he asked, the low rumble of his voice running through her chest.

Elizabeth could only nod, her heart was racing so rapidly. After a long pause, she raised her face, looked him in the eyes, and said, "You say the name three times and then try to place it as close to the person as possible."

Darcy twirled the satchel by the ribbon for a moment, gazing at the small object. Then he placed it in his palm and turned his full attention to her. Leaning close to the bars, fixing her with his deep, dark eyes, he said softly, "Elizabeth...Elizabeth...Elizabeth."

She leaned close to the window, staring at Darcy's lips as he formed her name—once, twice, three times. Her breath became unsteady as her body's strength seemed to drain away.

With their faces just inches apart, he asked, "Did it work?"

Gazing into his eyes, a smile on her lips, she replied, "No, it did not work."

Blinking in astonishment, Darcy began to pull away from the window.

Elizabeth reached under the bars and quickly clasped his hands in hers. The charm pressed into her palm as she continued, "For I have loved you since the very first moment I saw you, the moment you entered the library at Netherfield for your reading. You do not need to wish for what has been yours for this past year."

A startled look came across his face, almost pained at the realisation of her words.

"You mean to tell me...all this time...What a fool I am!"

"You will get no argument from me," she said with a mischievous flutter of her lashes.

"Do you forgive me?" he asked, clutching her hands tightly in his.

"Only with a proper payment."

"Anything you wish for, I will do all in my power to make it so."

Their faces were so close, a sigh of a breath away from each other. "A kiss, Mr Darcy. That is what I require."

Through the bars, their lips pressed together, light as a feather, but as fiery as a phoenix exploding from the ashes. Darcy pulled away, eyes dilated, sucking in a breath and clearing his throat. "Is there a way we could, perhaps, open the door to this little place?"

Elizabeth smiled and nodded. She leapt up, tore off her black cloak, smoothed her hair, and went to the ancient, thick, half-rotten wooden door. It was rarely opened, only a few times a year to retrieve sticks for the fireplace. Elizabeth grabbed the heavy key from the wall and turned it in the lock. She yanked on the handle, but the door did not budge.

"It is stuck, the rains have made it swell into place!"

She thought she heard a loud groan from Darcy on the other side.

"You pull and I will push," he said.

They both made a few unsuccessful attempts.

"Were you pulling?" he asked.

"Of course I was!"

"Stand back."

Elizabeth backed away and heard a loud thump and then a few colourful words. She could not help but place her hand over her mouth to suppress a giggle. There were several more loud bangs against the door. Elizabeth stepped farther back, eyes wide, as each impact caused the barrier to rattle. The door began to splinter and shake down with its own dust, moss, and rottenness. A last mighty bang caused it to collapse as Darcy rushed in and fell to the floor in a heap.

"Darcy," Elizabeth exclaimed as she knelt down beside him and placed her hand on his upper back. Quick as a flash, she found his arms wrapped tightly around her as he sat up and clutched her to his chest. She gasped as she felt his warm cheek press against her own.

"I think I finally did well enough," he said.

"Whatever can you mean?" she whispered back.

"Ever since I saw you at the Meryton assembly, every night, you have taunted me in my dreams that I would have to do better if I wished you to love me."

"You have indeed done well enough," she said quietly back to him with a smile in her voice.

He shuddered with apparent happiness as he traced his lips along her cheek and to Elizabeth's own, waiting lips. They kissed again and again as the chill of the day could find no crevice between their bodies to diminish the heat they felt. Finally, sensing the danger that their feelings, so long denied and misunderstood, could easily carry them away, Elizabeth reluctantly pulled her face from his.

Darcy slowly opened his eyes and said, "I think, perhaps, we should go to your father straightaway and ask him if he would be opposed to a very short engagement."

Elizabeth laughed as she pushed dusty, dishevelled curls of his hair back off his face. Her hand curved down and cupped his cheek. Looking in his eyes, she said, "I love you."

Darcy smiled contentedly, clearly cherishing her words, so long hoped for.

"Come," he said as he helped her to her feet, then they walked outside, hand in hand.

"My cards!" Elizabeth cried as she ran back to the outside window of the cottage to sweep the deck up in her hand. A sudden, unusually strong gust of wind whipped her skirts, her hair, and the deck scattered. The rectangles of paper twirled and danced around in the breeze. She grasped for them out of bushes and off the ground as Darcy helped her. Once they had picked up all they could find, she spread the deck before her in her hands. Elizabeth frowned.

"The King of Swords, he is not here," she exclaimed.

Darcy took her in his arms again and pulled her in close, kissing away the frown from her lips.

"I think we have seen enough of him," he said after their mouths parted. "He was a lonely, imperious fellow, too full of pride and too quick to insult that which is good and lovely around him."

"Oh, I do not know," Elizabeth replied breathlessly. "I was quite fond of him, really."

"Were you really fond of him? I was so unfeeling and rude. When I proposed to you in Kent, I was all that was insulting. I only spoke of my own interests and preference with no regard for what yours may be. I could not have belittled you and your family any more than I did."

"Your proposal in Kent was, perhaps, not the most well thought out for someone hoping to receive a positive response. But there was some truth in what you said of my family. As much as I love them, I cannot be ignorant of their shortcomings. And I think the false accusations that I spoke to your face in response were enough of a punishment for any rudeness that you can be accused of."

"But I did try to separate Jane and Bingley. You have forgiven me for that blunder as well?"

"If *you* had been the one who had to chaperone that pair for the last week, you would see that there was no harm done at all by that deception. Their love for each other is abundantly clear at every turn in the path. Truly! No matter how far back I fell in our rambles in which I had the very poorly executed duty of chaperone, by the time I caught up with them, they were as intertwined as vines of ivy climbing a wall. The more important question may be, has Bingley forgiven you?"

"I endured a full five minutes of his wrath at Pemberley. After we had accidentally encountered your sister, I confessed all. There were several rants, and he almost shouted in anger. But I was able to calm him quickly by instructing him to propose to Jane as soon as he was able."

"And I hear the vase population of Derbyshire may never recover."

They both laughed. Darcy stole a kiss from her lips as he took her arm through his, and they walked back in the direction of Longbourn.

In all of Hertfordshire, there could not have been a more shocked house standing. None of the inhabitants were even aware that Mr Darcy was in the neighbourhood. And that included Mr Bingley who was visiting with Jane. Added to that the fact that everyone had believed Elizabeth to be locked in her room, their appearance, walking up the path from the woods, caused many exclamations of amazement.

Arm in arm, the two entered the parlour, smiling broadly at everyone there. Darcy went to Mr Bennet and requested a private audience with him the moment the bedlam of greetings had been acknowledged and the loud questions from Bingley ignored.

Once Darcy and her father had retired to the study, Elizabeth had to suffer through several hissing questions from her mother. She attempted all manner of cheerful redirection that she could think of to distract Mrs Bennet from the shock and anger that the sight of Mr Darcy walking alone with her daughter could engender.

Finally, Elizabeth struck upon the perfect distraction for her. "Mama, I truly am having second thoughts about the menu for the wedding breakfast for Jane and Mr Bingley."

"Second thoughts? What can you mean, child? Second thoughts indeed. It is a very good breakfast, I can assure you. When you have daughters and weddings to plan, then you can tell me your thoughts on wedding breakfasts."

When Darcy returned, the room went silent as he muttered to Elizabeth that her father wished to see her. Elizabeth rose and went to his study.

After she was seated, Papa wasted no time in requesting her assurance that this was truly what she wished for. Elizabeth vowed to him that she did indeed love Mr Darcy and had loved him for a long time.

Brows raised in surprise, her father asked, "Have loved for a long time? You must be mistaken."

Elizabeth felt the justice of this comment as she reflected on how she was the most vocal in her denigration of Darcy. "I understand your confusion, sir. It has been a confusing time for me as well. I have loved him deeply since the earliest moments of our acquaintance. But I misunderstood his character to such an extent, and by his own admission, Mr Darcy was not behaving at his best during their time here in Hertfordshire. He had—other things upon his mind at the time."

Her father scrutinised her—puzzled yet amused—before waving a hand in the air as though done with a curiosity that had lost its lustre. He stood and leaned over to plant a single kiss on the top of her head, assuring her that he was happy that she had found a partner for her life who she believed would be her equal in feeling and thought.

After the gentlemen left, Elizabeth informed her mother and sisters of the happy news. Jane appeared surprised, but not so much that it might lead one to believe that she had no previous inkling of Darcy having a regard for Elizabeth. Their mama was at once ecstatic and humbled. To have two daughters so advantageously wed in such a short amount of time was beyond even her wildest expectations, which were significant, for her expectations could be truly wild. Elizabeth could only smile and let everyone express their amazement or congratulations as she surrendered any hope of a cosy, quiet conversation amongst intelligent company.

A tired, but warmly content, Elizabeth trudged up the stairs to her bedroom door that evening and found it would not budge.

'Tis locked! Because of my passage to the stone cottage this afternoon. My key is in the drawer beside my bed. I could wake Hill and ask her to find the key, but the likelihood of others having questions as to how this has come about is not at all what I desire. I must beg Jane for a corner of her bed.

Exasperated at her own lack of forethought, Elizabeth approached Jane's door and tapped lightly. She had been eager to enjoy the memories of her kisses with Darcy in her head until sleep overtook her, but the problem of finding a place to sleep took precedence.

"Come in. Lizzy! Is everything all right?"

Jane had been sitting up in bed, reading by candlelight.

"I seem to have locked my bedroom door and cannot get in. I would rather not rouse Hill and perhaps the entire house. May I sleep with you?"

"Of course. Slip into my old nightgown. I have not yet had time to mend it properly before passing it on to Mary."

Elizabeth undressed with a smile. "It is funny to think that we will soon no longer be plagued by the problem of which sister to pass down our clothes to."

"I had not thought of that. It is true. But I shall still mend my clothes myself and pass them on to one of the servants or to a family in the neighbourhood that is in need."

"Of course you will, Jane, I expect nothing less. It just struck me as odd that very soon it will not be a consideration for you and I and our sisters." She gave her sister a peck on the cheek as she snuggled under the blankets next to her. Jane blew out the candle. The fine light of the half-moon barely illuminated the room through the crack in the curtains.

"How did you lock yourself out of your own room?"

Elizabeth sighed dramatically as she leaned her head back on her arm and stared at the ceiling. "Would you mind terribly if I did not explain *all* of that tonight? It is rather complex, and I would rather dwell on a happier topic."

Jane smiled at her and, with a mischievous glint in her eye, asked, "And that would be?"

"Is Pemberley really as grand and beautiful as everyone says it is?"

"Oh, Lizzy!" The two sisters giggled. "Do be serious. I know you far too well to presume that Mr Darcy's estate had any influence upon your decision to accept him. But since you have never seen your future home, then I will say yes, it is the most grand and beautiful place I have ever beheld. It is the type of estate you would find particularly pleasing. Miles of woods, old but well kept up, and where beauty has taken precedence over a need to impress. Everything that you would approve of. There is a particular portrait of Mr Darcy that truly shows him at his most handsome. And Georgiana's playing on the piano... It is much like having a master giving concerts every night, she is so talented."

Elizabeth poked Jane in the arm and whispered, "Do not let Mary hear you say that or we shall never have a moment's respite from her determined rehearsing. Well, if Pemberley has been so fortunate as to garner your good opinion, then I suppose it will do for me."

"Lizzy, I must ask. It is plain that you *now* think well of Mr Darcy, but when did you begin to form feelings for him?"

"From the second I laid eyes upon him, Jane." Elizabeth stared up at the ceiling, remembering clearly the profile of his face as he looked into the library at Netherfield for his card reading. How her heart had wanted to tear from her chest. How much she wanted to smooth those lines of worry from his brow and kiss his cheek till he had forgotten whatever was ailing him.

"At the Meryton assembly?"

"Around that time, yes. I have so much to tell you that I do not know where to begin."

"You need not do it tonight. I am so happy to know that he has been so fortunate as to have had your regard for that long. I had thought you could not stand the sight of him. He was so rude at that very assembly."

"He *was* rude, I am in complete agreement. And I was so hurt that I cannot even begin to recall it without feeling low. So I tried, with every fibre of my being, to turn that love into hate. I talked so long and loud about how very much Mr Darcy displeased me that I think I was hoping to convince myself as well as all of those around me. My heart's dilemma calls to mind *Romeo and Juliet*, something about a 'Beautiful tyrant! Fiend Angelical!' I think that is what I was battling."

"Oh, Lizzy. I am sorry that you suffered so. I had no idea."

"It was a trying time. I was so positive that my dislike had defeated my love that I am certain that is why I refused his first proposal of marriage. Of course, it did not aid his cause that he was abominably rude in Kent."

Jane sat up in the dark. "His first proposal! You mean he proposed to you before today?" Jane cried out in surprise.

"Shhh! I want Mama to never hear a word of it. Can you imagine her fury at the notion that I turned down such a man as Mr Darcy of Pemberley? And that Lady Catherine de Bourgh paid us a call for the explicit reason to extract from me a vow to never accept a proposal of marriage from her nephew?"

"Lizzy! Is that why she visited here? I thought she was passing through the neighbourhood and felt obliged to call. Or that she conveyed to you a letter from Charlotte. What an awful time you have had. What did Lady Catherine say to you?"

Elizabeth could only giggle and shake her head. "You would be too shocked to sleep a wink if I recounted her scolding of me. If you would be so kind to me, dear sister, may we wait until a later time for me to explain?"

"Of course. You seem to have had so much that has been hidden from us all. I hope that you know that you may always rely upon me to give you comfort, and your secrets will always be safe with me."

"I know, I am sorry to have not been completely open. It was my fault in judgement. But I promise that I will tell all there is to know, if you are just patient with me. I *should* have consulted you more, for you were the only one in all of Hertfordshire who refused to condemn Darcy."

"It seemed to me that Charles, though forgiving in his nature, could not be *that* deceived by someone he held in such esteem."

"You were correct, as usual. Darcy and I—we both made mistakes in our judgement, we both were misled by our pride and discernment. It was made more difficult because we both consider ourselves to be terribly clever, so that made it all the more infuriating to admit that we were wrong."

The sisters laughed together at this humorous, but somewhat accurate, depiction of herself and Darcy.

"Oh, Jane," Elizabeth muttered as her eyes closed, "I will never attempt to sketch a character again. My abilities have caused me such sorrow this past year."

"Do not say that, you are skilled in it."

"Perhaps. But my many attempts to take the likeness of Fitzwilliam Darcy were miserable failures. Thank goodness they were."

Chapter 24

Extraordinary Sources of Happiness

The wedding was so lovely. The day was perfect with the weather being that sharp blend of sunshine and cold. The two couples marrying were genuinely in love with their future partners. The mother of the two brides properly vacillated between joy and sorrow in a highly theatrical fashion that entertained everyone present. It was really everything one could hope for.

Darcy was the happiest he could ever remember being in his entire life. His bride, his Elizabeth, was more exquisite than he could ever recall seeing her before. Even in the midst of all of the chaos, she managed to find moments to squeeze his hand reassuringly and whisper something amusing in his ear so that his natural gravity did not have a chance to take hold. Seeing his sister, Georgiana, standing near Elizabeth, laughing with her before enjoying some whispered giggling with Kitty Bennet, made the day even more perfect. Kitty and Georgiana were becoming fast friends, and Darcy approved of the development very much. He shook his head with a grin as he tried to even guess what they could be snickering about to each other so secretively.

He was just at the absolute limit of his ability to tolerate so much well-wishing. His jacket was beginning to feel too tight as he ran a finger between his cravat and his throat, hoping the added space would make it easier to breathe. So many people and so many words. Elizabeth walked up to him and touched his arm reassuringly.

"I have a small gift for you," she said as her eyes gleamed with a joke.

"But I have given you nothing today. I do have something special to give you later, when we reach London."

"My gift is not likely to be as fine as whatever you have in mind, but I think you will love it just the same."

She glanced around to make sure they were unobserved. Quick as a cat, she reached into the bosom of her gown and retrieved a card. Darcy, surprised, took it and turned it over.

A drawing of a man and woman, naked, lying with their limbs intertwined was on the card. Above them a childlike cherub with wings, his eyes covered with a cloth tied around his head, was pointing an arrow at the couple.

"Cupid," Elizabeth whispered to him as she pressed close, resting her hand lightly on his, "is blindfolded. Because we cannot control whom we fall in love with. Sometimes that can cause us to feel helpless and confused. It is The Lovers card."

Darcy looked back up into her eyes, his heart swelling, her scent filling his senses. He cleared his throat, attempting to sound nonchalant. "Perhaps we should leave soon for London. Now, even. If that would be agreeable. If you wish."

Her only response was a nod of assent and the pair soon found themselves in his carriage, racing along the roads to London.

The ride started with happy recollections of the day and a few laughs at the expense of Mrs Bennet. Good woman though she was, she had been something of a spectacle. Elizabeth hugged Darcy tightly.

"I am so glad you are able to laugh about it. You are too wonderful."

Elizabeth began to pull away, but Darcy was not about to let this moment slip past him. He pulled her onto his lap and pressed his lips to hers. His hand slid up under the skirt of her gown, caressing the outside of her thigh with gentle steadiness. The startled gasp from her lips made him that much more eager to get to London as quickly as possible. His arm around her waist held her tighter, as if some calamity or misunderstanding could tear her away at any moment.

Seeming to sense the anxiety in his tightened grasp, Elizabeth pulled her head back to gaze into his eyes and said, "I am here, body and soul. I am yours, my love."

"I keep wondering if it is too good to be true."

With a laugh, Elizabeth said, "I promise that you are stuck with me, sir. But, you should know that I have had several letters in answer to my enquiries across the sea. If we ever become too terribly vexed with one another, I may take a post as a governess there."

Darcy made a low sound of disapproval at that idea.

"Just a jest, I assure you."

She cradled his cheek in her palm. He turned his head and kissed her palm, then pressed his lips back to hers. Darcy brought his hand up to trace down the front of her neck and slid his fingers along to her shoulder. Gently, he slid the shoulder of her gown off and brought his lips to the skin at the base of her neck and kissed his way out to the end of her shoulder. The taste of her was exactly what he thought it would be. Sweet and sharply minty. He looked up into her face, her cheeks flushed and lips parted, and said, "I have wanted to do that since that very first evening I saw you at the Meryton assembly. All I could imagine was kissing you just here."

He kissed her shoulder again.

In a whispery voice, Elizabeth said, "You had a very peculiar way of showing an interest in me. Insulting me at the very same moment that you imagined kissing me in a most indiscreet spot. It is not the recommended way to woo a lady, I should think."

"Indeed, it is not something I would promote. It led to delay and—frustration."

"The delay is no more and the frustration—well, it will be at an end soon, I think. Though I would rather wait until we are in a less bumpy situation before that happens." She smiled at him mischievously as their lips came together again. The rest of the ride was spent in silence, with Elizabeth remaining on his lap, until they reached their home in London.

It was so late in the night that the entirety of London seemed to be in a deep slumber. Sleep came in intervals in the main bedroom of Mr and Mrs Darcy's residence. They lay together, happily entwined, on the grand bed. Two low candles were their only light. They were awake again, speaking softly to each other. The clock downstairs chimed three times. Darcy sat up suddenly.

"It is the next day and I have yet to give you my gift."

Darcy sprang out of bed, determined to make sure all was done in the proper way. He slid on his robe and retrieved the key from the top drawer of his desk. He went to the massive walnut cabinet, opened it, and knelt down. Finding the key hole for the strongbox was difficult in the dark, and his fingers ran along the metal in an attempt to locate it. Suddenly the interior of the cabinet was lit.

"Here, let me help." Elizabeth stood over him, holding one of the candles and with a large shawl wrapped around her.

"Thank you."

The key slid in and the lid of the black iron trunk swung open. Darcy picked up a flat, ornate wooden box and opened it. In it was a necklace of emeralds woven in silver. He lifted it from the box.

Elizabeth stared, transfixed. Then, letting the shawl drop to the floor with a mischievous smile, she took the finery from him and fastened the chain around her neck.

Darcy stood, eyes wide, as he beheld his wife. She was naked, dark hair cascading around her shoulders, with the necklace he had spent so much time selecting, resting on her chest just above her breasts.

"You are the most beautiful sight I have ever beheld," he muttered. Only then did he see the gooseflesh along her skin and rushed to envelop her in his robe. "I believe it is far too chilly for the kind of exhibition you are putting on."

Elizabeth nestled deep against his chest. She looked down into the strongbox and suddenly pressed away from Darcy. She took up the candle and wrapped the shawl over her shoulders again before kneeling in front of the box.

"I assure you, there is nothing else of interest in there."

"My fan! The new one I brought to the Netherfield ball," Elizabeth exclaimed as she pulled the flopping, grimy thing from the bottom of the box. "And here is the King of Swords! And my letter to Jane!" She gazed up at his face in surprise. "Why are they here? Under all these papers and boxes?"

Darcy blinked at her. "That is where I keep the most valuable items I possess. I know it was wrong of me to take the letter you had written to your sister. But when I read of how you played ships with your young cousins, it was the only happy thing in my life at that terrible moment. That image. I could not part with it. I needed it. I am sorry."

Elizabeth felt a smile of pure warmth spread across her lips. She replaced the items in the chest and blew out the candle. Taking her husband's hand and pulling him towards the bed, she said, "I think I need warming up, my love."

Elizabeth slid under the warm covers, still radiant from the heat of their bodies. Darcy paused.

"I forgot to add something to the chest."

He reached into his jacket from the day that lay across a chair and pulled out his gift from Elizabeth. The Lovers card joined the King of Swords card down at the very bottom of the strongbox. Darcy smiled as he closed the heavy, black iron lid, thinking with satisfaction that the king would never be lonely again.

Afterword

As some may have noted, I took an dash of inspiration from *Jane Eyre* by Charlotte Bronte, Chapter 19.

Historical precedent

From the August 1, 1809 London Chronicle-

The fashionable circles of Cheltenham have been much enlivened by the following circumstances;- At a magnificent ball and supper given by Lord Blaney, last Wednesday, a lady made her appearance, dressed in a most grotesque style. In a fanciful brown bonnet she wore a long green feather; she had a gown with a white sleeves; and a green body, and a purple petticoat, and red stockings finished her costume. She was totally unknown to all the company, passed herself off for a fortune-teller, and displayed much refined wit and a thorough knowledge of the most secret occurrences in high life, which happened during the last fashionable season in London. Her manners, though odd, were so engaging as to excite the greatest possible degree of interest. She retired, as she entered, without gratifying the extreme curiosity she had excited; her dancing was imitably graceful.

The history of Tarot cards is 'murky' at best. For quite a while, it was believed they originated in Egypt, but that seems to be a bit of a tall tale to add some spooky mysticism to their origins. The most widely accepted theory now is that they began as a complex card game in the 1400's in Italy and morphed into a form of divination. This tied in quite nicely to the priest's hole I added to Longbourn. I am intrigued by the idea that the cards themselves are portable little works of art—able to be passed down through generations or carried as your travel. Salvadore Dali painted a deck of cards that were supposed to be used in a Bond film, *Live and Let Die*. Other artists through time have taken a turn at painting a deck as well.

As to whether there is any *actual* magic in *Take His Likeness*, I leave that entirely for the reader to decide for themselves. I bought a tarot card set and did readings for the characters as I was writing this book. So, other than one—I can't remember exactly, but maybe the Wickham reading—all of the readings in this book are real readings that I did. They were incredibly accurate, especially the Darcy reading!

Something that has always fascinated me about Elizabeth Bennet is her apparent lack of some of the more conventionally accepted accomplishments for a lady and her enthusiasm for 'sketching characters.' I practically take this as a primitive form of psychology or personality assessment of the Regency era. I attempted to really expand on that idea, within the confines of the time, and show off how good and how terrible Elizabeth was at it, just as Austen did in *Pride and Prejudice*.

For history, I read and consulted:

Place, Robert M., *The Tarot: History, Symbolism, and Divination* New York: Jeremy P. Tarcher/Penguin, 2005

It's in the Cards(Catalog) by Maria Schurr; Metmuseum.org

Before Fortune Telling: The History and Structure of Tarot Cards by Tim Husband; Metmuseum.org

Acknowledgements

Thank you to my wonderful editor, Katie Jackson - Regency Editorial Services. She is awesome and makes me look better than I actually am.

Thank you to my wonderfully supportive beta readers- Jennifer Bolt, James Ferrell, and Sally Zeigler.

Thank you Jeremy Micheal Elder for a fantastic cover.

Again, thank you to Jane Austen. You have been my constant companion through good times and bad, I never weary of your spot-on humour and divine brilliance.

About the author

Lyndsay Constable has been a passionate reader since her early teen years and frequently selected books that could successfully be hidden behind the person sitting in front of her in class. Originally from North Carolina, she attended both North Carolina School of the Arts and SUNY Purchase. She currently lives in Virginia with her husband, child, dog, and cat.
Join my newsletter   https://lyndsayconstable.com/

Social Media
Facebook- Lyndsay Constable, Author
Instagram- authorlyndsayconstable
TikTok- authorlyndsayconstable

Also by

Lyndsay Constable

An Excellent Walker- A Pride and Prejudice Variation
Never Inconstant- A Persuasion Sequel
A Lover's Fine Eye- A Pride and Prejudice Variation Novella

The Puzzled Heiress- A Pomona Moriarty Mystery

Coming Soon!
2024
A Mortal Heart's Desire- A Pride and Prejudice Variation

2024 or 2025
The Cruise of Curses- A Pomona Moriarty Mystery- Book 2

Made in the USA
Coppell, TX
06 July 2024

34277847R00173